Fair Game

"Let us not beat about the bush, Mrs. Fairfield. I have proposed marriage, and now that your year of mourning is over, I have come for your answer."

Well, he was nothing if not direct, Emily thought. "You are still quite certain you wish me to be your wife, Sir Rafe?"

"Indeed, I am more sure than ever."

She was about to tell him she accepted, when something perverse rose through her, and instead she found herself asking a very unlikely question. "Do you love me, Sir Rafe?"

"I have always had affection for you, Mrs. Fairfield."

"You have always wanted me, sir, which is not the same thing."

The ghost of a smile touched his lips. "Very well, I have always desired you . . . and I yearn to enter your bed. Is that honest enough for you?"

"It is honest, sir, but I still hear no mention of love."

"Well, do you love me?" he countered.

She drew back. "No," she confessed.

A light passed through his eyes. "The future is in the lap of the gods, Mrs. Fairfield."

Easy Conquest

Sandra Heath

SIGNET
Published by New American Library, a division of
Penguin Putnam Inc., 375 Hudson Street,
New York, New York 10014, U.S.A.
Penguin Books Ltd, 27 Wrights Lane,
London W8 5TZ, England
Penguin Books Australia Ltd, Ringwood,
Victoria, Australia
Penguin Books Canada Ltd, 10 Alcorn Avenue,
Toronto, Ontario, Canada M4V 3B2
Penguin Books (N.Z.) Ltd, 182–190 Wairau Road,
Auckland 10, New Zealand

Penguin Books Ltd, Registered Offices:
Harmondsworth, Middlesex, England

First published by Signet, an imprint of New American Library,
a division of Penguin Putnam Inc.

First Printing, September 2001
10 9 8 7 6 5 4 3 2 1

Printed in the United States of America

PUBLISHER'S NOTE
This is a work of fiction. Names, characters, places, and incidents either are the product of the author's imagination or are used fictitiously, and any resemblance to actual persons, living or dead, business establishments, events, or locales is entirely coincidental.

1

There was no gentle way to say it, no simple method of lessening the blow. For the past six months Emily's usually sensible mother had been overspending to a fault, and it could no longer be tolerated. A line had to be drawn. Firmly.

"Mama, *neither* of us will be able to purchase new clothes this month, next month, or indeed for the rest of the summer. As for a gown for the autumn opening of the new assembly rooms at the Royal Oak, well, I am afraid you will have to wear the plowman's gauze you acquired for Bath two years ago."

"Mm? What was that you said, dear?" Mrs. Preston did not glance up from her sheet of music. She was seated at the harpsichord, and was framed against the lattice window that gave a view across the park to the Welsh hills. Her hour of morning practice was about to commence, and her thoughts were of Mozart, not country town assemblies. The half year of mourning she had elected to wear for Emily's late husband had ended a few days ago, and now she was pretty in mauve taffeta, with a lace shawl resting daintily over her dimpled arms. There was a frilled biggin cap on her head, and around her throat she wore a gold necklace with a jeweled "C" for her given name, Cora. At fifty-four she had become a little plump, but was still strikingly lovely, with hair a premature but very attractive silver, and eyes of the deepest blue imaginable.

Emily adored her mother, who as a rule was very prudent and practical. Reprimanding her was therefore not easy; but it had to be done. They *had* to discuss the disagreeable fact that the coffers at Fairfield Hall were almost empty. So Emily patiently repeated every unpalatable word.

This time a look of horror came over Cora's face. "Then

when *may* I expect the privilege of a new rag for my back?" she demanded.

"It would not be so bad if you were requesting a mere rag, Mama, but you have set your sights upon one of the best dressmakers in London!"

"Well, *je ne peux pas la sentir*. I can't stand her, but I suppose there is Mrs. Nicholls." It was a reluctant concession, Mrs. Nicholls being in Shrewsbury and therefore not regarded as a fashionable *couturière*. However, there was nothing unfashionable about Cora's French pronunciation, which was perfect enough for a Parisienne, even though she was English through and through.

Emily smoothed her black bombazine skirts exasperatedly. "Even Mrs. Nicholls is out of the question right now. We have to be frugal, Mama. Maybe when the rents are in next year there will be sufficient for . . ." Her voice died away wearily as she saw her mother's vexed expression.

"*Next* year? Oh, *c'est à ne pas y croire*! Which in case you do not understand, means it's beyond belief!" Cora was much given to sprinkling her conversation with French phrases, having spent her eighteenth year in Paris, and enjoyed every hour.

"I know it well enough, Mama. I could hardly grow up in your vicinity and *not* know French!"

"Nor will you have spent all that time with me and not understand that I cannot possibly wait so long for a new gown! I have Shropshire society to consider, so cannot possibly countenance turning out in anything less than à la mode. This is May 1805, and trains are no longer the thing, or had you not noticed? What will Temford town think if I turn out in my old frills from Bath? Worse, if *both* of us do that?"

"Mama, a Bonfire Night assembly is at issue, that means a traditional fifth of November junket at a country town inn, not a grand coming-out ball in London! The Royal Oak's new assembly room will open with what passes for a ball, however, followed by a display of fireworks as poor old Guy Fawkes is once again being burned in effigy on a bonfire, after which everyone will go home. But I will not be attending, so you need not fret on the score of both of us turning out in tired fashions."

"But your twelve months of black will be over by then."

"You may not approve of full formal mourning, Mama, but I do. Getting myself up in fínery to dance the night away on almost the very anniversary of Geoffrey's death simply does not seem appropriate to me. Anyway, that is beside the point. There is nothing to stop you attending, and I think you'll find your old gown will be all that is commendable. You haven't worn it since Bath, nor do I recall the county of Shropshire being present when you did. Even if someone was there and does recall, they are not going to think anything they do not think already. Everyone *knows* how reduced our situation has become."

Cora sighed. "Oh, this really is too bad, but if there is no alternative, I suppose I will have to wear the plowman's gauze. However, I still think you should attend, my dear. Close to the awful day or not, the occasion will be perfect for your return to society."

"I've already explained why I do not intend to go, Mama. If I change my mind, you will be the first to know."

"Hmm."

Emily was pricked. "Anyone would think this Bonfire Night frolic was the be-all and end-all of your existence!" she declared as she went to look out of the great bay window with its intricate sixteenth-century latticework. The tiny leaded lights distorted the view of the courtyard outside, fragmenting it like a broken mirror. Rain was falling again, and puddles had collected in the courtyard. A maid hurried across from the gatehouse to the kitchens, and one of the dogs pretended to chase her.

Fairfield Hall was a half-timbered medieval manor house, gabled and elaborately decorated, that was set in a fine park several miles outside the small Shropshire market town of Temford. It was built around three sides of a courtyard that was open to the north, and the whole building was encircled by a moat where water lilies floated and fish swam. The house rose three stories, each one projecting over the one below it, and its main entrance was by a stone bridge across the moat, then through an archway into the courtyard.

Over the centuries the foundations of the house had shifted and the timbers warped, giving the building an astonishingly drunken look, as if at any moment it would lurch to one side or the other, jump over the moat, then reel its way across the park. It was a miracle that it not only still stood, but was likely to do so for centuries to come.

The oak-paneled grand parlor was on the second floor, with the bay on one side, and windows facing toward the moat and rolling park on the other. It contained centuries-old furniture, tapestries, and paintings, the only recently acquired item in the room being the harpsichord Cora had purchased the year before her son-in-law's death.

The hall's parlous financial state had only come to light after Geoffrey Fairfield's demise, and now things were so bad that Emily had serious cause to fear she could no longer manage. She gazed unhappily across the park toward Temford, which clustered below the medieval castle that guarded the ford over the River Teme.

Cora's vexation had increased. "Oh, this lack of money is intolerable."

"I agree, but we have to manage as best we can." The little black ribbons on Emily's lace day bonnet fluttered as she turned to look back at her mother. "And I'm afraid that means the complete drawing in of our fashionable horns."

Cora didn't respond, but her shoulders drooped a little, and she lowered her eyes as if there was much she was leaving unsaid.

Emily relented. "Please understand, Mama. Wardrobes—or the lack of them—are only part of my problems, for I also have other things to consider. There is the running of the estate, at which I have very little experience, and there is also Peter's education and welfare to worry about." Peter was her thirteen-year-old son, at present away at Harrow, although for how much longer such an expensive education could be sustained remained to be seen.

Cora turned away. "Oh, the best laid schemes o' mice an' men gang aft a-gley . . ."

"I beg your pardon?"

"Mm? It's Burns, my dear. 'To a Mouse.' "

"I know that. I just wondered why you said it."

"It doesn't matter." Cora smiled briskly. "You must forgive me, my dear, for I know how tiresome I have been recently."

"Tiresome is your word, not mine."

Cora fiddled with her shawl, tweaking it one way and then the other. "It's just so hard to accept that we have lost nearly everything because of Geoffrey's unbelievable mismanagement. His financial foolishness was quite astonishing, but it might have been rectified if he hadn't expired so unnecessarily . . ."

"Geoffrey did not die deliberately, Mama." An edge had entered Emily's voice.

"No, of course he didn't, but he *did* accept Sir Rafe's challenge to that stupid horse race!" The circumstances of her son-in-law's death had always rankled with Cora; indeed most things about him rankled with her. Geoffrey Fairfield may have possessed one of the most respected names in Shropshire, but she regarded him as an artistic dreamer who thought more of gambling and his beloved portrait painting than he did of providing for his wife and child. As for his close association with abhorrent Sir Rafe Warrender, well, that was quite beyond pale as far as Cora was concerned.

She suppressed a grimace as she thought of Sir Rafe. He had purchased Temford Castle as his country residence about five years ago, and his land was separated from the more modest acreage of Fairfield Hall by the road that led west from Temford into Wales. He was forty years old and undoubtedly eligible, but there had never been a Lady Warrender to temper his excesses. Cora was certain this was because he was in love with Emily—or in lust with her was perhaps a more accurate way of expressing the emotion he felt. Emily's mother considered there to be no depth to which he would not sink in order to get what he wanted, and that he had only cultivated Geoffrey's friendship in order to attempt Emily's seduction. He had always been here at the Hall, Cora mused, even commissioning Geoffrey to paint his portrait, but all the time his hot, sly eyes had been upon Geoffrey's beautiful wife.

Emily wasn't quite ready to be drawn into a discussion about Sir Rafe, nor did she wish to discuss Geoffrey, whom she had loved very much in spite of his many flaws. "Don't say anything more, Mama, for I am not in the mood. We will have to agree to disagree about what happened. Sir Rafe has been in London these past six months, and seems likely to stay there for six months more, and poor Geoffrey isn't here to defend himself either, is he?"

"Defend himself?" Cora was withering. "My dear girl, Geoffrey Fairfield didn't even have the gumption to do *that*! If ever things did not suit him, he simply hied himself upstairs to the long gallery to paint! And although he protested to the contrary, assuming a veritable halo, it has since become as clear as crystal that when he slipped over to the castle for Sir Rafe's gaming parties, he was losing very heavily!"

"Please, Mama." Emily knew it was true, and did not need to be told.

Cora drew herself up. "Oh, very well, I will say no more, except to observe that we both proved singularly unfortunate in our choice of husband." She ran a finger sharply over the keys of the harpsichord, then rose in a rustle of mauve taffeta. She and Emily's father had not seen eye to eye on anything. He had been a bully who squandered her fortune on a tally of mistresses that would have put Charles II to shame, and his widow had not worn black at his funeral.

Emily was incensed to hear their respective husbands referred to in the same breath. "Mama, I trust you are not placing Geoffrey alongside Papa?"

"Well, neither of them was a shining example, was he?"

"Papa left you nothing at all. At least Geoffrey left this house."

"I daresay he did, but it would have been helpful if he had also left you sufficient funds to run it properly!"

Emily bit back a retort about unhelpful mothers who considered costly London dressmakers to be still in order.

Cora came to join her in the bay. "I concede Geoffrey was entirely unsuited to the business of owning and running an estate. However, I cannot forgive him for always putting himself first."

"He didn't!"

"Oh, yes, he did. He may have been the younger son and therefore grew up without expectation of inheriting the Hall, but once he *did* inherit, instead of indulging his passion for painting to the virtual exclusion of all else excepting gambling, he should have applied himself to business. And you, miss, should never have married a man who thought more of easels and portraits than he did of how he was going to care for his family. I know he was handsome, charming, sweet-natured, and generally good company, but such things alone are not enough. His selfish head was in the clouds, but it's your poor feet that are on the ground."

Emily gave her a wry look. "When it comes to heads in the clouds, Mama, yours has recently been as high as his, mayhap even higher. How can you expect me to provide you with a new evening gown when I do not even know if I can afford to send Peter back to Harrow next term?"

Cora gave a start. "It has become *that* bad?"

"Yes. In fact it has reached the point where Mr. Mackay now advises me to sell up and live somewhere more modest. Mayhap a town house in Temford." Mr. Mackay was their banker in the county town of Shrewsbury, and had been a tower of strength and help during recent months. He was doing all he could to stave off the creditors who would otherwise have been threatening legal action.

Cora was appalled. "A town house in Temford?" Her nose wrinkled with disdain because apart from the castle, Temford did not possess any houses she regarded as suitable for persons of their station.

"Mr. Mackay holds many of our debts, Mama. Well, *my* debts, since I am Geoffrey's widow. Anyway, with the best will in the world he cannot keep the wolf from our door indefinitely, so I have to consider what options I have."

"Options?"

"Yes, Mama. You see, there may be a way out of all this . . ." Emily trod with infinite care, for she knew her mother would not like what she had to say.

"What do you mean?" A suspicious note had entered Cora's voice.

"Yesterday I received a communication from Sir Rafe."

Cora froze. "And?"

Emily steeled herself. "He wishes to offer marriage when my twelve months of mourning are at an end."

2

"Marriage?" Cora repeated faintly. "Oh, this is my worst nightmare come true, the realization of every secret fear . . . Please say you jest, Emily."

"I would not jest about such a thing, Mama. Besides, if you do not believe me, I have it in writing." Emily met her mother's eyes frankly.

Cora's face had drained of color. "Sir Rafe Warrender is the most despicable man I have ever come across! Why, his motto is '*La fin justifie les moyens*,' the end justifies the means. I cannot think of anything more fitting for him!"

"He didn't choose the motto, Mama. It has been in his family for hundreds of years."

Cora ignored the comment. "Peter loathes him too, you know that, don't you? Oh, Emily, you cannot possibly be thinking of accepting him."

"I *have* to consider it, Mama. Our finances do not allow the luxury of dismissing it out of hand."

"Oh, how I wish that when I went to see Brockhampton . . ." Cora didn't finish, but turned away and pressed her hands to her cheeks.

Emily was mystified. "Brockhampton? Sir Quentin Brockhampton, you mean?" She knew that Sir Quentin was a prominent man of law in London, although what he had to do with anything she could not imagine. "I don't know what you're talking about, Mama. Why did you go to see Sir Quentin?"

Cora didn't answer, but moved weakly to the window and rested her forehead against the latticed panes.

"Mama?"

"There is nothing to tell you anymore, my dear. The best laid plans, and all that."

Emily was at a complete loss. "You're talking in riddles."

"A riddle is all I have left."

Emily was perplexed, and greatly concerned. "Mama, I have no idea why you have brought Sir Quentin Brockhampton into this conversation, but I *do* know that although you don't like Sir Rafe, his intentions toward me now are honorable."

"Honorable? Oh, you *gull*, Emily! How can you be so blind?" cried Cora, rounding upon her. "He was deliberately leading Geoffrey from the straight and narrow, and every time he came here to sit for that wretched, wretched portrait, he watched you with such burning eyes that I marvel he did not burst into flame! You were the only reason he bothered with Geoffrey. By luring him to the castle to gamble, Sir Rafe Warrender was making sure of a hold over him, and eventually over you!" Cora was in full flow now. "And do you imagine Sir Rafe *really* wanted his portrait painted? Geoffrey was accomplished, but he was not a genius like Mr. Lawrence, for whom Sir Rafe sat barely two years ago. The portrait by Geoffrey was a device to get beneath this roof, and if you do not know that, you are a great fool!"

"Mama!" Emily was thoroughly shaken.

"*Please* do not consider this marriage, Emily, for you cannot and must not entrust yourself and Peter to Sir Rafe Warrender."

Emily had to pause to compose herself, and when she spoke again, her voice was calm and level. "Well, since you mention Peter, let us speak of him. He is my responsibility, Mama, and so are all the unpaid bills I have been left with. I repeat, I simply cannot afford to cast Sir Rafe lightly aside."

"Peter would rather beg on the streets than see you unhappy. And you *will* be unhappy if you marry Sir Rafe, believe me."

"You are wrong."

"The private joys you knew with Geoffrey will be a very distant memory indeed! Sir Rafe Warrender will make you utterly miserable."

"Please, Mama . . ." Emily was embarrassed.

"Well, it's true. You are my daughter, and so I know you as well as I know myself. As a woman of the world I can tell you quite plainly, Emily Fairfield, that you need a virile, passionate man to demonstrate every night how much he adores you, and who will pleasure you as much as you pleasure him. Sir Rafe will use you for his own satisfaction."

Emily's cheeks flamed. "You really should not say such things," she said.

"Why not? We are alone, my dear, and a mother should be able to speak bluntly to her daughter. I made a terrible marriage, and I then allowed my true love to walk out of my life . . ." Cora's voice caught as the buried memory suddenly resurfaced.

"Your . . . your true love?" Emily repeated in astonishment, for this was the first she had heard of it.

Cora collected herself. "Yes, my dear, so I knew a thing or two about it when I advised you not to take Geoffrey Fairfield for your husband. He clearly wasn't the man for you, because even though I grant he knew a thing or two between the sheets, in every other respect he was selfish. Whether you admit it or not, I was right about your first marriage, and I am right again now. Sir Rafe Warrender could not be less suitable! All he has to commend him is money and a title, and what price either of those in the dark of night when you yearn for love? If he adored you, instead of simply desiring you, if he put your happiness before his own, if he had a single thought of Peter in his plans, I could forgive him much. But I know him for the devil he is."

"Mama, my days of yearning for love are over."

Cora was horrified to hear such resignation. "Emily Fairfield, you are thirty-three, not one hundred and thirty-three!" Catching her daughter's hand, she pulled her across the room to the carved stone fireplace, next to which a faded mirror had been set into the ancient dark oak paneling. "Look at yourself, my dear, and tell me what you see."

"There is no point in trying to reason me out of this, Mama."

"Humor me."

Emily sighed. "Very well. I see a hard-pressed widow whose happiness ended early last November when her husband was killed in a riding accident, and who has a young son to bring up alone. Oh, and who must also endure her own mother's complete lack of prudence."

Cora smiled a little. "Well, *I* see a lovely young woman with a great deal of happiness still to live for. I see a heart-shaped face of quite exquisite daintiness, golden brown hair that should never have been guillotined of its glorious long curls, and I see a pale skin that I would have rejoiced to possess in my youth. I see beautiful hazel eyes that are capable of turning most men's hearts over, and a sweet figure that is as perfect now as it was at sixteen. It certainly should *not* be hidden beneath black bombazine for a moment longer than necessary! I also see a gentle character that should never, *ever* be exposed to the awfulness of Sir Rafe Warrender!"

"You flatter me, I think, Mama," Emily murmured.

"No my dear, I merely speak the truth."

"Nevertheless—"

"I haven't finished yet," Cora interrupted. "Lastly, when I look at you, I see a warmth and vibrancy that needs a very special man, a once-in-a-lifetime man such as all women yearn for in their heart of hearts. I found mine, but I let him go. It was the worst decision I ever made, and not a day goes by even now when I do not regret it."

Emily turned in astonishment, longing to ask questions, but Cora made her look in the mirror again. "Look at yourself, Emily. Your once-in-a-lifetime man is out there, and I know you will find him. Believe me, his name is *not* Warrender! Wait and see what the future brings . . ."

"That is the whole point, Mama. How many times must I repeat that I cannot afford to wait? Our debts are accruing by the day, as Mr. Mackay has been reluctantly obliged to remind me."

Cora released her. "Your mind is made up, isn't it?" she said resignedly.

"I think it has to be, Mama."

"You will be throwing away your chance of happiness, just as I did all those years ago." Cora gazed wistfully at the rain. "Oh, I wish Felix were here."

"Well, Felix isn't here, and I really cannot see what difference it would make if he were," Emily said. Felix Reynolds was her mother's distant cousin, who was much older than she, and had spent most of his life abroad. It was a mystery why her mother always yearned for his advice in times of crisis, for he had never figured greatly in her life. He was an explorer of distant lands, and had last been heard of five years before, when a letter from him had been brought from Venezuela by a sea captain with whom he had struck up a friendship in Caracas.

The captain had come to the Hall and stayed for several weeks while Cora plied him with questions about Felix. All the talk of foreign climes and mysterious civilizations had so caught Peter's interest that from then on the boy had regarded Felix as the example he wished to follow. Emily could only hope it was a phase that would run its course, for the last thing she wanted was for her only son to set off across the world into the dangerous unknown.

Cora managed a smile. "You're right, of course. Even if Felix is still alive, he will be well on in his seventies now, and anyway I do not know if he changed his mind about . . ." She stopped speaking.

"About what?"

"He promised, you see. He said he would do something, but it seems he did not. Unless, of course . . ."

"Yes?" Emily prompted, heartily wishing her mother would divulge whatever it was.

"Sir Quentin Brockhampton, may have . . . Oh, there is no point in saying anything, for there is no proof at all, one way or the other."

"For heaven's sake, Mama, *explain* what you're talking about!"

Cora remained silent, and there was such a strange look in her eyes, a yearning for things lost, that Emily suddenly realized the truth. "Is Felix your once-in-a-lifetime man, Mama?" she asked gently.

"Yes," Cora whispered, tears welling from her eyes. "Oh, Emily, you will never know how much I wish I had gone with him when he begged me to."

Emily was startled. "Gone with him? Exploring, you mean?"

"Yes."

Emily recovered a little. "Well, I hardly think an exploring life would suit you, Mama. There are not many assembly rooms along the Amazon."

"That's all you think I am good for, isn't it? Indulging in a social diary that is as packed as possible? Well, let me tell you that my year in Paris as a young girl gave me what the Germans call *wanderlust*. As it happens, I have never been abroad since, because I married and then had you to consider, but I have never stopped *wanting* to go. If I could turn the clock back, I would not hesitate to fling caution to the winds. I'd have sailed the world's oceans with Felix. We belonged together, but I shrank from that final step because I was a wife and mother. I could hardly take a child exploring in South America."

Emily stared at her.

Cora gazed at the falling rain, seeing the forsaken happiness she could never regain. "If I'd thrown in my lot with Felix, it would have been the making of me. Oh, my love for him is no longer the great passion it once was, but it will never die completely. He will always occupy a very special place in my heart."

"I can't imagine you as an intrepid explorer, Mama. Could you really have clambered up the Andes, or carved your way through a tropical jungle? It just doesn't seem, well, you."

"It isn't the me I have become. It is certainly the me I might have been."

Emily felt guilty for criticizing her mother earlier. "I know I have sniped most horridly at you today, Mama, but I love you very much. You know that, don't you?"

"Yes, my dear." Cora patted her arm.

"Are you going to explain the mystery about Sir Quentin Brockhampton?"

"No."

Emily sighed, but nodded. "Well, I cannot force you."

"Nor I you, it seems. If your mind is made up about Sir Rafe, there is little more to say, except to beg you not to do anything precipitate. Wait as long as you can before finally accepting him."

"I will wait until the twelve months are up."

"And do not be hasty even then," Cora pressed.

"Mama, our debts will not permit it."

"But something might turn up!"

"And it might not. Sir Rafe has thrown a lifeline, and I will drown—we all will—if I do not seize it."

Cora struggled to maintain her composure. "Something *must* turn up, Emily. I will pray with all my heart that between now and November you will be saved from all threat of Sir Rafe Warrender!" Catching up her skirts, she hurried from the room.

3

That same day, on the other side of the world in Peru, John Lincoln—Jack to his friends—stood within the handsome enclosed balcony of the hillside hacienda overlooking Lima. "Do not ask me again, Felix, for you know I cannot possibly leave you now," he said quietly, deliberately not turning to look back into the shadowy but well-ventilated room, where Felix Reynolds lay propped up on the pillows of a huge rococo bed.

"But there is nothing more you or Cristoval can do for me, m'boy. Not even Cristoval's Indian servant Manco can speed my recovery with his Inca medicines and magic. I will be a long time recuperating from this illness, and while I languish here doing that, you and Cristoval should get on with your lives."

"We'll do as we choose, not as you see fit to command." Jack gazed steadfastly through the unglazed wooden lattice window, watching his and Felix's good friend Cristoval, the owner of the hacienda, issuing orders to the two Indians who had charge of the gardens. Don Cristoval de Soto was a Creole nobleman who could trace his ancestry to one of the original Spanish conquistadors. He had been a widower for twenty of his fifty-five years, and over the past twelve months had become a close companion of the two Englishmen. Over the past few weeks he had gladly placed his hacienda at their disposal because of Felix's poor health.

The hacienda was luxuriously decorated in the Spanish colonial style, with silk wall hangings, gilded furniture, and paved gardens of quite exquisite beauty. The month of May marked the onset of winter in this hemisphere, and Lima was obscured by the thick drizzling mist known as the *garúa,* or

Peruvian dew. If it were not for this, Jack would have been able to see not only the capital but also as far west as the port of Callao, some seven or eight miles away on the shores of the Pacific. Small earthquakes rocked this part of the world once or twice a week, and truly destructive earthquakes happened once or twice a century, so that nothing seemed permanent, except perhaps the snow-capped peaks and ancient Inca mysteries of the great Andes cordilleras.

Peru was an amazing country, but Jack now longed for England again. He was tired of being an exile. If there must be a mist, he wished it to be English mist, the sort that prevailed in a wood on a crisp autumn morning, with the luminous glow of imminent sunshine, not this soaking haze that never quite became rain. Felix, on the other hand, would never tire of Peru, and even now that his health had let him down, he did not yearn for the land of his birth. The old man had for some time been finding it increasingly difficult to climb mountain paths in search of remote Inca ruins, and eventually had been obliged to concede that he needed to rest. So the three friends had come to the hacienda, where Felix had promptly succumbed to the ague that was so very prevalent in the coastal regions.

Felix spoke again, his voice thin and weak where only a few weeks ago it had still been firm and strong. He was slightly built, and his hair, once dark, was now a mere tonsure of gray. His green eyes had become watery, but their gaze was still steady. "Admit you are homesick, Jack. The Swedish merchant vessel *Stralsund* sails from Callao next week, bound for Stockholm by way of Bristol with a cargo of silver, and you could be aboard her. Damn it all, man, can't you see that I *want* you to go?"

"Cristoval and I would now be at the bottom of Lake Titicaca if you hadn't hauled us out, so don't expect me to desert you." Jack smiled. What a strange trio they were he thought: an elderly English gentleman who chose to spend his life wandering, a young English gentleman who was an unwilling exile, and a lonely Creole nobleman who longed to wander but never had. A shipwreck on Lake Titicaca had brought them together the previous year. Until then Jack had been going his own aimless way, following a life that was filled with adventure but lacked purpose. Felix and Cristoval had given him a new outlook, and at last he wanted to return to England to pick up the pieces of an existence that had become little more than a dream vaguely recalled.

Felix turned his head to survey his young friend's silhouette against the latticework. "You're a stubborn fellow, Jack Lincoln."

"That makes two of us, I fancy," Jack replied as he came back into the room. He was thirty-five years old, tall and lean, but muscular too, with broad shoulders and slender hips. His eyes were the vivid blue of the southern ocean, and his skin was tanned from months in the Peruvian sun, which had also bleached his brown hair to blond. There was a ruggedness about him, a rough and ready air that marked him as one of life's adventurers, yet five years ago he had been an elegant man of fashion, a leading light of London's high society, and the darling of many a belle. And he had worn with measureless pride the great signet ring called the Agincourt ring, which had come into his family in 1415, when Henry V, who had worn it into battle, had presented it to Jack's ancestor in appreciation of conspicuous bravery.

That privileged society life—and the Agincourt ring—were now denied to Jack Lincoln because the courts had wrongly declared he was not after all the heir to his family's fortune. Instead, the law in all its majesty had found in favor of his deceitful cousin. Denied the right to appeal, Jack Lincoln was now penniless and cast adrift, robbed of the precious heirloom he had worn every day from the moment of his majority.

Now the Agincourt ring graced his cousin's thieving finger instead, and Jack was no longer clad in the latest modes. Instead, he wore leather breeches and a half-buttoned shirt, with an Inca necklace of solid gold around his throat. With his fair hair loose about his shoulders, he could not have looked less like an English gentleman if he had tried, yet a gentleman he was, and an honorable one at that; too honorable by far to countenance leaving a sick friend.

Felix continued to study him. "If I were well now, would you return to England?"

"That isn't a fair question, and you know it."

"Fair or not, I now know the answer. So Jack, if you won't

go willingly, maybe you will go if I beg you to do a favor for me?"

"A favor?"

Felix nodded. "I want you to help my daughter."

Jack looked at him in astonishment. "I didn't know you had a daughter!"

"She doesn't know it either. Her name is Emily, and she lives at Fairfield Hall, near Temford in Shropshire," Felix replied with a faint smile as he took something from beneath the pillows. It was a miniature of Emily that Cora had sent about ten years before. Geoffrey had painted it.

Jack gazed at the lovely face and the long golden brown curls that had been caught with a ribbon so that they tumbled in cascades to her shoulders. "She's very beautiful."

"She is indeed, and she has my eyes, I fancy." Felix looked at him. "Jack, I'm afraid I was guilty of bedding another man's wife, and enjoying every delightful damned second of it. Emily's mother, Cora, is a cousin of sorts, too distant for there to be any problem at all regarding consanguinity, which is just as well, because she is the most bewitching creature I have ever known. She married an oaf who did not deserve her, and in her unhappiness she turned to me for comfort. Even though I was a good generation older, I was more than willing to offer her that comfort, and Emily was the result. I begged Cora to leave England with me, so that we could begin a new life together, but she felt she could not because of Emily."

"Well, a life clambering over the Andes is hardly to be recommended for a woman and child," Jack pointed out, returning the miniature, then going to pour two glasses of the maize liquor known as *aguardiente*.

"Maybe not." A lump rose in Felix's throat as he thought of the family that should have been his. He gladly accepted the glass Jack pressed upon him. "I have seen Emily only once since I left, when I returned very briefly to England and managed to get myself to Fairfield Hall. She has a child of her own now, a boy, Peter." Felix paused to collect himself. "For obvious reasons I have never acknowledged my daughter or grandson, but I have followed their progress through Cora's letters. Emily believes she is legitimate, and for the sake of her reputation that is how her mother and I wished it to stay."

"I can understand that," Jack said.

"Cora wrote last autumn," Felix continued, "but the letter has taken until now to reach me, having gone first to Venezuela because that was where I was when last she heard from me. It seems Emily's husband died quite suddenly in a riding accident at the beginning of November, leaving her very poorly provided for, and Cora acted upon an arrangement she and I agreed upon many years ago. You see, I left a sum of money—not a fortune, but all I had in the world—in the safe-keeping of my then lawyer, to be used should either Cora or Emily ever find themselves in need. Well, they are both in need now, but when Cora went to the lawyer for the money, the scurvy knave told her he knew nothing about it."

"Presumably he pocketed it himself?" Jack leaned back against a table.

"Probably; indeed, I almost wish it were so, but the identity of Emily's neighbor leads me to suspect there is more to it. This neighbor is rather too interested in Emily for Cora's peace of mind, to the point that when she wrote the letter she expressed a strong fear that when the twelve months of mourning are at an end, Emily will be driven into his arms by financial need. The neighbor's name is Sir Rafe Warrender."

"Warrender?" Jack straightened sharply.

"Yes. The name is no coincidence, Jack, for it is the same man you have every reason to despise."

A nerve caught at Jack's temple, for Rafe Warrender was the cousin who had managed, with the aid of false evidence, to convince the courts that he, not Jack Lincoln, was the rightful heir to the family fortune.

Felix watched him. "Warrender succeeded over you because he has influence in high places. He moves among prominent politicians, and it is my guess that he knows many an awkward secret. If he didn't, his sleight of hand with legal documents in your case would not have passed unchallenged."

"It is a small comfort to know that," Jack replied dryly.

"I know. Anyway, although I knew of Warrender through you, this is the first I have heard of him from Cora. About five years ago, just after his victory over you in the courts, he purchased Temford Castle, which is adjacent to Fairfield Hall. Cora tells me that from the moment he arrived he clearly had a fancy for Emily, but she was a faithful, adoring wife. Now she is a widow, burdened with debts, and impoverished to boot. Cora envisages Warrender offering marriage to persuade Emily into his bed. How was it you once described him? As 'a silken serpent, agreeably patterned, but poisonous?' I cannot bear to think of such a man marrying my daughter, my only child . . . Jack, I want you to return to England to stop him."

4

"And how am I expected to do that?" Jack asked patiently.

Felix closed his eyes and sighed. "I don't know, Jack, but I want you to try; indeed, I *beg* you to try. If I—we—do nothing, Warrender might very well succeed in persuading Emily into wedlock, especially if she is in such dire financial straits."

"But if Cora mistrusts him so much, surely she will steer Emily away from—"

"Emily is a widow with many debts and a growing boy to consider. To her Warrender is security, not folly."

"Did her husband really leave her destitute?" Jack's face registered disapproval of such a circumstance.

Felix nodded. "According to Cora, Geoffrey Fairfield was a charming wastrel, a skilled lover, and a portrait painter of some merit, but he lacked common sense or business acumen. Cora mentions debts to the sum of forty thousand guineas."

"Forty thousand? Dear God above . . ."

"Now Emily must struggle to keep Fairfield Hall, provide for her boy, *and* give Cora a roof over her head as well, because believe it or not, Cora's wretch of a husband was an even worse provider than Fairfield! All in all, I am desperately afraid that Cora's fears are well founded, and that a timely offer from Warrender would be accepted."

"You mentioned your lawyer earlier, and seemed to hint at a connection with Rafe."

"Yes. You see, the lawyer I so unfortunately chose thirty years ago was Sir Quentin Brockhampton."

"But he was Rafe's lawyer at my hearing!" exclaimed Jack.

"I know that now, but he wasn't when I knew him." Felix drew a deep breath. "You see, it was because I learned from you that Brockhampton now acts for Warrender—at least, he did five or so years ago—that warning bells sounded through me from the moment I received this last letter of Cora's. Jack, I find it very suspicious indeed that Brockhampton denied all knowledge of the money I left in his charge. You know from bitter experience that Warrender likes to twist the law in order to get what he wants, so it is a little too convenient that my purse should disappear, thus ensuring that Emily and Fairfield Hall remain in jeopardy. I smell collusion."

"I think I do too." Jack ran an agitated hand through his long blond hair. He had been trying not to think of his thieving cousin Rafe, trying not to let bitter memories affect him, but this brought it all back. He drained his glass and placed it on the table. "Supposing I do go back to England, what exactly do you want me to do?"

"Time is still on our side, Jack, but it is beginning to run out. There are just over five months to go until this coming November, when Emily's year of mourning will be over. The voyage from here to England takes about five months too. If you leave on the *Stralsund* you could go to Fairfield Hall and try to find a way of rescuing them all from debt, and from Warrender." Felix held Jack's gaze. "If you are my friend, you will not refuse me in this."

"I fail to see how I can rescue them from forty thousand guineas of bills! And aren't you rather overlooking the small fact that Emily may not *want* to be rescued from Rafe? What if you and Cora are wrong anyway, and he has no designs upon Emily?"

Felix put a hand against his heart. "I know Cora is right, Jack. I fell it *here*." He paused, still keeping Jack's gaze. "I also know that you and Emily are right for each other."

Jack stared at him. "You think what?" he gasped.

"You heard me, my friend. If you set your mind to it, Emily will be an easy conquest. Marry her, Jack."

Thoroughly shaken, Jack continued to stare at him. "You take my breath away," he said at last, shaking his head incredulously. "First you tell me about a daughter you've never mentioned before, then—quite blithely—you add that you want me to solve her financial problems and make her my wife!"

Felix's countenance became troubled. "Jack, I have a deep

feeling that tells me that Emily should become Mrs. Lincoln. It's a feeling that is so strong that it has kept me awake every night since I received Cora's letter. I've wrestled with the demon of my conscience, and now I *know* I'm right about this. I want you to look after her, to be her lover, Peter's mentor, and Cora's protector. I need to know they are all safe under your capable wing. Can't you understand that? They must be shielded from the Warrenders of this world, and you are that shield, m'boy." He held out the miniature again, and pressed it into Jack's hand. "Look at her, man. Look at her! Can you tell me you will not love her?"

Jack looked at the lovely painted face. "No. Nor can I tell you that I will. Love does not come to order, like a new hat!"

"All I ask—no, all I *beg*—is that you at least go to Fairfield Hall for me. Will you give me your word on that? And if love should follow, as my heart tells me it will, then all well and good."

"Love will not be of any help at all where the debts are concerned. I am still the church mouse that I was when I left England," Jack reminded him.

"I know that, m'boy, but I still ask you."

Jack eyed him. "Is there something you aren't telling me?"

"No." Felix was all innocence.

"You are a tricky old devil, Felix Reynolds."

"I know it, sir, I know it."

Jack smiled resignedly. "Very well, I promise to go to the Hall and do all I can, which to be truthful I anticipate will not be much. Neither do I know under what pretext I can go there."

"The last is easy. I have written to Cora and want you to deliver the letter, just as the sea captain did from Venezuela. No, no, keep the miniature, for I wish you to have it. Look at it whenever you doubt your purpose. You and Cristoval will leave on the *Stralsund* next week."

"He's coming as well?" Jack was surprised.

"Yes. I have already discussed all this with him."

"Including your wishes regarding a marriage between Emily and me?" Jack did not know whether to be indignant or not.

Felix cleared his throat. "Er, yes, as it happens."

"So the truth of it is that you are sending him along to see that I keep my word?"

"Certainly not. He has always longed to see the world, but has never had the temerity to leave Peru. How better to realize his ambition than by sailing with you to England? I doubt if he even intends to go to Fairfield Hall, but plans instead to tour the country, commencing with London. Look, be totally honest, Jack. There is no point in either you or Cristoval staying with me now, for I will simply lie here each day getting grumpier." Felix paused, expecting a rude comment, but none came, so he continued. "A muleteer has already been engaged to carry all the baggage to Callao. Manco has the arrangements well in hand. Er, by the way, as I understand it, Manco will be going with you as well."

"Will he indeed? At the very least he'll frighten the horses." Jack hardly dared imagine the stir Cristoval's Indian manservant would cause in England! Manco played his flute whenever the mood took him, danced if he judged the gods to desire it, and every dawn and dusk he sang loudly in praise of Viracocha, supreme God of the Sun. He was very proud of his Inca ancestry and lived by Inca laws and practiced Inca magic, in which he was very skilled indeed. If summary justice seemed necessary, Manco did not hesitate to carry it out. Woe betide anyone who crossed him, for he was apt to be very free with bow and arrow, blowpipe, sling—and sorcery. From time to time he also indulged in the ancient Inca pleasure of coca-chewing, which gave him boundless energy and brought out his mischievous side. Nothing amused him more than to slip the tricky herb into others' food, just to see what happened. There was no doubt that all these traits, together with his red-and-yellow poncho and brightly patterned woolen hat, which had a pointed crown and flaps over the ears, would make the British populace sit up and take notice!

Felix grunted. "Frighten the horses? Let him, for they are foolish creatures. Give me mules or llamas any day."

"Unfortunately, there aren't many llamas in England."

Felix eyed him, suddenly needing reassurance. "So we are *definitely* agreed upon all this, Jack?"

"Yes. I've given you my word, and I will stand by it."

The sick man smiled and drew something else from beneath

his pillow. It was a purse, which he pressed upon Jack. "Take this. It does not contain the crown jewels, but the coins it does contain I estimate to be worth around five hundred pounds. Enough to provide you with a suitable wardrobe when you arrive in England."

"Felix, there is no need—"

"No? I thought you were a church mouse."

"I am."

"Right, so take this purse. I happen to know that you don't possess any fashionable clothes these days, just things that are suitable for exploring the Peruvian hinterland! That being so, you can hardly grace the grand parlor at Fairfield Hall looking as if you have just wandered out of a jungle or descended from the cordilleras."

Jack looked into his eyes. "Which once again raises the obvious point that my lowly financial circumstances hardly make me a suitable husband for Emily. My honor forbids me to court her, Felix. Geoffrey Fairfield left her impoverished, and I cannot improve upon his record, so I will be doing her no favors by—"

Felix interrupted. "Trust in fate, Jack."

Something in the older man's eyes prevented further argument, so Jack accepted the purse. "All right, I'll take it, but only in order to give it to Emily or Cora. I shall tell them it is a gift from you. I have my pride, Felix, and I also have sufficient money to buy my own clothes when I reach England. Five hundred pounds will not make much of a dent in forty thousand guineas, but it will help to put food on the table at Fairfield Hall."

That night, as Felix slept, Jack donned a warm brown poncho made of llama wool and woven with a design of serpents and condors, then went out into the garden at the rear of the hacienda. The night air was very cold but clear, the *garúa* having lifted for a while, and as the full moon slid briefly from behind a cloud, the snowy peaks of the Andes were revealed in all their magnificence.

Manco was seated on the ground by a fountain, playing a gentle Inca lament on his wooden flute. His bow, quiver, and capacious vicuna wool purse lay on the ground beside him.

Heaven alone—and perhaps Viracocha—knew what that purse contained, for it was bulging and heavy, and the Indian never went anywhere without it. All that Jack could say for certain was that it held Manco's sling and some stones, but there was much else besides, secret things that the Indian used for his Inca sorcery. Manco's other weapons, his knife and blowpipe, were always secured to his belt.

He was a short man in his mid-fifties, deep-chested and strong, with brown skin and a broad hairless face, and he too wore his red-and-yellow poncho against the night chill. Discs of gold stretched his earlobes, which were just visible beneath the flaps of his knitted hat, and his short hair was combed forward in a fringe. His dark eyes were set deep above a prominent hooked nose, and his expression was impassive; his music, however, was filled with emotion.

Don Cristoval de Soto leaned against the trunk of an evergreen molle tree, gazing toward the distant cordilleras, but he straightened as he saw Jack approaching. "Ah, my friend, you too feel the need for the night air?" He was a slender, darkly handsome man about the same age as Manco, with a mane of iron gray hair that swept back from a point low on his forehead. His brown eyes were quick, and his Spanish ancestry very evident. Unlike Jack's, his clothes were fashionable and European, as were those of all Lima's high society.

Jack joined him beneath the tree as they listened to Manco's flute. The music died away at last, and the Indian looked solemnly at Cristoval. "I definitely go England, Capac Cristoval?" *Capac* or "lord" was a form of address he used both for his master and the two Englishmen.

"Yes."

"Pizarro day today," Manco stated. Pizarro had been the hated sixteenth-century Spanish conquistador who had commenced the downfall of the Inca nation, and thus his name had become Manco's favorite insult. Today the Indian had been hoping that there would not be a bowing to Felix's wishes about going to England, a country Manco had no desire to see, so the fact that Jack had given in meant that the day was indeed a Pizarro day.

Cristoval smiled and nodded. "Yes, for you today is indeed a Pizarro day, Manco."

"And for Capac Jack." The Indian grinned unexpectedly and gave Jack a sly look. "You go England to make Palla Emily your wife?" *Palla* meant "lady."

Jack wasn't best pleased to realize Manco was apparently in on the plan as well. "Yes, not that it is anybody else's business."

"Manco not told, Manco just know," the Indian explained, then looked at him again. "England have llamas, Capac Jack?"

"I fear not."

"Hmm. Pizarro land."

"You may be right."

"Hmm." Manco was about to resume his flute playing when something caught his eye, a small, stealthy movement along the top of a low wall. It was a rat. The Indian reached for his purse and felt inside, then flicked his fingers toward the rat, which was all of thirty feet away. The rat gave a squeak, jumped up in the air, then leapt away on the other side of the wall.

Jack stared, then looked at the Indian. "How do you do that?" he demanded, for it wasn't the first time he'd witnessed such a thing.

Manco gave a mysterious smile. "Inca magic. Manco have favor of Viracocha," he said, then raised his flute to his lips.

As the music rippled over the garden again, Jack looked inquiringly at Cristoval, who shrugged. "Do not ask me, my friend, for I do not know either."

5

It was just after dawn on Thursday, October 31st, Halloween, five days before the betrothal, when the *Stralsund* made landfall in the Bristol Channel. The weather was fine but cold, with a brisk breeze that filled the sails and whipped white tips upon the waves. Seagulls soared and screamed as Jack, Cristoval, and Manco stood on the starboard deck, watching the shore of North Somerset slip by. Five months had passed since the vessel set sail from Caliao, and Peru seemed so far away that it might as well have been on the moon.

During his years in exile Jack had almost forgotten the war in Europe, but the reminders had started almost from the moment the *Stralsund* reached the Atlantic. A Royal Naval frigate had tracked the Swedish vessel on the final few days of the voyage, for which they had reason to be thankful when a French man-o'-war loomed on the horizon. But the Frenchman hadn't come near, and not a shot had been fired.

Jack's thoughts turned to the promises he had made to Felix. How on earth was he going to carry them out? It was one thing to give his word to do all in his power to solve Fairfield Hall's financial difficulties and at the same time save Emily Fairfield from the possible designs of Rafe Warrender; it was quite another to actually achieve either aim.

All he had was Felix's letter, and the purse of five hundred pounds he intended to give to Cora Preston. What if both were gratefully accepted and he was immediately but politely shown to the door? What could he possibly do then? He needed to be close at hand if he was going to do anything; ideally he needed to be actually at Fairfield Hall. Otherwise how in God's own name was he going to know what was going on and be able to take any necessary steps? There was another aspect of it all that he had yet to consider properly, and that was the thought of coming face-to-face with Rafe again.

"Pizarro land," Manco said suddenly, his face and voice devoid of expression. As far as he was concerned England was already a grave disappointment. There weren't any real mountains to be seen, not a single snow-whitened peak or summit lost in cloud, and he did not like it at all. He tugged his hat down by its flaps, then drew his poncho more closely around his body.

Beneath the poncho the Indian was clad in a brown tunic that was lavishly embroidered with Inca symbols, and his loose cross-gartered dark blue trousers reached down to his ankles. His waist belt was hung with his bulging purse and small arsenal of weapons, and in his arms he clutched a plaited-reed box containing certain Inca medicines, and a variety of spices and herbs with which to give his food what he considered to be acceptable flavor. To Jack's uncomfortable knowledge, it also contained a supply of coca, which Manco had administered to a fellow passenger, a Flemish pastor who had been instantly transformed from a religious bigot into a singer of bawdy songs, which he bellowed from the top of the mainmast during a storm.

The Indian looked hopefully at Cristoval. "We go home again soon, Capac?"

Cristoval smiled as his mane of gray hair streamed in the wind. He wore a heavy cloak over a crimson coat and fawn breeches, acceptable attire that certainly would not cause the stir his servant would on disembarkation. The wind had played havoc with his neckcloth, and the Atlantic winds had long since convinced him it was foolish to wear a tall hat on board ship. "We will return in due course, Manco. Now remember, there are things that simply will not do in England."

"Things, Capac?"

"You must not shoot birds or anything else with a bow and arrow, or bring down a horseman with your sling."

Manco scowled, but said nothing. Cristoval was referring to an alarming incident when an albatross had escaped unscathed, but Captain Gustavus of the *Stralsund* had lost his tricorn! It was fortunate that Gustavus had a sense of humor, otherwise Manco knew he would have been put ashore at the next port of call.

Cristoval continued. "Nor must you use your knife to threaten anyone who displeases you, or poke ladies who don't happen to be moving quickly enough to suit you."

The Indian raised an eyebrow. "Lady too slow."

Jack grinned. "Ladies are allowed to be slow, Manco, especially when they are negotiating a difficult hatchway, as this one was. But whatever they are doing, you are not allowed to prod their posteriors."

"Hmm."

Jack sighed. "And while we are speaking of such things, the British do not eat guinea pigs."

"No?"

"No. And if I catch you offering the wrong people a chew of coca, so help me I will dispose of your entire supply. Pious Flemish pastors are definitely the wrong people. I want your word about this, you are not to give it to anyone, is that clear?"

Manco looked as if he had just been requested to drink ditch water, but nodded. "Manco gives word."

"Good."

The Indian scowled at the shore again.

Jack's attention returned there as well. His own feelings about England were mixed, for he was a stranger here now. His sun-bleached hair fluttered around his shoulders, his poncho flapped as fiercely as the sails overhead, and his gold necklace shone against his tanned throat. An English gentleman? Who would believe it to see him now? Emily Fairfield certainly wouldn't, for he looked more fit for piracy on the high seas than for sipping tea in an elegant drawing room! But he intended to undergo the desired transformation before he met her for the first time. He'd wear fashionable clothes, have his hair cut in the latest style, and be all that was acceptable in polite circles.

He drew the poncho more closely around him, and as the wind gusted and spindrift flew on the roaring air, something in his heart began to lighten. He was home again, and it felt good.

While the *Stralsund* was sailing the final leagues to Bristol, Emily was on her own at Fairfield Hall, waiting for Sir Rafe

Warrender to call. The skies of Shropshire were as clear and blue as those over the Bristol Channel, but there was no wind at all. It was one of those absolutely perfect fall days, timeless and mellow, when the last of the apple harvest hung plump and rosy in the orchards, and smoke from chimneys floated vertically toward the heavens.

Sir Rafe had returned to Temford Castle the day before, and sent word that she should expect him that morning. The moment Cora and Peter learned he was coming, they made plans to be elsewhere. Directly after breakfast Peter had gone out roaming in the park, as he did most days, and Cora had gone in her chariot to the stores in Temford market square in search of new trimmings for her evening gown, Bonfire Night now being less than a week away.

Peter had been removed from Harrow several months before, and made no secret of being bored and resentful. He had become a moody, difficult boy, quite unlike his usual self, and one of his principal ways of passing the time was to stalk people. He was like a predator creeping after its prey, and no one was safe from his activities. It was most irritating to go out in the sunken topiary garden, where one liked to feel cozy and private within the centuries-old enclosing wall, only to become aware of a furtive figure slipping from shrub to tree to shrub behind one! Or to sit at one's desk, composing a pleading letter to a creditor, only to realize that Peter had tiptoed into the room to hide behind the curtains.

This all conspired to convince his mother that marriage to Sir Rafe was her only option. Apart from the need to defray her enormous burden of debt, Peter needed a father's steadying influence. There was no reason to believe her mother's low opinion of Sir Rafe was correct. After all it was not a crime for a man to desire another man's wife, nor was it a crime for him to invite that man to attend gaming parties. Or challenge him to a race on horseback.

Emily had vacillated during the five months since the May confrontation with her mother. Sometimes she had felt that come what may she would remain a widow and try to cling to everything as it had been during Geoffrey's life. At other times she had been so lacking in courage and resolve about the future that several times she had almost written to Sir Rafe in London, accepting his offer of marriage without further ado.

Now the vacillation was at an end. Peter's resentful presence day after day had concentrated her mind remarkably, making her face the fact that Sir Rafe wasn't just *her* salvation, he was her son's as well. Peter needed his life to be safe and settled again; he needed to return to Harrow and his many friends there, and be able to go on with his life as before. His anxious mother's only way of providing all that was to marry Sir Rafe Warrender.

The minutes seemed to drag unconscionably as Emily waited nervously for the promised visit, and she went up to the long gallery on the top floor to watch for Sir Rafe's approach. For the first time in almost exactly a year she was wearing a pretty color again, heather pink. Strictly speaking there was still another day to go before her twelve months of mourning was actually at an end, but she had decided not to wear anything subdued for this meeting. It would surely have been hypocritical to garb herself in even half mourning for an interview that would center upon her definite decision to remarry. Nevertheless, she felt awkward, as if she were letting Geoffrey down, mayhap even beginning to dismiss him from her mind.

The gown she had chosen was three years old, and consequently had a train that was now even more unmodish than it had been last May when her mother had brought things to a head by asking for new togs from a London *couturière*. The heather pink was made of finely woven merino, long-sleeved and high at the throat, and it bestowed a deceptive glow to her cheeks, as if she felt eagerness for the forthcoming meeting. But she wasn't eager at all, just resigned to the only solution to her troubles.

She paced restlessly up and down the gallery's uneven wooden floor, wishing today was over and done with. A brown-and-white cashmere shawl dragged behind her, and after a year of black and gray, she was very conscious indeed of the gown's color. Should she change after all into something more restrained? The olive green dimity perhaps? Oh, she didn't know what to do . . . Why hadn't Sir Rafe arrived yet? she wondered. Had he undergone an eleventh-hour change of heart? Maybe he had met someone he wanted more, another bride who wouldn't bring him just herself, but a fortune as well. Doubt after doubt beset Emily, and with each one her stomach knotted a little more. She felt cold, and every now and then her teeth chattered slightly. She was so filled with nerves that she felt quite ill!

The gallery was seventy-five feet long, and occupied the entire third floor of the west wing. There was no ceiling, just the heavy beams and trusses of the roof, and windows took up every side except the eastern end so that the sun shone in almost all day long. With so much light it had been the perfect place for Geoffrey to do his painting.

His things were as he'd left them on the day he died. It would be a year ago tomorrow she mused, yet seemed a lifetime away now. Paints, brushes, rags, stacked canvases, all lay just as if he had slipped out for a while and would be back at any moment. But he *had* intended to return quickly that November 1st, having only gone out because he and Sir Rafe had a wager about riding each other's horses to the old disused gatehouse on the boundary of the Hall's land and back again. But when it came to horsemanship, Geoffrey was mediocre, and Sir Rafe's black thoroughbred was barely manageable.

Emily drew herself up and took a deep breath. She didn't want to think about the race now, not when she was about to give her hand to the owner of the horse. Geoffrey's death hadn't been Sir Rafe's fault; indeed Sir Rafe hadn't even seen the accident happen, having lost all track of Geoffrey in the boundary woods. He had reached the old gatehouse, found no trace of Geoffrey, then returned to the Hall, thinking himself outridden. He had been distraught with guilt afterward, saying he should never have entered into the wager. But neither should a less than adequate horseman like Geoffrey.

Beset with a sudden feeling of disloyalty, Emily glanced around the gallery. Samples of Geoffrey's work graced every inch of paneling, especially the windowless eastern wall, where he had hung portraits of her, Peter, her mother, and even some of the servants. There was also a fine self-portrait of Geoffrey himself, the eyes of which had seemed to follow her from the moment she entered the gallery.

She went closer to look at it. "Oh, Geoffrey, I miss you so," she whispered, gazing at the sensitive, almost beautiful face. There was French blood in the Fairfields; indeed they had once been called the Beauchamps, and in Geoffrey that Gallic strain seemed to have come to the fore. He was matchless, the dark-eyed, dark-haired personification of French romance, sometimes melancholy, sometimes joyous, always loving. He could caress her with a glance, arouse her with a whisper, and take her to the edge of ecstasy with a single kiss. And he possessed more passion in his fingertips than Sir Rafe Warrender probably had in his entire body. There was not a day when she did not miss Geoffrey; as for the nights, they were more empty and lonely than she had ever imagined possible. She would continue to miss him even if she married Sir Rafe, whose unfinished likeness was still on the easel at the other end of the gallery, where the great south-facing window had always given Geoffrey the best light of all.

Reluctantly, Emily walked the length of the gallery to look at Geoffrey's last work. Sir Rafe gazed haughtily down the canvas, as if demanding that she compare him with the man she had lost. But they were too unalike, both in character and looks. She studied Sir Rafe. His head was almost fully painted, but the rest of him was a pencil sketch that was at once casual and detailed. He had an oval face and even features. It was an oddly expressionless visage, with wide, finely shaped lips, and light blue eyes that seemed almost secretive beneath their heavy lids. His hair was pale chestnut, thinning a little at the temples, but although he was forty, his figure was still slender, with no sign as yet of any thickening at the waist.

He was pictured standing beside a chair that was still in the corner of the gallery. His beautifully drawn hand rested upon the gold-embroidered upholstery—except it didn't simply rest there; it grasped the rich fabric as if proclaiming ownership of every last stitch. Geoffrey had captured him well, for Sir Rafe Warrender grasped everything like that. Soon he would grasp her too. What would it be like to be taken by such a man? In spite of what Mama said, had his considerable experience made him a skillful lover? Or would his lovemaking be perfunctory, an efficient coupling like one of his stallions with a mare? Did it matter? Why concern herself with such things when her heart was not involved? She was using Sir Rafe as a means to an end, so could she in all conscience complain if he used her in the same way?

6

While waiting for Sir Rafe, Emily was in an agony of nerves and unanswered questions, but her thirteen-year-old son Peter was lying idly along a branch overhanging a pool in the woods that cloaked the northern boundary of the park. He dangled a fishing line into the water below. Starlings sang piercingly in the trees, and the guttural tones of a pheasant came from somewhere among the autumn-shaded ferns that covered most of the clearing. The mirrorlike pool was dotted with leaves of yellow, crimson, amber, and brown, and every now and then he could see fish darting like quicksilver in the green depths.

The woodland air smelled of autumn, that strangely invigorating blend of fading vegetation and smoke from garden fires, in this case from a single garden fire, that of the gatehouse, which lay several hundred yards away on the road from Temford into Wales. Directly across that road stood Sir Rafe's castle estate, the armorial gates of which opened impressively from the town square of Temford.

Emily's boy was very like his father, with the same dark hair and rather French features, but he had her hazel eyes, Felix Reynolds's eyes . . . Peter wasn't very tall, nor was he well built, but his boyishly good-looking face promised a handsome man to come. He wore a maroon short-tailed coat, beige breeches, and top boots that had been newly polished when he set out from the house, but were now wet, mud-stained, and very scuffed.

Peter was very conscious of his slight build, and of his unimpressive physical accomplishments. Mentally he was very quick and agile, but when it came to running, riding, or anything that required strength and endurance, he did not show up at all well. He wished he were more like the gatehouse keeper's burly son, Archie Bradwell, who could run like a hare, ride like a cossack, and heave weights that Peter Fairfield could barely move an inch. Archie was also an able fisherman. If he were lying along this branch right now, his sack would be full of fat fish; Peter knew his sack was empty. It was *always* empty. There was no doubt that if they were both marooned on a desert island, Archie Bradwell would survive; Peter Fairfield would not. What point was there in being fluent in Latin if one died of hunger because one couldn't catch a fish!

Only yesterday there had been another humiliating encounter with the gatehouse keeper's son. It had happened in the narrow valley by the rapids, where the River Teme, which flowed through the Fairfield Hall estate, squeezed swiftly between rocks. Peter had been stepping carefully from boulder to boulder, but had missed his footing and fallen into the river. He didn't know Archie was watching from the other bank until he heard the roar of laughter as he hauled himself out by the packhorse bridge a little way downstream. Peter had been so mortified that he ran all the way home. Archie Bradwell was his pet aversion, and if he could best him even once, he'd be very happy indeed!

Right now Peter was too hungry to think about his rival. All he had to eat was an apple he'd stolen from the gatehouse garden about half an hour before. What he really fancied was a toasted currant bun, which he knew he could have if he returned to the Hall, but nothing would drag him back there until Sir Rafe Warrender had been and gone. So the apple would have to do. He hoped it was a good one after all the trouble he'd had stealing it!

He'd had to clamber over the garden wall in view of the gatehouse, and the Bradwells' vicious lurcher had spotted him just as he was making his getaway. The wretched dog had managed to leap up and sink its teeth into his boot, hanging on so grimly that it had been at least a minute before he'd managed to shake it off and drop down to safety outside the wall. Unfortunately, the animal's teeth had punctured the boot leather, so that copious amounts of brackish water had soaked his right foot when he'd run across the swampy area between the gatehouse garden and the edge of the woods. Now his stocking was cold and soggy, and his foot felt quite horrid. As if that was not bad enough, Bradwell had seen the apple thieving in progress, which meant Mama, or maybe Grandmama, would be told of the young master's latest misdeeds. He would be ticked off again, as he had been yesterday when he crept up behind Grandmama just as she decided to check that her garter was secure. It wasn't his fault that she'd raised her skirts and shown her stocking top! Nor was it his fault that people were stupid enough not to like it when he stalked them.

With a sigh, Peter sat up and wriggled into a more comfortable position. More leaves floated down to the pool, landing without a sound and creating gentle concentric circles on the water. A fish plopped, disturbing the patterns, then glided away again, almost as if taunting him. Peter was resentful. If fish could laugh, these were undoubtedly curled up with mirth.

He took the stolen apple from his pocket, polished it on his sleeve, and began to eat. He wished he didn't feel so restless, fed up, and generally bad-tempered all the time. He knew he was upsetting his mother, but he just couldn't help himself. At school he'd soaked up lectures about antiquities and geography like a blotter absorbing ink; now he had nothing to do all day. He had grown up on this estate and knew every inch of it so well that there was nothing left to intrigue him. He itched to travel like Grandmama's distant cousin Felix, who had ventured to exciting places on the far side of the world. How could anyone be satisfied with Shropshire when there was South America to explore? Somewhere as provincial and insignificant as Temford could *never* compare with the wonders of the Incas and the Aztecs!

He finished the apple, and tossed the core away, wiping his hand on his breeches. Then his gaze slid away from the pool toward an old fallen tree that lay in the center of the clearing, its gnarled trunk covered with moss and bracket fungi. Even now he could hardly believe his father had died because his head struck it when he was thrown from Sir Rafe's horse. Tomorrow was the anniversary of that horrible day, yet Mama was wearing pink *today*. It wasn't right, especially not for Sir Rafe!

Tears shone in Peter's eyes. He missed his father so much

that it hurt, and he was so angry about it all that he often felt like going up to the long gallery at the Hall and destroying every last brush and canvas. He blinked the tears away furiously. He wouldn't cry, for he was the man of the family now, and would remain so even if Mama married Sir Rafe! He bit his lip. To have such a stepfather thrust upon him was surely every boy's worst dream. Please let Mama have a change of heart, he prayed. Let her come to her senses and find another way to put everything right.

He began to clamber down from the tree, but paused as he heard a horse approaching. Quickly he scrambled back up to his branch and lay along it to see who it was. Archie maybe? He hoped so, for there might be an opportunity to get back at him somehow for the debacle at the rapids. But it was Sir Rafe Warrender who rode into the clearing, mounted on the same raw-boned black thoroughbred of a year ago.

The horse was still as difficult a creature now as then, tugging at the bit and fighting its rider every inch. Sir Rafe reined in by the fallen tree and slipped lightly from the saddle, keeping an iron grip on the reins. He wore the pine green coat and cream breeches that gentlemen of fashion regarded as de rigueur for riding, and his auburn hair was bright in the autumn sunshine.

Peter remained quiet as a mouse as Sir Rafe began to search for something by the tree. He was very thorough, even going down on his hands and knees to feel underneath. What was he looking for? the boy puzzled. Whatever it was it eluded Sir Rafe, for with a foul oath he scrambled to his feet again, then bent to brush leaves from his breeches. He stood there for a moment, then plunged his right hand into his coat pocket and drew something out, which he looked down at in his cupped hand. Something small and white lay in his gloved palm. His fingers closed convulsively over it, and he closed his eyes for a moment, then replaced whatever it was in his pocket.

After that he widened his search a little, pushing the ferns and poking the moss and leaves with the tip of his riding crop. The minutes passed, and still he did not find what he was seeking. At last he took out his fob watch and looked at the time. Another curse escaped him, and he remounted the impatient horse to ride swiftly away in the direction of the Hall, which lay well over a mile to the south.

Only when the sound of the hooves had died completely away did Peter come down from the tree. He was filled with curiosity as he hurried over to the fallen tree, where the prints of Sir Rafe's boots and horse were plain in the soft ground. After examining what seemed like every nook and cranny and finding nothing, Peter stood with his hands on his hips, surveying the tree as if suspecting it of willfully concealing what Sir Rafe had sought. How the boy wished he knew what had been searched for. And what the small white object was that the master of Temford Castle kept in his coat pocket.

Peter's stomach grumbled suddenly. The stolen apple hadn't even taken the edge off his appetite. Sir Rafe or not, there was nothing for it but to go home. With luck he could slip unseen into the kitchens, where the cook would give him something to eat. Maybe some toasted currant buns! Turning, he ran from the clearing.

7

Emily hastened down from the long gallery the moment she saw Sir Rafe riding toward the house. She had assembled her embroidery in readiness in the grand parlor, and seemed the very picture of industrious composure when he was shown in a few minutes later.

"Why Sir Rafe, how good it is to see you again," she declared, setting her needle down as if she had been stitching away for some considerable time. Then she extended her hand, which he swept gallantly to his lips. His touch was cold, she thought, and she had to remind herself that he had just ridden through the early autumn chill.

"My dear Mrs. Fairfield, how very charming you look," Sir Rafe murmured, gazing into her eyes and continuing to hold her hand in a way that reminded her of his portrait.

"It is kind of you to say so, sir. Would you care for some refreshment?" She summoned a smile and politely withdrew her fingers from his grasp.

"A measure of brandy would do nicely after the ride here."

"Then please help yourself, sir." She indicated the decanter on the table behind the sofa.

He went to pour a large measure. "I trust I find you well, Mrs. Fairfield?" he said, and after a pause went on. "It is good to see you out of black, and a day early at that. May I presume to feel honored?"

She smiled again, but a little awkwardly, and avoided answering. "Er, how was London?"

"Well enough. Pitt is ill again. A surfeit of port. It is believed he will not last another year."

"I hope that is not true, for Mr. Pitt is a great man. Britain needs him at the helm against Bonaparte."

He glanced at her, but did not reply.

She cleared her throat. "Er, have your Foreign Office friends any news from Europe?"

"Sir Lumsley Carrowby says there are conflicting rumors. Some say the French have scored an astonishing victory over a huge Austrian force; others are adamant that not even the inept Austrians could have lost so resoundingly."

"Where is it supposed to have happened?" she asked.

"Somewhere called Ulm, I believe. I cannot say for certain, but if the rumors are true, the French are now advancing on Vienna. Carrowby seemed to think there was truth in it."

Emily had met Sir Lumsley Carrowby, who was a close friend of Sir Rafe's and often stayed at the castle. His position in the Foreign Office meant that there was very little about the war that he did not know, and he was sometimes a little indiscreet with information that might have been better kept secret. "And what do you think, Sir Rafe? Do you agree with Sir Lumsley?" she asked.

"I do not know, Mrs. Fairfield, but I have little faith in anyone's ability to take on the Corsican and win."

She did not approve of praise bcing directed toward Bonaparte. "We will take him on and win, sir, that you may count on. The rest of Europe may flounder and fail, but Britain will stand firm. Mr. Pitt will stand firm. Lord Nelson will drive the French from the seas, and our army will drive them from the land."

He smiled. "How very fierce and patriotic, to be sure," he murmured.

"Of course, sir, for I do not hold with Bonaparte at any price. Nor does my mother."

"Ah, the peerless Mrs. Preston. How is she? Also keeping well, I trust? And your son?"

"They are both in fine fettle, Sir Rafe. Peter has gone out in the park as usual, and Mama has some urgent shopping to attend to in Temford this morning."

"Urgent shopping?"

"Well, no doubt you would not consider it thus, Sir Rafe, but to a woman the trimming of a gown is all important. With only a few days to go to the opening of the new assembly rooms at the Royal Oak . . ." Emily's voice died away awkwardly, for it was clear he knew her family was avoiding him. She shifted a little uncomfortably.

He came around the sofa to stand directly in front of her. The smell of horse clung to his clothes, and she noticed some moss stains on the knees of his otherwise pristine breeches. "Mrs. Fairfield, the absence of your mother and son is of no real consequence, for they are not the ones I have come to see, are they?"

His directness disturbed her, and she felt color warming her cheeks. "No, I suppose they are not," she admitted.

He swirled his glass, and the light from the windows caught the Agincourt ring on his fourth finger. There was a design cut into the gold, a rose badge—actually blue—she knew he had adopted as his own five or six years ago when he came into a contested inheritance through his mother's family. Sir Rafe had not only become a much richer man as a result of this good fortune, but had acquired the ring as well, and the badge engraved upon it now graced his writing paper and flew from the turrets of Temford Castle. Emily could only imagine the resentful thoughts of the relative he had successfully disinherited.

Sir Rafe slid his hand into his right pocket to finger the smooth white quartz pebble he always kept there. It was his lucky charm, and he did not go anywhere without it. If fate was to favor him, then the pebble had to be touched. Yet fate had not favored him in the clearing, when he needed it most . . . He pushed this disagreeable fact from his mind and held the pebble tightly as he spoke again, interrupting Emily's thoughts. "Let us not beat about the bush, Mrs. Fairfield. I have proposed marriage, and now that your year of mourning is over, I have come for your answer."

Well, he was nothing if not direct, Emily thought. "You are still quite certain you wish me to be your wife, Sir Rafe?" Her heart wanted him to have changed his mind; her head willed the opposite.

His pale glance moved over her. "Oh, yes, Mrs. Fairfield; indeed I am more sure than ever."

She was about to tell him she accepted when something perverse rose through her, and instead she found herself asking a very unlikely question. "Do you love me, Sir Rafe?"

The brandy stopped swirling, his fingers clenched over the pebble, and he stared at her. "I beg your pardon?"

"I wondered if you have any affection for me, sir."

He exhaled slowly. "I have always had affection for you, Mrs. Fairfield."

"You have always wanted me, sir, which is not the same thing."

The ghost of a smile touched his lips. "I see that you do not beat about the bush either. Very well, I admit it. I have always desired you. I envied Geoffrey his nights, and I yearn to enter your bed. Is that honest enough for you?"

"It is honest, sir, but I still hear no mention of love."

"Well, do *you* love me?" he countered.

She drew back. "No," she confessed.

A light passed through his eyes. "The future is in the laps of the gods, Mrs. Fairfield. One thing I can promise you, I will not be tardy between the sheets. I have wanted you for so long that you may count upon my being ardent." His fingertips stroked the pebble . . .

She got up quickly to hide her agitation, and went across to the other side of the room to look out over the park. The thought of Sir Rafe's ardency filled her with dismay. She didn't want him to touch her at all! The realization was an icy shock, freeing an avalanche of cold fact that plunged down over her resolve and buried it. What could she say? What could she do?

He watched her, and sensed something of her thoughts. "My dear, you do know that I have your well-being at heart, don't you?"

The new note in his voice made her glance uneasily back. "Yes, of course . . ."

"And that I would never willingly do anything to harm you."

"Yes." She looked intently at him, wondering what he was coming around to.

He did not leave her on tenterhooks. "I fear there are things about Geoffrey that you do not know, important things that have a bearing now."

"Things? What things?"

"To begin with, he had many gambling debts of which you do not know, debts that are over and above the forty thousand you already face. Lady Luck was seldom, if ever, on his side."

Emily's heart stopped within her. "Over and above?" she whispered.

He nodded. "His IOUs were, er, somewhat well known, shall we say? I myself have a considerable number of them. I have been able to prevail upon the other gentlemen involved to stay their demands for the time being, but their patience will not last forever."

Emily gazed at him in alarm. "What are you saying, Sir Rafe? How much did my husband owe?"

"You do not need to concern yourself with that, my dear."

"But I do! Of *course* I do! If these IOUs are called in, they will become my responsibility!"

He smiled a little. "If you are my wife, they will be *my* responsibility, my dear, and I am more than able to pay." In the darkness of his pocket, his thumb smoothed the surface of the pebble, imploring it to work for him.

As far as Emily was concerned, he could not have made things more clear. Marry him and *all* Geoffrey's debts, including those of which she had only this minute learned, would be entirely removed; decline, and her situation would worsen to a degree she had hitherto not even imagined.

He replaced his glass by the decanter and followed her to the window, then drew a slip of paper from the same pocket as the pebble. "Please examine this, my dear. It proves that I am telling you the truth."

She took the paper unwillingly. Geoffrey's spidery writing was unmistakable, bearing witness to the fact that he owed the sum of fifteen hundred guineas to Sir Lumsley Carrowby. "Fifteen hundred guineas?" she whispered.

"You may rip it up, Mrs. Fairfield, for I have settled with Carrowby."

"So I am now in debt to you instead of Sir Lumsley?" She looked out again, just as Peter emerged from the boundary woods and began to run back toward the house.

"Please don't view it in that light, my dear. I am telling you this as proof of the immense regard in which I hold you. If you will marry me, I will gladly settle every IOU Geoffrey ever wrote. And there were many, believe me." He paused, clearly considering whether or not to say the next thing on his mind.

She solved his quandary for him. "Please go on, Sir Rafe, for I can tell there is something else of import you think I should know."

"There is indeed something else of import, but I shrink from mentioning it for fear you will misunderstand. I do not wish to appear as if I am, er, blackmailing you into marriage."

"Blackmailing?" She felt suddenly cold. What else had Geoffrey done? What else *could* he have done?

He cleared his throat. "This is a matter of great weight, Mrs. Fairfield, and believe me I do not pass it on lightly, but I wish you to know that I am at pains to be honest on all fronts."

"Please tell me what it is, Sir Rafe."

"Very well. You know that Sir Lumsley Carrowby is in the Foreign Office, and many of my other guests at the castle are politicians as well, among them even cabinet ministers. All of them are men of the highest importance, patriotic men who would lay down their lives for their country. Unfortunately, Geoffrey's loyalty to Britain was perhaps not as complete as it might have been."

Emily's heart turned to stone. "What are you saying?" she whispered.

"That there was a little too much French blood in your late husband's veins. On the night before he died he attended one of my gaming parties at the castle, and I caught him going through Carrowby's private papers. I made him replace the documents as he found them, and I requested him to leave the castle immediately. For your sake, and Peter's, I did not raise the alarm."

Emily's hand crept wretchedly to her throat. "No!" she breathed. "No, I will not believe it of Geoffrey . . ."

"It is the unpalatable truth, my dear. I came here the next day to confront him. He admitted his treachery, but declined to discuss anything in the house, for fear that you or your mother might overhear. The wager about racing each other's horses was concocted as a flimsy excuse to leave the house without arousing undue suspicion. When he set off like the wind on my thoroughbred, I confess I thought he was going to make a run for it, but my mount was no match for the black thoroughbred. I lost him in the woods. When I came back to the Hall and there was no sign of him, I became quite convinced he had decamped rather than face the scandal of exposure. He hadn't of course, for he was dead because he had fallen from my horse."

Emily stared, so stunned by what he was saying that she could not utter a word. She didn't believe it, *wouldn't* believe it. Not of Geoffrey. And yet, there *had* been times when he had voiced support for some of the French objectives. To hide her anguish, she turned to look out of the window again. Peter was coming nearer and nearer to the house. The wind blew his hair, his coattails flapped, and now and then he kicked out at a tuft of grass in that way boys have. He looked so very young, so very defenseless . . .

Rafe set asidc his empty glass, then slipped his hand into his pocket again, touching the pebble a little uneasily. *Work for me! Be my aid!* "Er, have you nothing to say?"

She swallowed, feeling so close to tears that she struggled to find her voice. "I . . . I find it very hard to accept that Geoffrey would do this awful thing, Sir Rafe."

"Of course you do, my dear; indeed, it would not be natural if you did not find it so. But, painful as these facts are, they *are* the truth." Standing behind her, he took her gently by the arms. "Geoffrey's activities are at an end now, and no good can come of raking over the ashes and spreading them on the world's hearth. I have only told you because I do not wish to have secrets from you. I want you to know that I will protect Peter from the ignominy of knowing his father was a bankrupt traitor. A clean slate, Mrs. Fairfield—Emily . . ."

It *was* blackmail, she thought, no matter how much he pretended it wasn't. He had closed the trap around her as neatly as any poacher, and now, whatever her opinion of him, she *had* to do as he wished if her son was to be shielded. Her gaze did not move from Peter, and as the boy disappeared around the corner of the house she nodded. "Very well, Sir Rafe. I accept your proposal."

She heard his breath escape on a long sigh. "Ah, my dear, you have just made me the happiest of men."

And made myself the most unhappy of women, she thought, knowing that she now despised the man she had just consented to marry.

He took his hand from his pocket and moved away. "I think it best if we announce the match in public, don't you? The Royal Oak assembly on Bonfire Night will be the perfect occasion."

"Oh, but I . . . I wasn't going to attend . . ." she began, her thoughts still a wild confusion of opposing emotions.

"Well, perhaps you should reconsider."

Again she felt the cold caress of blackmail.

"The year is at an end," he continued smoothly, "and you have discarded mourning. Think on. A goodly portion of the county will be there, so it will be the perfect occasion. Then we can be married by special license a week after that."

She began to feel as if she were careening downhill in a runaway carriage. "No! I . . . I mean, the betrothal can indeed be announced at the assembly if that is your especial wish, but I would like to wait awhile before the marriage itself takes place."

"But why? Surely your debts need settling without delay?" His eyes had cooled.

Emily could not have been made more aware that financial salvation and the avoidance of horrendous scandal hinged upon bowing to his will. "Yes, they do need settling, Sir Rafe, but it is my birthday on Christmas Eve, and I would dearly like to remarry then."

His expression cleared, and he smiled again. "A Christmas Eve wedding? I had no idea you were of such a romantic inclination, Emily."

"You do not know me at all yet, Sir Rafe." *But I begin to know you, and what I know I find abhorrent . . .*

"Just Rafe will do," he stated.

She gave a quick laugh, then turned away. "It, er, feels a little strange not to use your title."

"We are to be intimate, Emily, so have no need of titles between us."

Intimate? Geoffrey was the only man with whom she had ever been that . . .

"It is agreed then? We announce the match at the Royal Oak on November 5th, and then arrange the wedding itself for Christmas Eve?"

"Yes." She forced herself not to shudder as his fingers touched her hair.

"Just one thing, Emily. While it is obvious that we do not wish Geoffrey's treason to become common knowledge, I also think it best if we keep the IOUs secret as well. It is our business and ours alone, and for Peter's sake I think it best not to harm Geoffrey's memory in any way at all."

She managed to nod.

8

Cora had just returned from Temford with her purchases when she found Emily waiting for her in the low-ceilinged hall, which was directly below the grand parlor. A bowl of chrysanthemums stood on the octagonal table in the great bay window facing the courtyard, where the coachman was carefully turning her chariot in order to take it around to the stables. Firelight danced in the stone hearth and cast moving shadows over the oak paneling and green-and-white painted medieval plasterwork.

Cora's footsteps sounded on the stone flags as she put her packages on the table. Her glance rested shrewdly on her daughter's face. "You've accepted him?" she asked as she teased off her gloves. She was dressed in a pelisse and matching gown, coffee trimmed with wine red, and there was a flouncy ostrich plume in her hat.

"Mama, you knew that was why he was coming here today."

"Nevetheless, I still hoped . . ." Cora broke off, for Peter had appeared in the doorway that opened into the passage from the courtyard through to the knot garden at the rear of the house. He stood there, his face very pale and still, and although Cora knew she should tell him to go away, she did not have the heart. After all, this concerned him as well. So she continued to speak to Emily. "Yes, I knew why Sir Rafe was coming here today, but I confess I rather hoped it would not happen."

"It is done now. The betrothal will take place at the Royal Oak assembly."

"I see." Cora surveyed her. "Are you pleased with your decision to take such an odious creature as your next husband?"

"Pleased is hardly the word I'd choose." *Resigned is more appropriate*, Emily thought.

Cora eyed her. "Answer the question, Emily. Are you pleased with your decision?"

"I'm satisfied it is the right one. And before you start wagging your finger and telling me that my once-in-a-lifetime man is waiting somewhere for me to find him, let me remind you that a lifetime can be very long. I might not find this paragon until I am in my dotage, by which point I will be past caring how wonderful he is!" Catching up her skirts, Emily turned toward the doorway, then immediately halted as she saw Peter. "I suppose *you* are about to berate me as well?" she said.

His eyes—so like Geoffrey's—were accusing. "Only if you are really going to be Lady Warrender. Please say you will look for another way to—"

"Have either of you paused for a single moment to consider what is going to happen if I do not do this?" Emily broke in.

"We can manage, Mama," Peter said.

Cora backed him. "Yes, I'm certain we can, Emily. Why, we can close half the house, sell some—"

"We *can't* manage!" Emily cried. "Do you honestly imagine I would be considering this marriage if I didn't have to? Things are far worse than you know—worse than even I realized until a short while ago!"

Cora looked urgently at her. "There is something new, isn't there, Emily? Something you aren't telling us?"

Emily faced her. "Nothing that you did not know already," she said untruthfully. "The matter is settled, and I will not hear any more argument. The match will be announced at the Royal Oak on Bonfire Night, and the marriage will take place on Christmas Eve." Gathering her skirts again, she fled into the passage and then out into the garden.

No one followed. For a long, long moment there was silence in the hall, broken only by the ticking of the longcase clock in the corner. Cora closed her eyes to compose herself. When she opened them again, her gaze fell upon Peter, who had not moved from the doorway. "Well, young man, you are about to wish you had scuttled off when you had the chance."

"Oh?" he looked warily at her. Which of his sins was he to be upbraided for now?

"On my way back from Temford, I was waylaid at the gatehouse by Mr. Bradwell, who informed me that you have been stealing his apples."

"Only one!" the boy protested indignantly.

"One, two, or a dozen, the crime is the same. You are not to do it again, is that clear?"

"Yes, Grandmama." His lower lip jutted. "Are you going to tell Mama?" he added.

"Not this time, for I think she has enough to think about right now."

"I'm not doing any harm," Peter grumbled.

"You are, sir, for you are stealing. And when you insist upon creeping around after people, spying on them, you are intruding most grievously upon their privacy. I daresay you think nothing of it, but I'll warrant you would not like it if someone followed you to the privy, mayhap even spied upon you through a knothole!"

"That's different!" he cried indignantly.

"Is it? Where do you draw the line between what is acceptable and unacceptable? I'm told you watched the maid Betsy meeting her sweetheart in the stables last night. Is it true?"

He didn't reply. There were tittle-tattlers at every corner in this horrid house!

"Ah, the eloquent silence," Cora said. "Clearly you did do it. It has come to something if young lovers cannot meet after their duties for the day are over without being observed by a Peeping Tom. It is not to happen again, do you hear? Either you behave like a responsible young man, or you will rue it. That is all. You may go."

He turned on his heel and dashed away before she could change her mind. "Oh, Peter, Peter what has come over you of late?" she murmured sadly.

9

That evening found Jack Lincoln dressed modishly again for the first time in years. It was after dinner, and he leaned against a brightly lit streetlamp on Bristol's Broad Quay, wearing a caped dark green greatcoat over a pale gray coat and cream breeches. A top hat rested at a nonchalant angle on his head; there were gloves on his hands, and he carried a cane. The figure he presented now was a far cry indeed from the Jack Lincoln who had boarded the *Stralsund* at Callao.

One of Bristol's finest tailors, on being offered a handsome bribe for his trouble, had produced from a storeroom two outfits and a greatcoat that had already been made for another customer. The garments had just been completed for a gentleman who had fallen ill and therefore would not be able to attend his final fitting for another month or more. The tailor knew he could easily make the clothes again within that time, and so parted with them most willingly, well satisfied with such unexpected and lucrative business.

Jack had then purchased shirts, neckcloths, hats, gloves, night attire, and all the other accessories a gentleman of fashion might require. Now he was once again the stylish English gentleman—except perhaps for his hair, which he had not been able to bring himself to have cut. Instead, he had tied it back with a length of black corded-cotton ribbon. He felt he needed to retain some part of him that was unconventional.

Darkness had fallen several hours before, and Broad Quay, known as the Street of Ships, was quiet at last. The night air was cold, and his breath was visible in the lamplight, but he didn't feel the chill. The quay had grown up along a channel of the River Avon that reached into the heart of the city. Here the tide rose and fell between twenty-five feet, accommodating even the largest seagoing vessels. The masts and rigging of what seemed like a hundred ships formed an almost impenetrable forest on the water, among them the *Stralsund.* Because the tide was out, her deck was well below the level of the quay. Earlier, when the tide was in, the decks had been too high to see onto.

Jack's greatcoat was unbuttoned, and his thumbs were hooked over the waist of his breeches as he surveyed the scene. Opposite the moored vessels was a line of shops, inns, and gabled houses, and between these and the water's edge was an area of cobbles where casks of molasses and rum were piled beside drums of tobacco and bales of silk.

Children's laughter made Jack glance over his shoulder. Turnip jack-o'-lanterns bobbed as some little boys, faces blackened, ran past dressed as mummers. The mark of Halloween was all around, even in so busy a port, and most of the houses on the quay had lanterns in the windows. The flickering faces had greatly alarmed Manco when he saw them just after dinner. An explanation about All Hallows' Eve had not helped. A festival of the dead? Of wicked spirits roaming the night? Manco knew enough wicked spirits of Inca origin without encountering those feared by the Christian church as well! He fled to his attic bed at the inn, and vowed not to emerge again before the safety of daybreak.

Footsteps sounded on the sturdy wooden plank that stretched up to the quay from the *Stralsund*, and Captain Gustavus came ashore. Jack called out to him. "Good evening, Captain."

The Swedish captain turned, then came over to him. "Good evening, Lincoln," he said in his impeccable English. "Are you longing for the *Stralsund* already?" He was a short man, broad-shouldered and ruddy-complexioned, with keen blue eyes and a gruff voice. He did not so much walk as roll, which strange gait resulted not from his years at sea but rather from the fact that one leg was very slightly longer than the other. He was dressed for traveling, in a fur-edged cloak and new tricorn.

Jack grinned too. "Damn it all, Gustavus, I've had enough of your leaking old scow to last me a lifetime."

"I will have you know she's one of the best vessels on the ocean."

"Then heaven help the rest."

The captain laughed and tugged on his gloves. "I am going to

London now, where I intend to live well for a week or so before continuing to Stockholm. Then I fear it is Lima again for me."

"You ply the same route all the time?"

"It is tedious but profitable." Gustavus drew a deep breath. "So I take it I will not have the pleasure of your company when we sail?"

"No."

"What of Don Cristoval and that Indian fellow he has in tow?"

"Ah, well, that I cannot say. Don Cristoval has not indicated how long he intends to stay, but Manco is already keen to go home. He decided that England was not to his liking before we even entered the Avon."

"I hope he stays here, for he is one of the *last* passengers I desire to see again." The captain tapped his new tricorn as he remembered the fate that had befallen its predecessor.

Jack gave a chuckle. "Once seen, never forgotten, that is Manco," he murmured. The Indian had caused the anticipated astonishment when he came ashore because he proceeded to sing a loud paean in praise of Mother Earth, whom he called Mama Pacha. He then brought the quayside to a complete standstill by performing a stately dance of thanksgiving for the safe passage. Only then had he consented to accompany the others to the Queen of the Indies inn, which Captain Gustavus had recommended.

The captain turned as a carriage rattled along the quay and halted in front of a nearby chandlery. "Ah, my post chaise has arrived. I'll take my leave then, Lincoln. *Alt god lyckan.* Good luck." The two men shook hands, then the Swede hastened away.

As the sound of the chaise died away into the night, Jack fell to pondering again. It was good to be on terra firma, especially English terra firma. And it was good to taste English food once more. Only here were to be found such delights as beefsteak pie, with hot yellow mustard and light-as-a-feather puff pastry that had risen to over an inch thick. Oh, how he had enjoyed his dinner tonight, starting with smoked mackerel and horseradish sauce, then the beefsteak pie, and finally apple tart made with the sharpest codlings and served with sweet custard. When he thought back to the times he had sat by a campfire under an Andean moon, longing for just such a meal . . .

Cristoval had enjoyed the repast as well, but Manco, needless to say, had disapproved of everything. He had produced his plaited-reed box, taken out a selection of spices and herbs, and proceeded to "doctor" every dish placed before him. The result appeared most unappetizing, but he had eaten it all.

"Looking for some company, sir?" inquired a seductive female voice. Jack turned to see a lady of easy virtue standing there in a pink muslin dress and white woolen shawl. Her hands were provocatively on her hips, and there was an inviting smile on her painted lips. She was in her early twenties, he supposed, and pretty enough, with straw-colored hair and a curvaceous shape that was too scantily clad for such a cold night. He could see how she tried to hide her shivering.

"No, thank you," he replied.

She didn't walk on, but permitted her glance to move saucily over him. She liked what she saw, and his long blond hair attracted her too, for it made him interestingly different, a little exciting even. "Are you sure, sir? I know how to please a man . . ."

"I said no, and I meant it," he said firmly, but fished in his pocket for a coin. "Here, take this and get yourself something warm to eat. You look half frozen."

She hesitated, but then took the coin. "I can come to you later if you like," she offered.

"I have other things on my mind tonight."

"Who is she?"

"She?" He looked blankly at her.

"Whoever is on your mind. It has to be a woman."

Jack smiled. "I was thinking of beefsteak pie, as it happens, but if a lady had been on my mind, her name would have been Emily."

"She's lucky, your Emily." Turning, she hurried away.

His Emily? Jack smiled. How could she be "his Emily" when she didn't even know he existed? Well, he supposed she'd know soon enough now, for he had engaged a post chaise to convey him to Shropshire the next day. It would take two days to reach Fairfield Hall. And while he was thus engaged, Cristoval and Manco intended to go on to London. He did not know when he would see them again, or indeed if he ever would.

10

Jack was still en route to Fairfield Hall when Cristoval and Manco reached London, where they immediately repaired to the nearest coffeehouse for some refreshment after the journey. At least, Cristoval repaired to the nearest coffeehouse; Manco remained outside. By now the Indian was convinced that the British made coffee that was as undrinkable as their food was inedible, so he chose to drink fresh water from a nearby horse trough. This action caused some surprise among passersby—and aroused no little indignation from the horse that happened to be drinking from the trough at the same time.

After this, Manco sat cross-legged on the pavement next to the coffeehouse doorway. He took out his flute and began to play in praise of Viracocha, whose bright orb was beaming down from a flawless blue sky. Immediately, a crowd of onlookers began to collect, including some ragamuffin children who clustered around giggling and staring. Several passing carriages drew up at the order of their gentlemen occupants, who observed with curiosity the strange figure in the colorful hat and poncho.

Cristoval tried to pretend he had no connection at all with the Indian. He found a quiet corner table, the last unoccupied one in the room, placed his copy of *The Times* before him, and smiled up at the bonny serving girl who brought him a large cup of dark, sweet coffee. Then he settled to relax for a while after the long hours on the road from Bristol. Except that relaxation was not easy to come by when there was an increasing commotion both inside and outside the coffeehouse. Everyone was fascinated by the brightly dressed Indian, and the crowd on the pavement grew by the moment so that before long the street itself was almost completely blocked. A bootmaker, whose premises were next door to the coffeehouse, became greatly incensed by the interruption to his trade, and came out to ask everyone to move on. When they wouldn't, he sent his boy to find a parish constable. Manco played on regardless, so lost in his Inca melodies that he seemed totally unaware of what was going on around him.

Cristoval wasn't unaware, however. He was fast becoming weary of the trouble Manco caused wherever they went. The Indian had been a liability on the *Stralsund*, at the Queen of the Indies in Bristol, and when they had paused briefly in Bath, where he prostrated himself in a puddle on being confronted by a gouty invalid in a sedan chair. As far as Manco was concerned, only great Inca nobles were conveyed in such litters, so the astonished invalid was treated to a grave and respectful display of subservience.

After that there had been a stir of one sort or another at every stage of the journey. At Chippenham he had been bitten by a disagreeable dog belonging to an equally disagreeable Wiltshire farmer. Manco had promptly bitten the dog in return, and when this provoked outrage from the farmer, the Indian warned him *he'd* be bitten as well if he didn't take his Pizarro dog and go away. Fortunately, the farmer had seen the wisdom of obeying. Now there was this fracas in London.

With a sigh, Cristoval sipped the coffee, which was surprisingly good. All heads in the room were craned toward the goings-on in the street, where the parish constable had now arrived to sort things out. He was a plump, officious fellow, potbellied and self-important, and brandished a cane with which he gestured to the crowd to stand back. Manco played on regardless. Cristoval was sorely tempted to put the Indian on the first ship back to Peru, but feared that Manco would not reach the end of the voyage without provoking someone to murder!

Cristoval was so lost in his thoughts that he hardly glanced up as a gentleman asked if he minded sharing the table. "No, no, be seated by all means," Cristoval replied, waving the newcomer to the chair opposite.

"It is always busy here," said a thin, rather nasal voice.

"If they always serve such excellent coffee, I can well understand why," Cristoval said, looking at his companion at last. The gentleman was about his own age, stooping, and very sallow, with a long nose upon which spectacles were perched. He wore a powdered wig and dark clothes, and held a bundle of letters and legal documents that he placed carefully on the table.

The man smiled. "I am fortunate to find a place at all with all the fuss going on outside. Some savage fellow with a pennywhistle."

Savage fellow with a pennywhistle? Manco *would* be flattered, Cristoval thought.

The man made himself comfortable. "London is becoming a terrible place, sir. There is always something to cause a nuisance."

Cristoval smiled, then indicated the papers. "You seem a busy man, sir."

"I am indeed, but do not complain. The law is a demanding profession. Today, however, I could have done without quite so much to do."

"Today in particular, sir?"

The man nodded. "I suddenly find myself about to embark on an unexpected journey. It is a great inconvenience." He realized he should introduce himself, and extended a hand. "Sir Quentin Brockhampton, your servant, sir."

"Don Cristoval de Soto," Cristoval replied, taking the proffered hand, but his thoughts quickened. *Sir Quentin Brockhampton?* The name rang a bell . . .

Sir Quentin looked up at the serving girl, who appeared at the table. "Your finest Turkish coffee, and some ratafia biscuits to settle my stomach for traveling."

Suddenly, Cristoval remembered why the man's name was familiar. Sir Quentin Brockhampton who suddenly knew nothing of the money Felix gave him to keep for Cora Preston. Surely London could not harbor two men of law of the same title and name?

Sir Quentin looked curiously at him. "By your name, appearance, and voice, I know you cannot be English, sir. May I know from where you hail?"

Cristoval hesitated, for some reason disinclined to answer truthfully. "I am from Spain, sir," he replied.

"Ah, Spain. Land of excellent wines."

"I am honored that you think so, sir."

The Turkish coffee and ratafia biscuits were brought, and Sir Quentin reached for the cup, but as he did so, his sleeve brushed the bundle of documents, which slithered to one side. Some fell to the floor, and Cristoval bent to retrieve them. The very first letter he picked up was addressed to Sir Quentin at his chambers. It had been written by Sir Rafe Warrender of Temford Castle. Yet another name that was only too familiar! With lightning presence of mind, Cristoval slipped the letter inside his coat, then straightened to hand the other papers he'd recovered to Sir Quentin, who was grateful.

"You are most kind, Don Cristoval. I fear we legal fellows are always trying to carry too many documents around."

"Better too many than too few, Sir Quentin."

"Ah, indeed, indeed," murmured the other.

Outside, the disturbance centering on Manco was still in progress. The increasingly furious parish constable had not met with assistance when it came to clearing the street. The crowd was in an obstinate mood and Manco's flute playing had now become far from melodious, consisting of about six notes played in sequence, over and over again. He had risen to his feet and was performing a jerky little dance, lifting his feet in time to the notes.

People caught up in the jam of traffic were becoming impatient, shouting angrily for clear passage, when a small black-and-white terrier appeared from nowhere and began to bark at the top of its lungs. The constable laid about the little dog with his stick, and Manco's music broke off mid-note. The Indian felt in his purse for whatever it was he kept there, then flicked his fingers at the parish bully, who sat down with a jolt that almost knocked the breath from his body.

This was greeted with a roar of laughter, no one realizing they had witnessed Inca magic. They simply thought the constable had fallen over, and as they didn't like him, they applauded his plight. The terrier became more excited than ever, and rushed to and fro snapping at his ankles. The constable tried to get up, but couldn't. He uttered a curse and lashed out with his stick, which promptly flew out of his hand and landed on top of one of the carriages in the street. The terrier began to leap up and down, trying to get at it, which in turn frightened the horses. They set off along the street before the coachman had a chance to get them in check, and the crowd parted hastily.

A whistle sounded as two Bow Street Runners came upon the scene, and there was pandemonium as people scattered in all directions, not wishing to be apprehended for being involved in a disturbance. The parish constable at last managed to haul himself to his feet, then took to his heels, knowing that something rather unpleasant and exceedingly untoward had just happened to him.

The Bow Street Runners disappeared in pursuit of some known pickpockets who had been busy in the crowd, and gradually the street returned to a semblance of normality. Manco calmly resumed his place on the pavement, put his flute to his lips, and began to play a gentle, soothing tune. This time no one paid any attention to him.

Everyone in the coffeehouse had observed events with interest, and now a babble of chatter broke out, drowning the sound of the Indian's music. Sir Quentin looked at Cristoval. "How astonishing," he declared.

Cristoval gave a genial smile, less interested in Manco than in finding out all he could about the lawyer whose name figured in both Jack Lincoln's past and Emily Fairfield's present. "You mentioned an inconvenient journey?" he prompted.

"Yes. To Shropshire."

Cristoval was hardly surprised; indeed, he'd almost expected it.

Sir Quentin went on, "I have to see a gentleman by the name of Sir Rafe Warrender. It is a matter of some urgency."

"Not bad news, I trust?"

"Well, I'm not sure if it is bad or not; in fact I cannot even be sure that it is the truth, but nevertheless I feel it is information I should pass on because I believe the person from whom I received it to be reliable."

"Then you must act upon your conscience, Sir Quentin," Cristoval declared, dearly wishing he knew what the information was.

"I shall do, Don Cristoval, I shall do." Sir Quentin sipped his coffee. "Mind you, in one way the journey is not inconvenient at all."

"Oh?"

"There is a lady . . ."

"Ah." Cristoval sat back. "A matter of the heart, Sir Quentin?"

The lawyer hesitated, then nodded. "Indeed so, Don Cristoval, although I fear my stock is not all that high in this instance. I have met her only once, and on that occasion the news I had to impart was not at all to her liking. However, I sincerely trust I will have the opportunity to renew the acquaintance when I am in Shropshire."

"I wish you luck, sir," Cristoval murmured. "Does the lady have a name?"

"She does indeed. Preston, Mrs. Cora Preston."

Half an hour later, the two men parted amicably, although Cristoval had not managed to elicit any more information from the lawyer. Cristoval waited until Sir Quentin had gone, then took out the purloined letter to read.

> Temford Castle, Shropshire. December 14th, 1804.
>
> My dear Brockhampton,
>
> It is with great pleasure that I enclose a draft upon my bank to the value of two thousand guineas, in payment for services rendered. I am in your debt, and will show my gratitude still further when the lady is mine. In the meantime I will be grateful if you will continue to use all the means at your disposal to tighten the financial noose around GF's estate.
>
> You may be sure you will not regret your decision to assist me in this.
>
> I am, yours etc. Warrender.

Cristoval gazed incredulously at the sheet of fine paper, which had at the top the blue rose badge that really belonged to Jack Lincoln. The letter had been written six weeks after the death of Geoffrey Fairfield, who was surely the GF mentioned in the text. That also meant it had been written not long after Cora Preston had gone to see Sir Quentin about the money Felix had deposited with him before leaving England. Clearly the lawyer's denial of any knowledge of this money was the news that was not at all to her liking.

What "services rendered" might Sir Rafe Warrender be referring to? The timely disappearance of Felix's money? Pressure from Geoffrey Fairfield's debtors and duns? The letter on its own proved nothing, but suggested much. Oh, to have learned the important news the lawyer felt was urgent enough to warrant an immediate departure for Temford Castle.

Cristoval folded the letter again and put it in his pocket. Pure chance had brought him together with Sir Quentin Brockhampton in a London coffeehouse, and Cristoval de Soto was not a man to ignore such strokes of fate. The lawyer was suddenly not the only person for whom a visit to Shropshire seemed advisable. Without further ado, Cristoval left the coffeehouse.

Manco rose quickly to his feet. "We go see Capac Jack?" he said, his tone a statement rather than an inquiry.

Cristoval nodded, not bothering to ask how the Indian knew.

11

While this was going on in London, Jack had driven down through Temford and over the River Teme to take the road that led west into Wales. The fine rolling acres of Temford Castle lay immediately to the north. To the south lay Fairfield Hall, hidden behind its screen of boundary trees. The chaise passed the disused entrance to the Fairfield estate, a dilapidated Tudor gatehouse that was considered beyond repair. A notice on the gates advised callers to go on to the next entrance, about half mile farther on.

As the chaise continued its journey, the woods thinned suddenly, and for a moment Jack was able to see the astonishing half-timbered mansion. He immediately lowered the glass and ordered the postboy to halt. With an irritated curse the man complied, managing to bring the travel-stained vehicle to a commendably smooth halt at the roadside, where the hedgerow was bright with scarlet and black berries and clouds of wild clematis.

Jack alighted and found a gap through which he could see the house. Like others before him, he could only marvel that such a seemingly rickety building had withstood the arduous test of time. As he looked, he saw a woman in emerald green riding toward the woods, who then disappeared behind the trees. Was it Emily, or her mother?

He removed his top hat and ran his fingers through his long blond hair, which was untied now for comfort. Then he returned to the chaise and instructed the postboy to drive on. With a gruff command, the man kicked his heel and urged the tired horses into action again.

The woods were thick and impenetrable at the second gatehouse, beyond which the leaf-strewn drive disappeared among the trees. The gatehouse keeper, Bradwell, came out when the chaise halted. He was a big, rather porcine man, balding, with a pink face and a nose that could only be likened to a snout. He looked up suspiciously as Jack leaned out of the vehicle and addressed him. "My name is Lincoln, and I have a letter for Mrs. Preston."

"I will deliver it, sir," Bradwell said, coming to the chaise door.

"I am charged to give it to the lady in person," Jack replied, then added, "I have come from Peru."

"Peru? Where's that? Down Cornwall way?"

"A little farther, I fear. The other side of the world, in fact." Jack smiled, then noticed a curtain twitch at an upstairs window as a boy looked out. He was tall and well built, with a country face, open and amiable.

Bradwell's eyes had widened. "The other side of the world?"

"That's right."

"Well, I er . . ."

"I think you had better open the gates, don't you? Or is it your job to say who can and cannot call at the Hall?"

The warning tone had the desired effect, and Bradwell hastily flung the gates open and waved the chaise through. The team came up to pace again, and fallen leaves scattered as the vehicle left the road and set off along the drive.

The rider Jack had seen was Emily, and she had reached the edge of the clearing where Geoffrey died. She could see the fallen tree lying among the ferns and the pool overhung by the oak from where she knew Peter liked to fish. She could not bring herself to ride any farther.

Echoes of the past rang painfully through her—Geoffrey smiling at her, making love to her, teasing her, holding her hand as they walked in the gardens, praising Bonaparte as a genius. Rafe's voice whispered slyly inside her. "*. . . there was a little too much French blood in your late husband's veins. On the night before he died he attended one of my gaming parties at the castle, and I caught him going through Carrowby's private papers. I made him replace the documents as he found them, and I requested him to leave the castle immediately. For* *your sake, and Peter's, I did not raise the alarm . . .*" Was it true? Had Geoffrey been spying for the French?

Without warning a pheasant burst noisily from the undergrowth, flying up past the mare's head with all the whirring clatter that such a bird can make. The mare reared, and the sunlight was blinding through the canopy as Emily lost her balance. She fell with a scream, jarring herself so heavily on the ground that she began to lose consciousness. Her hat had rolled away, only stopping when its scarf tangled in the ferns.

She lay there, unable to move. Her short golden brown hair stirred gently in a breath of wind that crept idly across the clearing. The daylight began to fade, and the last thing she remembered was something very small and bright shimmering on the fallen tree. Then she knew no more.

Her riderless roan mare cantered out of the woods, directly cross the path of Jack's chaise. The startled postboy was forced to swerve to avoid a collision. Jack was flung forward. "What the dickens—?" he exclaimed, then opened the door and jumped down. "What happened?" he demanded.

The rather shocked postboy had already dismounted from the lead horse and was endeavoring to calm it. "A bolting horse, sir. It crossed the drive about ten yards in front of me."

"Bolting?" Jack repeated, immediately thinking of the woman rider.

"Yes, sir. A roan mare. Sidesaddled," he added.

Jack recognized the description. "Where did it come from?" he demanded, scanning the autumn-hued woods for a glimpse of emerald green.

"Somewhere that way, sir." The postboy pointed.

Without further ado, Jack dashed into the trees and soon found the mare's prints in the soft ground. He followed them, pausing now and then to cup his hands to his mouth and call. "Hello?" But there was no response. The prints led farther and farther into the woods, so that when he glanced back he could no longer see the drive or the chaise. He called again, then listened carefully. Still there was nothing.

But Emily had heard him. His voice crept faintly into her unconsciousness, and she stirred. Her eyes opened. The ferns seemed to tower above her, and beyond it the soaring trees which looked as if they scraped the sky itself. Where was she? What had happened? she wondered.

A man's voice sounded in the distance. Or was it nearby? She couldn't tell. "Hello? Can you hear me?"

"I . . . I hear you," she murmured.

"Hello?"

"I'm here," she said. Her voice seemed loud enough to her, but in reality it was little more than a whisper. At last she came to properly. "Here! I'm here!" she cried, struggling to pull herself up into a sitting position. The woods seemed to spin, and she closed her eyes quickly.

"Keep answering!" the man shouted.

"I'm at the edge of the clearing, over here," she called back, and was relieved to see him hurrying toward her, past holly bushes where the berries were already Christmas bright.

Jack ran the last yards and knelt on the ground beside her. He recognized her immediately from the miniature, even though she had cut her hair. Her fragile loveliness almost stopped his breath, and he stared at her, unable to take his eyes away. She was exquisite, vulnerable, and more desirable than any woman had a right to be. No wonder Rafe wanted her. Realizing he was staring, he managed to find his tongue. "Are . . . are you all right?"

"I think so," she said, wondering who he was. She noticed his fashionable clothes but strangely long hair. He was a contradiction, like a Viking invader in Saxon clothes to fool the enemy, or a corsair sailing under false colors. She found him fascinating, and more than simply handsome, for there was something about him, a hint of danger, of the unknown . . .

He brushed a leaf from her cheek. "Do you think you may be injured?"

"I don't think so. I just fell very heavily."

"What happened?"

"A pheasant flew out of the undergrowth right by my horse's head." As if to confirm her words, another pheasant called nearby, a raucous, grating sound that seemed at odds with the woods. As the sound died away, she looked at Jack again. "May I know your name, sir?"

"Lincoln. Jack Lincoln, your servant, Mrs. Fairfield."

Surprise lightened her eyes. "You know my name, sir?"

"I, er, have seen your portrait." He was conscious of her spell weaving subtly around him, trapping him more with each second that passed. Who was the easy conquest now?

"My portrait?" Geoffrey had painted her on a number of occasions, and sold some of them, so this Mr. Lincoln might have seen her anywhere. But what was he doing on her land?

Before she could ask him, he spoke again. "Can you stand?"

"I . . . I'll try," she replied.

He got up and held out his hand, which she took hesitantly. His fingers closed reassuringly around hers, and he pulled her gently up from the ground. She swayed a little, and he caught her quickly around the waist. She smelled of lavender, and it suited her, he thought. "It's all right, I have you," he said gently.

"This is silly—my legs feel as if they don't belong to me."

He picked her up to carry her into the clearing, where the fallen tree seemed to offer a perfect place for her to sit and rest. But as she realized what was in his mind, she was filled with sudden panic. "No! Not there!"

"Why? What's wrong?" He halted, tightening his grip a little, as if by that he shielded her from whatever it was she feared.

"It's where my husband, Geoffrey, died," she whispered.

"Forgive me, I . . . I had no idea," he replied, wanting to crush her close and protect her forever. He glanced swiftly around and saw a mossy bank where he knew there would be primroses in the spring. As he carried her toward it, he could not believe that such an incongruously, foolishly romantic thought had passed through his mind. Because of the glance of a pair of incredible hazel eyes, Jack Lincoln the adventurer had become Jack Lincoln the lovesick swain! But what role did Rafe Warrender play in her life? he wondered. Did she see him as a black-hearted villain or a knight in shining armor?

Emily smiled gratefully as Jack laid her gently down, then looked unhappily at the fallen tree. "Geoffrey fell from a horse here in this clearing, just as I did today, except that I have been more fortunate. Maybe a pheasant caused his accident too; we will never really know. He was simply found by that old tree. He'd struck his head against it as he fell." Something occurred to her then, and she looked at Jack in puzzlement. "How is it that you have come to search for me, Mr. Lincoln? If anyone, I would have expected men from the estate, not a complete stranger."

"Your mare bolted across the path of my chaise."

"Out on the road? Oh, no . . ." She was immediately anxious for the animal.

"Please don't fear for her," Jack replied swiftly. "I wasn't on the road when it happened, but on the drive, going to the Hall."

Surprise lightened her eyes. "To the Hall? Who exactly are you, sir? And what brings you here?"

"I have a letter to deliver."

Oh, no, surely he wasn't another dun! She couldn't help leaping to such a conclusion, because the only letters that arrived at the Hall these days were demands for payment of one sort or another.

He saw her alarm, and so was at pains to put her mind at ease. "Please don't fear it is a disagreeable missive, Mrs. Fairfield, for nothing could be further from the truth. The letter is for Mrs. Preston from Felix Reynolds."

"Felix?" Her eyes cleared.

"I had the good fortune to meet him in Peru about eighteen months ago, and I spent a year in his company. When I left to return to England, he gave me the letter for Mrs. Preston, and a gift for her as well."

"I trust he is well? It is so long since Mama last heard from him that she has been most concerned."

"His health hadn't been of the best before I left Lima, but he was making a steady recovery."

"Have you any pressing plans for the coming days, Mr. Lincoln? Or will you be able to stay with us for a while?" she asked suddenly. "Mama will wish to pump you quite disgracefully about Felix, as she did the last messenger he sent. She would not let the poor sea captain escape for over a month!"

Was it really going to be this simple to place himself beneath the roof of Fairfield Hall? Jack wondered. It was almost *too* easy . . . "Well, I have nothing in particular that demands my presence elsewhere," he replied.

"Then I insist that you are our guest, sir. Besides, I am in your debt." Their eyes met, and she found herself blushing a little. Feeling awkward, she looked away. "Please don't misunderstand, Mr. Lincoln, for it isn't my custom to ask strangers to stay. It's just that Felix means a great deal to Mama, and . . ."

"There is no need to explain, Mrs. Fairfield, for I *do* understand. Your mother means much to Felix as well. Of course I will stay for a few days."

She wondered how much Jack knew about Felix's past. Enough to be aware of his past affair with her mother? His eyes gave nothing away, except . . . She thought she saw something in his glance, an awkwardness, perhaps, as if he knew something of which he did not care to speak. Yes, perhaps he did know that Felix and her mother had been lovers, she decided.

Jack sought something to end the silence that had fallen between them. "Er, are you feeling better now?"

"Yes, although I confess the fall has made me feel a little weak."

"My chaise isn't far away. I'll carry you to it."

"There is no need, for I am sure I can manage."

"I insist," he said, giving her a look that brooked no argument.

Their eyes met again for a long moment, then she gave in. "If that is what you wish, sir . . ."

"It is."

In a moment he had lifted her into his arms again, and as he held her, he was aware of never wanting to let her go, least of all into the embrace of a serpent like Rafe Warrender. Felix had spoken of a feeling that she should become Mrs. Jack Lincoln; Jack Lincoln now shared that feeling . . .

Emily liked being held by him because he made her feel safe for the first time since Geoffrey's death. Rafe did not have this effect because the safety he offered was given a price by his thinly disguised threats. Her husband-to-be did not stir her senses or her body, but this man did—this exciting Viking corsair who had swept her up into his arms as if she were weightless. For the first time since Geoffrey died she was aware of herself, of her feelings and needs, of her desire.

12

The chaise arrived to find the Hall's courtyard a scene of consternation. Emily's riderless mare had just returned, and some men were on the point of setting out to comb the grounds for her.

Peter had already rushed off to the stables for his pony, and Cora was hovering anxiously by the archway as the men mounted their horses. She wore a cream dimity gown, and was distractedly twisting the fringe of her cream-and-brown shawl as she imagined all the awful fates that might have befallen her daughter. Then the chaise swept into the courtyard, and she burst into tears of relief when she saw that Emily was unharmed.

Jack stepped quickly down from the chaise, and lifted Emily out in order to set her carefully on her feet. She smiled appreciatively and accepted his supporting arm. Cora hurried to them, hardly glancing at him in her concern for her daughter. "Emily, dearest! What happened? When your horse returned without you, I—"

"I'm quite all right, Mama," Emily broke in reassuringly. "A pheasant frightened my mare and I fell, but Mr. Lincoln has been my Good Samaritan."

"Mr. Lincoln?" Cora looked gratefully at him, at last pausing sufficiently to notice his fine clothes but unexpectedly long hair. What an intriguing paradox, she thought, wondering who on earth he could be and how he had come to Emily's rescue.

Emily turned to the waiting men. "You may return to your duties, for as you see I am all in one piece."

They nodded and touched their caps, then led their horses out of the courtyard to go back to the stables, which lay behind the house.

Emily quickly introduced Jack. "Mr. Lincoln, this is my mother, Mrs. Preston, for whom you have brought the letter."

"Letter?" Cora repeated.

"Mr. Lincoln met Felix in Peru," Emily said.

Cora's eyes brightened with joy. "Really? Oh, *tout vient à point à qui sait attendre*!"

Emily smiled. "Yes, it seems that in this instance everything does indeed come to him—or rather, her—who waits."

Cora was quite overcome. "Is he well, Mr. Lincoln? Do tell me he is."

"When I took my leave of him, he was on the road to recovery after contracting the ague that is so very prevalent on the coast near Lima."

"But he was definitely recovering?"

"Yes."

"Dare I hope that he received my letter? The one I wrote to him late last year?"

"Yes, and he was anxious to reassure you that he *did* honor the, er, arrangement I understand he had with you." Jack did not wish her to think he was party to her great secret, and so was at pains to pretend that he wasn't. "I, er, do not know what the arrangement concerned, of course, but Felix did instruct me to tell you that if there is fault, it lies not with him but with Sir Quentin Brockhampton."

She was both glad and angry at the same time. "Oh, I'm so glad to hear you say this, Mr. Lincoln. I feared it was a case of *loin des yeux, loin du coeur*."

"Out of sight, out of mind? Not where Felix was concerned, I assure you." Jack drew out the purse. "He wished you to have this. I fear it will not by any means banish all the debts I know beset the Hall, but it was all Felix had, and may help a little."

Cora accepted it and pulled open the strings. Her lips parted as she saw the money inside. "I . . . I do not recognize the coins, sir. Their value is meaningless to me . . ."

"My estimate is that if you exchange it all for sterling, you will receive in the region of five hundred pounds."

She turned shining eyes upon Emily. "Oh, my dear, with this we can stave off the irate tradesmen of Temford *and* settle one or two of the more urgent matters at the bank!"

Jack realized he hadn't given her Felix's letter, so hastily produced it. "I almost forgot . . ."

She pressed it to her breast, her eyes shimmering with tears. "Mr. Lincoln, you will never know how much this means to me. It has been so long since I've heard from him that I was beginning to fear . . . Well, no matter, for at least I now know he was well some while back, and he didn't change his mind all those years ago." She closed the purse. "Would that this was sufficient to keep the Warrender wolf from my daughter's door, but I fear that is far from the case."

Emily gave her an uncomfortable look. "Mama . . ."

Cora was defiant. "A wolf is how I see him, my dear."

"Financial salvation is financial salvation," Emily replied shortly.

Jack read much from this exchange, and his heart sank. Cora's fears about Rafe's intentions had clearly come to fruition, but what was Emily's attitude? Did she regard Rafe with fondness, or resignation? It might not seem from her remark about financial salvation that she thought of him with warmth, but it wouldn't do for Jack Lincoln to make assumptions without really knowing. One thing *was* certain, however—Rafe Warrender was a definite element in the picture that was Fairfield Hall.

Cora spoke again. "Well, I shall not allow the likes of Sir Rafe to spoil my pleasure in Felix's letter and gift. I will send word to the inestimable Mr. Mackay, requesting him to come here at the earliest opportunity." She looked at Jack, feeling she ought to explain. "Mr. Mackay is our banker in Shrewsbury and has been doing all he can to help us. Now then, you must both forgive me, but Felix's letter burns my hand. I simply must go to my rooms to read it." Without further ado she hurried away into the house.

Emily was mindful of her manners. "I trust you have not changed your mind about staying, Mr. Lincoln, for you see how happy you have made Mama."

"I have not changed my mind," he assured her.

She smiled. "Good. I will have the servants unload your things from the chaise, and you will be shown up to a guest room the moment one has been made ready." She began to take a step toward the house, but suddenly felt oddly light-headed.

Instinctively, she stretched out a hand to Jack, and in a moment he had caught her up in his arms again. "A doctor should be sent for, Mrs. Fairfield," he said as he carried her into the house, where the slight, dark-haired figure of Emily's Welsh maid, Gwyneth, was just hurrying downstairs.

Gwyneth became upset on seeing Emily being carried. "Madam? Oh, madam . . . !" she cried, her brown eyes widening with alarm.

"I'm all right," Emily insisted, feeling a little foolish for being so weak.

But Jack did not think she was all right. "Take no notice of your mistress," he said to the maid. "Have someone bring a doctor without delay."

"Yes, sir." Gwyneth bobbed a curtsy, then caught up her gray woolen skirts to hurry away toward the kitchens to find someone to ride to Temford.

Jack carried Emily toward the staircase. "Direct me to your rooms," he ordered, and she meekly did as he said. A minute later he put her gently down on the huge velvet-hung four-posted bed she had once shared with Geoffrey Fairfield. Jack gazed down at her, thinking she looked so lost and alone against the gold brocade coverlet that he wanted to gather her to him and kiss away her unhappiness. The urge to do just this was so strong that he stepped quickly back, as if there was safety in even a few feet of distance. He gave a quick smile. "I, er, should not be in here with you like this, so I will leave you. No doubt Gwyneth will return in a moment."

But as he turned to go, she caught his hand. "Mr. Lincoln . . . ?"

"Yes?"

She looked up into his sea green eyes. "Thank you for all you've done today."

"I've done very little, Mrs. Fairfield."

"It may seem that way to you, but I see it differently."

"I—" He broke off because at that moment Peter ran into the room.

"Mama? Oh, Mama! When your horse returned like that . . !" The boy flung himself down into his mother's arms.

Jack withdrew and closed the door gently behind him. Then

he returned to the head of the staircase, where he paused. The house felt welcoming, as if it wanted him to be there, or so it seemed anyway. But he was at Fairfield Hall because he had promised Felix to do all he could to free Emily from debt—and from Rafe Warrender. How he was going to do it he still hadn't the slightest clue, especially when Emily's feelings were an unknown quantity, but at least he had some days in which to plan a course of action—some days to spend in Emily's fair company . . .

He was about to go downstairs, where his baggage was being brought in from the chaise, when he happened to look back along the passage behind him. He had not noticed before that Cora's rooms lay that way. Her door was slightly ajar, and he could see her seated on a window seat with Felix's letter on her lap. She was gazing across the park toward Temford Castle, visible above the hillside in the distance.

There was a faint smile on her lips. It was a knowing little smile, almost like a secret shared, and it made Jack feel strangely uncertain.

13

The doctor reassured Emily that she had not come to any harm in the fall from her horse, and that all she required was a little rest. He was sure that she would be quite well enough to come down again for dinner, and that by the next day she would be as right as rain again.

After the doctor's departure, Cora made such a great fuss about remaining with her daughter to be certain she was all right that it was left to Peter to entertain Jack. Not that the boy found this an imposition; on the contrary, the moment he realized Jack had traveled so far and wide in the world, especially to mysterious Peru, he became very eager to spend time with him.

The autumn afternoon was drawing in as Jack and Peter walked in the sunken topiary garden, which had been there since the time of Elizabeth. It was a peculiarly private place, made intimate by a surrounding high brick wall, and even though it could be looked into from the house, to walk its path was to feel quite removed from everything. Long shadows stretched across the paths between the carefully clipped evergreens, and the pervasive autumn smell of woodsmoke drifted from the bonfire of leaves the gardeners were burning behind the glasshouses to the south of the house, beyond the moat.

Peter's face was so animated with interest about Jack's travels that from time to time Jack could see Felix's restless spirit in his eyes. The boy was not his father's son, nor indeed his mother's, but almost seemed to be his grandfather's young self, filled with the same urge to wander and explore. Jack knew that this corner of Shropshire would never hold Peter Fairfield, nor would Britain itself; only the entire world would do for someone with such a need to discover more. Above all it would be Peru that drew Emily's boy, and that was because of the Incas.

Manco's ancestors and the wonders they had left behind were of such paramount interest to Peter that he made no secret of his huge disappointment that the Indian had not come to the Hall with Jack. The thought of meeting someone who was actually descended from the Incas was too exciting for words. Peter took in so much about the snow-topped Andes, hidden valleys, lost ruins, and strange rites that Jack doubted the boy would be able to sleep that night.

They sat awhile on a bench in a little stone summerhouse that faced over the garden. It was only about a hundred years old, and had a domed roof supported on Ionic columns. Inside there was a stone bench that looked a little like a low sarcophagus. The setting sun was vivid, and the coming of winter was in the air.

Peter looked hopefully at Jack. "Do you think Don Cristoval and Manco will come here?" he asked hopefully.

"I fear not."

"Oh." Peter heaved a long sigh. "If . . . if I ask Mama and she agrees, will you invite them to come?"

Jack smiled. "Don't forget, I am here for only a few days—"

"I know but if you stay longer?" Peter interrupted.

"I have not made any plans to get in touch with them, Peter, but if I do stay here longer, if I do hear from Cristoval, and if your mother and grandmother are agreeable, you have my word that I will extend such an invitation."

Peter gave him a broad grin. "That would be splendid! Oh, I *would* like to meet Manco. Just think, a real Inca . . ."

"An Indian of Inca descent," Jack corrected.

"That's close enough," Peter replied with a grin, then he shivered. "I say, it's chilly tonight, isn't it?"

"You need a poncho," Jack replied.

"A poncho? That's a sort of cloak, isn't it?"

"Yes, and a very warm garment it is. I have mine with me if you would like to see it."

"See it? Oh, yes, please!"

Jack smiled again. "It is yours, Peter, a gift from Peru."

The boy was overwhelmed. "Do . . . do you really mean that?"

"Of course. It isn't Inca, mind, for it is far too modern. However, I do have something that is truly Inca." Jack undid his neckcloth and unbuttoned his shirt to reveal the gold necklace he still wore.

Peter gazed at it with shining eyes. "Oh, I say, how absolutely first-rate! One day I will have such a necklace. I will go to Peru and find treasure that eluded the conquistadors. Maybe I will even find a forgotten city!"

Jack wondered what Emily thought of her son's ambitions. "I'm sure your Mama will not like you to go so far away."

Peter's jaw jutted mutinously. "Mama will not care, for she will soon be married to Sir Rafe."

"Oh?" Jack's heart lurched. He had already guessed that a marriage was in the air, but to hear it actually said . . .

"Grandmama and I hate Sir Rafe, for he is odious in every way, but Mama wants the match. They are to be betrothed at the Bonfire Night assembly at the Royal Oak, then the wedding is to be on Mama's birthday on Christmas Eve."

Christmas Eve? Jack felt unutterably stricken. *Ye gods above*, he thought, it was as if the dearest thing in all the world had been wrenched from his arms. Yet he barely knew Emily Fairfield! He had gazed upon her for the first time a matter of hours ago, but already he knew he loved her. How the wheel of fate did turn. Instead of Emily herself being the easy conquest Felix had predicted, it was Jack Lincoln whose hitherto inviolate heart had submitted without struggle. He was Emily's captive, her prisoner, to do with as she pleased; but it pleased her to marry Rafe Warrender . . . "Er, your Mama must love Sir Rafe very much if she is prepared to marry him in spite of how you and your Grandmama feel," he ventured.

"No, she doesn't love him. Grandmama says it will be what the French call a *mariage de convenance*."

Jack almost felt like leaping to his feet with a cry of triumph! She didn't love Rafe! All was not lost! But all he said was, "I see."

The rather ridiculous rush of victorious emotions subsided almost immediately, for the definite existence of a match meant that Rafe was bound to call at the Hall, where he would come face-to-face with Emily and Cora's unexpected guest. This unavoidable fact was something Jack had been pushing to the back of his mind, and now he wished he hadn't; indeed, he wished he'd owned up to the kinship the moment Rafe's name had been mentioned. But it was too late now. The moment had passed, and he'd inserted himself beneath the roof of the woman who was to be Lady Warrender! He would have to cross the bridge of his meeting with Rafe when he came to it, and in the meantime concern himself with his promise to Felix.

Peter and he returned to the house shortly afterward, for the sun had almost gone down and the air was decidedly chilly. After resting awhile in the comfortable third-floor bedroom he had been given, Jack then got ready for dinner. Before going downstairs, he studied himself in the mirror, thinking how far away now was the rover who had explored the streets of Cuzco and sailed upon Lake Titicaca. Tonight he was respectable again, and with his long hair tied back and thus invisible when he looked directly into the glass, he could see once more the Jack Lincoln who had been one of the most sought-after men in London.

He supposed such clothes as these suited him, for he could not find fault in the way the black silk coat and white silk breeches showed off his tall, leanly muscular figure. It was the vogue to have evening coats too tight to be buttoned, thus exposing the white satin waistcoat and lace-trimmed shirt beneath. It was also the vogue for the line of the coat to taper away to the tails at the back, thus revealing how his silk breeches clung to his hips and thighs, as well as to another more private portion of his anatomy. He smiled a little wryly, for since his return to England he had heard much comment about immodest female fashions, but not a great deal about male fashions, which to his mind were just as shocking.

As he made his way down to the dining room, he encountered Cora at the head of the staircase. She was wearing a bottle green silk gown and pretty embroidered shawl; a little ivory fan dangled from her white-gloved wrist, and there were pearls at her throat. A hint of rouge warmed her lips and cheeks, and she had placed an aigrette in her silver hair. Her beauty still shone out, and Jack could well understand why Felix loved her so very much.

"Why, Mr. Lincoln, how every elegant you look," she declared, inclining her head gracefully.

He bowed. "In spite of my regrettably long hair?" he replied with a smile.

"Well, it suits you, to be sure." She toyed with her fan. "Felix writes very highly of you, Mr. Lincoln."

"Then I am honored, Mrs. Preston, for I regard him as the finest man I have ever known."

"Oh, I do too, Mr. Lincoln, I do too." Cora paused. "It is strange that he does not mention the purse in his letter."

"Oh?" Jack met her eyes.

"Well, I suppose it does not matter. The mere fact that he sent it is sufficient. I have already written a note to Mr. Mackay, instructing him to come here as soon as he can. I will send someone with it in the morning, and imagine we will receive a visit the day after." Cora smiled again. "Did Felix speak much of me, Mr. Lincoln?" she asked suddenly.

"Yes, with the greatest affection and longing," Jack replied honestly.

"I appreciate your candor, sir."

Candor? He knew he was tiptoeing around the facts like a ballet dancer!

Cora held his gaze. "And did he speak of Emily?" she asked lightly.

"I . . ." Jack squirmed, then ran his fingers through his hair. "Yes, Mrs. Preston, he did."

"So you know . . . ?"

"Yes," he said quickly. "But if you fear I will say anything, please be assured that your secret is safe with me."

She searched his face. "I know it is, Mr. Lincoln, for Felix would not praise you so highly if you were anything less than a paragon."

"A paragon is something I definitely am not, Mrs. Preston," he replied with feeling.

"Oh?" Their eyes met. "Is something wrong, Mr. Lincoln?"

The question concentrated his mind. "Er, no, of course not, Mrs. Preston."

"You seem a little . . . Well, I'm not sure what you seem, but you seem it, nevertheless." There was a small smile on her lips.

"Perhaps it is just that I am nervous about the meal ahead."

"Nervous? Whatever for?" She was taken aback.

"It is some time since I dined in the company of ladies."

She tapped his arm with her fan. "Sir, you have no need at

all to be nervous; indeed you will not have time to be nervous, for you will be too busy satisfying our endless curiosity about Felix and foreign climes." She slipped her hand over his sleeve. "Let us go down now, sir. And remember, *vouloir, c'est pouvoir*. Where there's a will, there's a way."

14

Dinner was at an end, the cloth had been removed, and liqueurs and fruit had been served. The room was warm from the fire that danced warmly in the hearth, and candlelight glowed on the faces of Jack's three companions as he told them all about his travels in distant lands.

The meal had commenced with watercress soup, followed by whiting, and then roast pork. It ended with a deliciously light tart made with bottled gooseberries. All simple fare, but beautifully presented and garnished. Jack had enjoyed the occasion in spite of his conscience about not having admitted he was Rafe's cousin, but pangs of guilt reached through him as he played the perfect guest.

Cora and Peter were full of questions about Peru, but Emily did not seem to share their interest; at least, perhaps that was not entirely true, more was it that she deliberately refrained from showing an interest. Jack was sure that the reason lay in the excitement that animated Peter's face. She was afraid that her son, like Felix, would leave England and seldom—if ever—return. So she listened politely enough to the conversation around the table, but asked no questions of her own. Wearing a long-sleeved crimson velvet gown, with diamond earrings that glittered in the candlelight, she watched Peter's enthusiasm with all the inevitable pain of a doting mother who could suddenly see the future more clearly than before and did not look forward to it.

Jack felt he understood, so when Cora and Peter were talking to each other—or rather arguing with each other about the height above sea level of Lake Titicaca—he leaned across to her. "Most wanderers return, Mrs. Fairfield. Felix is the exception that proves the rule."

A self-conscious blush colored her cheeks. "You can clearly read minds, Mr. Lincoln."

"On this occasion it was not difficult."

She smiled a little wryly. "No woman likes to be told she is an open book, sir."

"Not an open book, Mrs. Fairfield, just a loving mother."

"If Felix is the exception that proves the rule, Mr. Lincoln, where does that leave you?"

"Me?"

"Well, correct me if I'm wrong, but have you not just spent a number of years abroad?"

"I did not leave this country willingly," he said after a moment.

"Oh?" She had visions of duns in hot pursuit, for that was the usual reason gentlemen quit England's shores.

Again he read her mind and smiled. "Nor was I forced to flee in order to stay out of jail. I left because I had nothing to stay for. I was a bitter man, Mrs. Fairfield, and perhaps I still am."

"Bitter?"

He paused again, acutely aware of his glaring omission about Rafe. "I, er, was cheated out of my inheritance."

She was appalled. "How dreadful. Is there no hope of regaining it?"

"Not as things stand at present," he replied, wondering if he should use the moment to explain.

"Who cheated you?"

Rafe's name blistered on Jack's lips, but something held him back. "Oh, it is too long a story, Mrs. Fairfield."

Cora and Peter had resolved their difference over Lake Titicaca, and were now listening to the conversation across the table, so Emily tactfully changed the subject. "We are a little out of the way here in Shropshire, Mr. Lincoln, and the latest news takes a little time to reach us. So please, tell us what you heard in Bristol. I'm sure there must be a great deal to relate. Of the war in Europe, perhaps?"

"Well, it's said there has been a great French victory over the Austrians . . ."

"Ah, yes, at somewhere called Ulm, I believe?"

He smiled. "You are abreast of the news after all, Mrs. Fairfield."

She smiled as well. "I only know because Sir Rafe mentioned it, and he had just come from London."

Again he felt he should explain about Rafe; again he did not. "Maybe he knows more, having been in the capital. I confess it was unsubstantiated talk in Bristol. The only other thing I heard was that there *may* have been a naval engagement off Cadiz. Lord Nelson's command."

Cora sighed. "Ah, Lord Nelson. When it comes to naval matters he is matchless; privately, of course, he is to be reprimanded most considerably. He and that great lolloping Hamilton creature are a disgrace!" She looked at Jack. "Let us speak of something *interesting*. Is there no gossip from Brighton, Mr. Lincoln?"

Emily laughed. "Mama, I hardly think the port of Bristol was rife with that kind of chitter-chatter."

"Oh, I suppose not. I'm just interested to know what Mrs. Fitzherbert is wearing now."

Emily eyed her mother. "I would rather know whether or not the lady is to be our next queen. After all, the Prince of Wales does seem to have married her *as well as* the Princess of Wales, which rather makes him a bigamist. Is that not so, Mr. Lincoln?"

"If it's true, then yes, it does," Jack replied.

Cora's lips twitched. "I hope it *is* true, for at least Mrs. Fitzherbert is a lady. Caroline of Brunswick is another great lolloping creature like Lady Hamilton. Quite appalling."

Jack felt he had to speak up. "Maybe so, Mrs. Preston, but surely the qualities of the two ladies in the Prince's life are not the question. Rather should we consider the qualities of the Prince himself. Is a man who can overlook a first wife in order to marry a second really desirable as a future king?"

Cora smiled. "Why, Mr. Lincoln, are you stirring up sedition over the walnuts?"

He laughed. "The whiff of revolution must have accompanied me from Lima."

Peter's lips parted. "There is revolution in Lima?" he gasped.

Cora groaned. "Oh, no, please do not let us start on Peruvian politics as well!"

Emily smiled. "I agree, Mama. Mr. Lincoln, I daresay you are wondering what you will do to pass the time while you are here—when you are not being ruthlessly pumped for information, that is. Let me assure you that we will look after you. Our social calendar is not full to the brim, but on Bonfire Night there is to be an assembly at the Royal Oak in Temford. Most of local society will be there, and I am sure that you will enjoy the evening if you accompany us."

Cora cleared her throat. "Mr. Lincoln may enjoy it, Emily, but I certainly will not."

"Please do not start, Mama—"

"You will be making the greatest mistake of your life that night! The bonfire will not be the only thing to go up in flames, for your happiness will as well."

Emily flushed. "Mama!"

"*Il n'y a que la vérité qui blesse.*"

Jack knew the French phrase. "It is only the truth that hurts."

Cora looked at him. "Emily intends to be betrothed at the assembly to Sir Rafe Warrender, who is the worst insect that ever lived and breathed."

Emily's gaze rested reproachfully on her mother. "This is very ill done, Mama, and if you think I will allow the conversation to continue in such a vein, you are very much mistaken."

Cora was cross, and deliberately addressed Jack. "Mr. Lincoln, if you should happen to go up to the long gallery, which is at the very top of the house, you will find my late son-in-law's, er, studio, I suppose one would call it. He was an artist of some talent, and there is an unfinished portrait of Sir Rafe on the easel. The odious fellow has been captured well, for the nasty little eyes are most indicative of the mean character within. It is my opinion that there is nothing to which Sir Rafe Warrender would not stoop in order to get what he wants." She cleared her throat a little awkwardly, realizing she had expressed a rather more heated opinion than was polite to someone who was little more than a stranger. "Er, forgive me, sir, and please disregard all I have just said. Emily is to marry him, and I must make the best of it. Peter and I both must," she added, glancing across the table at her grandson.

The boy pulled a face.

15

Emily had a dream that night. She was in Geoffrey's arms again, abandoning herself to the passion she had missed so much since his death. His kisses were fierce and yearning, and his body hard and urgent. Her fingers curled richly in his hair as she was swept along on waves of gratification. But the pleasure was greater than she remembered, becoming so intensely erotic and wanton that she felt carried to the edge of control. Her flesh felt as if it would melt, and she ached with desire. Then came the joy, delirious, wonderful joy that flooded over her existence. She cried out, and the sound of her voice awoke her.

The joy scattered, disappearing into the darkness and leaving her feeling empty and confused. For several moments she lay there in bewilderment, unsure of herself or her surroundings, but then she knew it had been only a dream. Disappointment cooled her skin. She was alone in the bed. Geoffrey had gone forever and could never come to her again.

She hid her face in her hands, waiting for her emotions to subside, then slowly she pushed the bedclothes aside and got up to go to the window. A low mist hung over the park, but the sky was clear, with a waxing moon gliding across the starlit heaven. She heard a vixen screech in the distance and saw a barn owl, white and ghostly, swoop toward the stable loft. The dream still touched her, like a sweet echo, faintly heard. But there was something wrong about that echo, something she could not take hold of and bring closer. What was it?

The fire had burned low in the hearth behind her, and the room was cold and shadowy, but she still felt warm because the voluptuous dream still wound treacherously around her, reminding her of the physical joy she was now denied. Her nights were so lonely, and she knew that they would remain so even when she married Rafe, because she didn't desire him as she had Geoffrey, didn't long to feel his arms around her or his lips upon hers. "Oh, Geoffrey . . ." she whispered, blinking back the tears that often came in these small hours. Suddenly, she needed to look at his portrait again. Turning, she donned her lilac woolen wrap, held a candle to the fire, then slipped out of the room.

If it had not been for the cat, she would not have made a sound as she hurried toward the landing, but the animal darted from behind a heavy curtain, where it had been watching a mouse hole. Emily was so startled that she gave a loud gasp and almost dropped the candle, but then she recovered and continued on her way.

Jack was lying awake in his nearby bedroom. He heard nothing until that single gasp. Curious, he immediately got up and went to the door, opening it in time to see the flicker of candlelight disappearing toward the landing and then up the staircase to the floor above. As it faded away, his curiosity increased. The long gallery was up there, or so Cora had said. Who would go there at this hour? A thief, maybe? He would investigate, for it was better to be safe than sorry. He was naked, and so put on the new russet paisley dressing gown he had purchased in Bristol, then took a small pistol from its case in his portmanteau and left the room.

Emily had reached the long gallery, where the light of her candle hardly seemed to stretch at all. The other paintings seemed to be watching as she made her way toward Geoffrey's self-portrait. Moonlight shone palely through the numerous windows and lay in latticed patterns on the wooden floor. There were odd sounds, the scuffling of mice in the walls, the shifting of the house on its ancient foundations, but she heard nothing as she held the candle up to the portrait and gazed once more upon her husband's handsome face. A face she might not know as well as she once thought.

Was there any truth at all in what Rafe said? She would not have doubted Geoffrey for a moment if it had not been for his freely expressed admiration for the French cause. Had there been more to that admiration than mere words? Why had he really gone to Temford Castle? The gambling was an attraction, certainly, but had the political company been of even more interest? Had treason been his true purpose? If only she knew the truth. She wanted to believe him innocent, but there was a sliver of doubt, a tiny splinter that had begun to fester amid memories that were otherwise entirely good. Well, maybe not entirely, for there had always been the pressure and worry of finding the money to meet bills.

As she stood there, her dream echoed once again, reminding her that in spite of all the pleasure—more pleasure than she ever recalled in fact—something had not been quite right. It wasn't to do with Geoffrey's possible treason, but something else completely. Her brow wrinkled as she tried to recall, but it eluded her.

The staircase creaked, and she whirled about in time to see a man's silhouette draw swiftly out of sight. "Who's there?" she cried in alarm.

Jack hesitated, in half a mind to hurry back to his room and have done with it, but he knew he'd frightened her, so he continued up the staircase. "It's only me, Mrs. Fairfield."

"Mr. Lincoln?" She was relieved to know his voice.

"Forgive me, I didn't mean to give you a fright. I saw your candlelight coming up here and thought I should investigate in case it was an intruder." His gold necklace caught the light from her candle as he paused at the top of the stairs.

Her alarm subsided. "No intruder, sir, just a widow dwelling on the past," she said, looking at the portrait again. "This is my late husband," she explained.

Jack joined her, and became conscious once more of the lavender scent she wore. It was fresh and delicate, as she herself was. He studied Geoffrey Fairfield's likeness. "He was a very handsome man."

"Yes."

"You obviously loved him very much."

She nodded. "I did." Even a short while ago she would have corrected him to the present tense . . . but that had been before she accepted Rafe Warrender's offer of marriage. It wasn't love for Rafe that now tempered her heart toward Geoffrey, but the feeling of trapped helplessness that had grown steadily worse over the past twelve months. The match with Rafe had made the entrapment complete, and—heaven help her—she blamed Geoffrey. Perhaps that was what had been wrong in her dream. There could not possibly be such pleasure now because she had fallen out of love. The realization shook her.

The candlelight revealed the emotions passing through her hazel eyes, and Jack became concerned. "Is something wrong, Mrs. Fairfield?"

"Wrong? I . . ." Her breath escaped gently. "No, not wrong, just rather sad."

He wanted to touch her, but suddenly she seemed beyond his reach.

"Mama thinks I made a mistake when I married Geoffrey. Maybe she was right. Maybe not. He had many faults, but are any of us perfect? I know I am not."

Jack tried to interpret the light in her eyes as she gazed at the portrait. Was it anger? Bitterness? No, perhaps neither of those. Just reproach. He felt awkward, and knew he was intruding. "Forgive me, Mrs. Fairfield. This is your home, and you came up here to be alone with him. I am encroaching upon your privacy."

She smiled. "I can hardly find fault in your presence, sir, for you came to check that there wasn't an intruder in the house."

"And now that I know there isn't, perhaps I should return to my bed." Lavender drifted seductively over him. It was a fragrance that had never affected him before, but on her it was almost unbearably arousing.

She glanced at him. "You are a very tactful man, Mr. Lincoln."

"My thoughts are not tactful, I assure you."

"Your thoughts?" She looked curiously at him.

"It's none of my business I know, but I cannot help wondering if you will be happy in a marriage of convenience with Sir Rafe Warrender."

"You have been listening to Mama, sir. And probably to Peter as well. They do not care at all for my decision, as was made only too clear at the dinner table." She moved away, and the candle flame fluttered in the draft so that shadows leapt and shrank. "Sir Rafe and I will do well enough together," she said then.

Jack remained by the portrait. Who was she trying to convince? Him? Or herself? "But do you love him?" he suddenly found himself asking.

The question reached a nerve, and she turned quickly, defensively. "You go too far, sir."

"Perhaps because I am concerned for your happiness."

"You hardly know me, Mr. Lincoln."

"I realize that, but—"

"And my happiness is none of your business," she interrupted quietly.

He flushed in the candlelight. "I stand corrected," he murmured.

"I do not wish to sound rude or ungrateful, sir, but on less than a day's acquaintance I can hardly be expected to . . ." Her words died away, then she met his eyes again. "Suffice it that you do not know me, Mr. Lincoln, nor do you know Sir Rafe."

The moment was perfect for telling her he knew Rafe better than anyone, but even as he hovered on the brink of confession, she walked along the gallery to the easel at the other end, then held the smoking candle up to the unfinished canvas. "This is Sir Rafe, Mr. Lincoln. Come, tell me what you think."

Jack went to her and looked at the likeness of his cousin. Candle shadows moved over the despised face, making it seem almost demonic. Geoffrey had picked out the essence of the man, making him no less real for being in oils and pencil outline instead of the flesh. It was Rafe to the very "T." Sly, untrustworthy, and scheming; the serpent in the Garden of Eden. And for Jack Lincoln, the supreme touch was the Agincourt ring. Except that it wasn't a very accurate rendering of the rose badge . . . The thought was severed as Emily spoke again.

"Mama wishes I would wait for some imagined true love, but if I wait, all I will be united with is bankruptcy. The Hall and this estate are Peter's birthright, but both will have to be sold, and *still* there will be debt." She looked away. *And scandal of a magnitude I cannot bear to consider . . .* She inhaled deeply. "You know about losing your birthright, Mr. Lincoln, so you of all men must understand the implications for Peter. It is for his sake that I have accepted Sir Rafe. But to be frank with you, there is much I am not telling you."

"Do you wish to tell me?" he offered quietly, guessing that whatever it was had as much—if not more—significance than anything mentioned so far.

"I cannot, sir. Shall we just leave it that I have overriding reasons, things that even Mama does not know. And I do not simply speak of debt." She put the candle down on a nearby windowsill.

Jack sensed Rafe's manipulative hand in things. He longed to coax her into confiding more, but knew the subject was closed. So he moved to a different tack. "But what if Mrs. Preston is right, and true love does indeed come your way?" In his mind's eye he could see her surrendering to that love. He felt his body begin to awaken, responding to the erotic images his thoughts were conjuring. *Oh, that it could be Jack Lincoln she surrendered to, Jack Lincoln that she loved . . .*

"If it comes my way at all, sir, it will do so far too late, for I will be Lady Warrender. And grateful for it." She couldn't help glancing at his necklace as it shone in the moving light. The gold looked so rich and vibrant against his tanned skin. She was aware of his lean but muscular figure, of the broadness of his shoulders and slenderness of his waist, of the softness of russet paisley cloth against his hard contours. Naked contours, virile, exciting, and masculine.

"Grateful, but discontented," he murmured, willing his loins not to betray him too visibly.

Their eyes met, and she looked away first. "I perceive that Mama has made an ally of you, sir."

"My words are my own, Mrs. Fairfield. From all you have told me tonight, I too think you will be making a mistake if you proceed with this marriage. You will be settling for less than you truly desire. You knew love once, and in your heart you wish to know it again. On your own admission, you have not found it with Sir Rafe Warrender."

"On my own admission I haven't *yet* found it with Sir Rafe. When we are husband and wife, who knows how things may turn out?" But the words were hollow, and she knew it.

Things will turn out horribly, Jack thought, wanting to tell her all about dear Rafe, but not knowing how to now that he had allowed so much to be said. Everything he had done since coming to this house had been based on things unsaid, and right now it was made all the worse because suddenly she looked back toward Geoffrey's portrait again and tears sprang to her eyes. "Why must everything be so complicated, Mr.

Lincoln? Why did Geoffrey have to die and leave me like this? I need to speak to him again, need his reassurance that . . ." Her voice broke, and she bowed her head.

It was too much for Jack to bear. He went to pull her into his embrace and held her close. She began to push him away, but the comfort was too welcome. She needed a man's strength and tenderness, and Jack Lincoln gave both.

He could feel her trembling through her nightgown and wrap; he could also feel the sweet pliancy of her body. His own body told tales on him, refusing to remain quiescent. Desire ached at his loins. To make love to her now would be to enter Paradise itself! He closed his eyes as he struggled to quell his rising virility. He must think of something else, anything else . . .

For a moment—the mere span of a heartbeat—Emily clung to him, femininity cleaving to masculinity, need to need. Such intimacy hid no secrets, and she pressed to his arousal. She couldn't help herself. It was the starving response of a warm-blooded woman who had been without physical love for the past year. Wild sensations darted over her, making her feel more alive and essential than ever before. She longed to raise her lips to his, so close, so temptingly close. The pleasure . . . oh, the pleasure . . .

Suddenly, she knew what had been wrong in her dream. The man with whom she had been making such abandoned love had not been Geoffrey, for he did not have long, sun-bleached hair, or eyes as blue-green as the sea. The knowledge snatched her breath away, and she wrenched free of his arms and ran from the gallery.

16

When Jack awoke the next morning, his first thought was of Emily. And his second, and the one after that. She filled his senses as he washed and dressed, and she was still lingering pleasantly in his mind as he paused to look around the room before going down to breakfast.

Situated beneath the long gallery in the west wing, it was a pleasing chamber that was so very Tudor in atmosphere that he almost expected to find fresh herbs strewn on the floor, or hear a madrigal being sung. Rich paneling clad the walls, and an old livery cupboard stood next to the stone fireplace. Apart from all the dark oak, the predominant colors were gold and white, from the painted design on the beamed ceiling to the hangings at the window and on the bed.

Through a low doorway and down a steep step that had become necessary because the house had shifted so much over the years, there was another room containing a wardrobe and washstand. The floor of the dressing room was surprisingly level, but that in the bedroom had a definite downward slope from the door to the window. This meant that at some time the feet of the great tester bed had been raised on one side to keep it comfortable for anyone who slept there. Jack was thankful for this because it meant that he had eventually been able to sleep quite well. *Eventually* was the appropriate word, because after his encounter with Emily in the long gallery, it had been some time before he'd been calm enough to sleep.

Morning sunlight filled the room, and the air was warm as he went to look out of the north-facing window. A horseman was riding along the drive toward the house. For an awful moment he wondered if it was Rafe paying an unexpected call, but as the rider drew closer, it was clear he was too ordinarily dressed—and mounted—to be the master of Temford Castle. Jack thought no more of it as he left his room and walked toward the staircase, nor did he remark anything amiss when he saw that Cora had descended just ahead of him. She was crossing the entrance hall toward the dining room, but halted and turned when a serving girl hurried in from the courtyard with a note that the horseman had just brought.

"For whom is the message, Betsy?" Cora inquired.

"It is for Mrs. Fairfield from Sir Rafe, madam," the girl said, dipping a curtsy.

"I will see that she receives it."

"Yes, madam." Betsy surrendered the note, then hastened away. As soon as the maid had gone, Cora glanced cautiously around without observing Jack on the staircase, then broke the seal on the note and read it. After a moment she refolded it and pushed it into the bodice of her cinnamon-colored morning gown. Then she caught up her skirts and walked on to the dining room.

Jack followed in her footsteps, and was in time to hear her greet Emily and Peter, who were already at the table. "*Bonjour, mes enfants!*"

Peter's chair scraped as he rose. "*Bonjour, Grandmère,*" he replied in a commendable French accent.

"I trust I find you both well?" Cora was saying as Jack entered.

Peter had been about to sit down, but hastily straightened again as Jack appeared. "Good morning, sir," the boy said. He was wearing a maroon waist-length coat, gray breeches, and top boots, and his neckcloth was knotted as neatly as an adult's.

"Good morning, Peter. Ladies." Jack bowed, his glance drawn to Emily as if by a thread. Her short golden brown hair caught the light from the window, and she was neatly dressed in a high-throated gown made of blue-and-white striped muslin, with full sleeves gathered at her wrists. Self-conscious color marked her cheeks, and she avoided his eyes. Awkwardness beset him as well, and he made much of assisting Cora to sit down.

Breakfast at Fairfield Hall was all Jack could have wished of an English country house. The food was excellent, and the helpings generous. Cora made no mention at all of Rafe's note, and at first Jack thought she had forgotten it, but then he saw her fiddle a little with the folded paper because it was digging into her. She hadn't forgotten at all; she simply wasn't going to mention it!

But she rattled on about anything and everything else under the sun, including religion. "Are you a churchgoing man, Mr. Lincoln?" she inquired.

"Er, not really. At least, I haven't been in recent years. Why do you ask?"

"Well, today being Sunday, morning service is of course required. Fortunately, this being the first Sunday of the month, the Reverend Johnson will come here after his service in Temford."

"Here?"

"Yes. We have a small chapel off the courtyard, and morning service is held there once a month. It is a way of keeping it in use—a tradition, if you like. Everyone in the house attends, as well as all the people on the estate. I trust you will join us?"

"Of course."

"Excellent." Cora's attention then moved smartly on to Peter's education, or lack of it. *"Eh, bien, mon petit brave!* After service, I shall be attending to you," she warned, deftly slicing the top off a boiled egg.

Peter looked up warily. "Me?"

"Yes. You are at a loose end, young man, rambling aimlessly in the park every single day when you should be keeping up with your lessons."

He scowled, thinking it wasn't *his* fault that he was here instead of Harrow!

Cora was undeterred. "I have therefore decided to help you with your studies, commencing today, directly after morning service."

Emily lowered her cup in astonishment. "You? Mama, you are many things, but certainly not a scholar."

"Maybe not, but I consider myself fluent in French."

Peter gave her a look. "I think Mr. Lincoln has probably noticed," he said dryly.

Emily frowned at him.

Cora turned to Jack and explained. "I spent a year in Paris a long time ago. *Les jours les plus heureux de ma vie.*"

Emily smiled. "They may have been the happiest days of your life, Mama, but I still cannot picture you instructing Peter in French. Fluent or not, you are too much of a scatterbrain."

"I will make you retract those words, *ma petite*," Cora said tartly. "Peter and I will commence directly after breakfast."

Peter was keen to avoid any such thing. "But what of your harpsichord practice, Grandmama?" he reminded her slyly.

"Mm? Oh, no dear, not on a Sunday."

He knew there was no escape, although why French lessons were acceptable on a Sunday but music practice was not, he failed to understand.

Emily was suspicious. Her mother was scheming at something. But what, that was the question.

Cora obliged her curiosity by suddenly gasping, as if something of import had just occurred to her. "Oh, my! How remiss of me!"

"Remiss?" Emily inquired, stepping innocently into her mother's trap.

"I will be teaching Peter, and cannot therefore attend to our guest. We cannot neglect Mr. Lincoln after morning service, my dear, so I will place him in your capable hands."

Jack felt a little awkward. "I'm sure there is no need to worry about me, for I am quite able to amuse myself."

"Nonsense!" Cora declared. "Emily will look after you in my stead, sir. She has nothing pressing to occupy her time, and it will do her good to get out and about more."

"Out and about?" Emily repeated. "Clearly you have something particular in mind."

"Yes, my dear. I was going to take Mr. Lincoln to see the rapids. I know our little River Teme cannot compare with the majestic falls he was no doubt accustomed to in Peru, but I think it pretty enough for all that. I would like you to take him there, Emily."

Seeing Emily's expression at the prospect of having to ride alone with him, Jack spoke up hurriedly. "Much as I appreciate your thoughtfulness, Mrs. Preston, I fear that I do not have any riding clothes with me. When I arrived in Bristol, I only possessed my Peruvian garb, and although I managed to acquire two sets of togs, this one and the evening garb you saw last night, neither of them are suitable for riding."

Cora had an answer for everything. "Well, I'm sure Emily will place Geoffrey's wardrobe at your disposal, Mr. Lincoln. He was about your height and build, and the clothes are doing nothing but hanging in his dressing room. Is that not so, Emily?"

Emily forced a smile. "Yes, of course," she murmured.

"There, you see? As they say in France, *tout est bien qui finit bien*, all's well that ends well," Cora declared, then set her napkin aside and got up. "I perceive that it is some time yet before morning service, so Peter and I will make a start now. Come along, Peter. You need to put in a great deal of effort with your verbs. Your conjugation is really quite dreadful, you know. I cannot imagine what manner of person is teaching French at Harrow, but I doubt if he has ever been across the Channel." She ushered her reluctant pupil away, the message from Rafe still unmentioned.

Jack and Emily found themselves alone. The longcase clock ticked into the silence, and the fire shifted, but the flames were as nothing to those that flared in Jack's heart. Just looking at Emily aroused his desire once more, so he did not dare to look at her. His glance rested here, there, everywhere, except upon her; and yet she was the one thing in the room that he longed to feast his eyes upon.

Nor were Emily's thoughts as innocent as they ought to have been. She was acutely conscious of everything about him, and her gaze stole secretly toward him across the table. He hadn't tied his sun-lightened hair back this morning, and she loved the way it curled down, so pale and golden. And then his eyes . . . oh, his eyes. They were the color of the summer sea, and as inviting. Her surreptitious gaze moved farther down, to his body, now so properly attired in pale gray coat and cream breeches. She remembered the night. All he had worn then had been a thin, russet paisley dressing gown, through which she had been able to feel absolutely everything she should not.

The trembling seconds ticked by, then suddenly they looked at each other and spoke at the same time.

"Mr. Lincoln, I'm sure—"

"Mrs. Fairfield, there is no need—"

They both broke off in confusion, then he managed a smile as he deferred to her. "Ladies first, Mrs. Fairfield."

"I . . . I was going to say that I'm sure you have no real desire to see the rapids. As Mama said, you will find them rather trifling after the cataracts you must have observed in the Andes."

He held her eyes across the table. "On the contrary, Mrs. Fairfield, I am looking forward to seeing what your Shropshire river has to offer. Unless, of course, you would prefer not to go."

"It will do me good to ride again, Mr. Lincoln, especially after the fall yesterday. They do say that it is best to return to the saddle as quickly as possible, or run the risk of losing one's nerve." She cleared her throat a little and began to fold her napkin.

Jack immediately got up to go around the table to draw her chair out for her. She rose to her feet and turned to thank him. Their hands brushed, and she snatched hers back as if the contact burned her. Lavender enveloped him, bewitching him still more. It would be so easy to simply reach out and pull her to him again, to find her lips . . .

She felt the charge in the air, like that breathless moment between lightning and thunder. Time itself seemed to hesitate. Images shimmered before her—being carried in his arms, making love in her dreams, the embrace in the long gallery . . . Oh, the embrace in the long gallery. Somehow she managed to murmur that she would see him in the courtyard after morning service, then she hurried from the room.

But as she closed the door behind her, she knew how dangerously alluring and erotic were the sensations that enveloped her now. She could easily have put a stop to the ride; indeed, feeling the way she did, she *should* have put a stop to it. Instead, she was allowing herself to be swept along by the virile excitement of Jack Lincoln. It was excitement that was forbidden to her because she had pledged her hand to Rafe.

She took a huge breath to steady herself. "This won't do, Emily Fairfield," she whispered. "If you carry on like this, he'll think you the most easy conquest in all the world!" She began to walk toward the staircase, but as she passed the little silver plate on the hall table, she noticed that even though it was Sunday, a letter had been brought. She recognized the by now familiar hand of Sir Quentin Brockhampton, who acted for Lord Fitchett, one of the more pressing and impatient of Fairfield Hall's creditors. With a sinking heart she broke the seal and read. It advised that either she paid the seven hundred and fifty guineas owed to his lordship, or—regretfully, of course—court action would be taken.

Common sense rushed soberingly over her, and she glanced back at the dining room door. The reminder of her debts and responsibilities came none too soon. She had to keep an iron grip on her emotions—and make sure Jack Lincoln stayed at arm's length.

17

Sir Quentin Brockhampton, author of the disagreeable communication Emily had just received, was almost at the end of his journey from London. Exhausted from a night of being bounced and jolted over the highways of England, he had fallen into a fitful sleep by the time his traveling carriage reached the square in Temford. He was huddled in his warmest ankle-length greatcoat, with a shawl around his shoulders and a rug over his knees, and his top hat had slipped forward over his face as he swayed to the rhythm of the vehicle.

Because it was Sunday morning, the square was almost deserted, two sides lined with houses, shops, and the church of All Saints. The third side was occupied by more shops and houses, and by the Royal Oak inn, a large, newly painted white building, three stories high, gabled, with a central archway that led into a large yard. At the rear of this yard stood the newly completed assembly room, where the long-awaited Bonfire Night gathering was to take place.

The fourth side of the square was a tall, impenetrable hedge of yews, with grand armorial gates through which could be seen the medieval splendor of the castle. A Yorkist stronghold during the Wars of the Roses, it was now a gracious and much improved residence, where the white rose of York had given way to the blue rose that Sir Rafe Warrender had stolen from his kinsman.

The carriage rattled toward the castle gates, which remained firmly closed across its path because the man at the lodge did not admit visitors before Rafe's usual breakfast hour. As the vehicle swayed to a halt and the coachman called out the identity of the caller, Sir Quentin awoke with a jolt. He had been dreaming he was on trial for his life at the Old Bailey for the crime of eating ham. His jury consisted of farmyard animals in gentlemen's clothes, and the foreman was a Gloucester Old Spot pig with a very mean and vengeful expression in his little eyes.

Sir Quentin sat up on the carriage seat and took out his handkerchief to mop the beads of perspiration that stood out on his forehead. Dear God above, he vowed mentally, he'd never touch ham again! Or bacon! Or pork! He became aware of the voices outside and lowered the window glass. "What's going on?" he demanded.

The coachman leaned down. "This fellow says he is not permitted to admit anyone this early, sir," he explained.

Sir Quentin's gaze swung to the gatekeeper, who took the precaution of doffing his hat, but made no move at all to opening the gates. He was a thin, weedy fellow with a receding chin, but nevertheless had a very determined look about him. By this time Sir Quentin was cold, stiff, hungry, thirsty, and bad-tempered enough to draw a pistol from inside his coat and level it at the man. "Now look here, fellow," he growled, "I have urgent business with Sir Rafe. Open these gates immediately, or so help me I will puncture you between the eyes!"

The man's jaw dropped, and even Sir Quentin's coachman gaped, but in a moment the gates had been flung open and the carriage was permitted to pass. Its wheels crunched on the scrupulously raked gravel beyond, and the horses snorted and tossed their heads as once again they reluctantly came up to a trot. Peacocks paraded noisily on the lawns, and a flock of doves rose from the ivy-covered battlements as the vehicle approached the barbican. The moat had long since been filled in and the bridge replaced with a turning area of gravel because a peculiarity of the castle's design made it far too awkward for vehicles to actually enter the inner ward. Sir Quentin therefore alighted outside the walls, in the cool shadow of the formidable gatehouse.

Rafe was in the middle of taking breakfast in a small chamber off the great baronial hall. He was dressed in a scarlet quilted silk dressing gown with a large shawl collar trimmed with black fur. It was buttoned at the waist, and beneath it he wore his shirt and breeches. At first he frowned when informed that a visitor had called, but his annoyance turned to unease when he learned the visitor's name.

"Sir Quentin Brockhampton? Show him in immediately," he declared, tossing his napkin aside and getting up to go out into the hall, where every sound echoed and not even two roaring fires could warm the chilly air. Grimacing gargoyles gazed down from the hammerbeam roof high above, and a number of suits of armor stood around, as if intent upon eavesdropping.

Sir Quentin's footsteps echoed loudly as he hastened toward Rafe. "Ah, Warrender, I'm relieved to find you at home."

"Where else would I be at this unconscionably early hour?" Rafe replied rather churlishly, then turned to go back to his meal. "I'm taking breakfast, so you'd best join me."

"Eh? Oh, yes . . ." Sir Quentin followed him.

"Are you hungry?" Rafe asked, gesturing to him to sit down, then resuming his own chair.

Sir Quentin was a little distracted. "Er, yes, damnably so."

Rafe snapped his fingers at a footman. "A little of everything for Sir Quentin."

"Sir." The man bowed and moved to the nearby sideboard, which was covered with silver-domed dishes. Far too many for one man, Sir Quentin thought.

Rafe indicated the coffeepot and toast. "Help yourself in the meantime, dear fellow. Now then, what the devil brings you here like this?"

"Well, two things really. Yesterday I had occasion to go to my club in Pall Mall. One of the other members had a Swedish sea captain along as a guest, a fellow by the name of Gustavus, who is the captain of a merchantman out of Lima, the *Stralsund.*"

"I trust this is leading somewhere, dear fellow?" Rafe murmured wearily, getting on with his sausages, bacon, and scrambled eggs.

"Er, yes." Sir Quentin fell silent as the footman brought him a mountainous plate of food. "Good God, do you usually eat this well on your own?" he asked.

"Mm? Yes, as it happens."

As the footman withdrew from the room and closed the door, Sir Quentin surveyed the plate, which was topped with a thick slice of streaky bacon. The memory of the foreman of the jury lingered unpleasantly, and he knew he couldn't eat it, or the pork sausages, or the delicious black pudding. He even shrank from the kidneys in case they came from a pig! Instead, hungry as he was, he would content himself with the eggs, mushrooms, and fried bread.

"Well, get on with whatever it is you have to tell me," Rafe prompted irritably.

"Eh? Oh, yes. You see, when I realized that Gustavus had just returned from Peru, I asked on the off chance if he had heard anything of Felix Reynolds. Oh, I know South America is vast, and the chances of—"

"And *did* he know anything?" Rafe interrupted.

"Yes, as it happens. At least, he knew of *a* Felix Reynolds, but only through a third party, a Peruvian doctor friend. And since I hardly imagine there is more than one Felix Reynolds in South America, I can only believe it is *the* Felix Reynolds. Anyway, the doctor informed him that Reynolds is not going to recover from a recent illness."

"Not going to recover?" Rafe put his knife and fork down slowly, then slid his hand nervously into his dressing gown pocket, where nestled the quartz pebble.

"Yes. I pressed Gustavus on the point, but the doctor had apparently been adamant. Apparently Reynolds did not wish to distress his friends with the truth, and so pretended that he was getting slowly better. Gustavus was certain he must have passed away by now."

Rafe's eyes began to gleam, and he took his hand from his pocket. "What else did your informative captain have to say?"

"About Reynolds? Nothing."

"But he was absolutely certain of his facts?"

"He could not have been more so."

Rafe breathed out with satisfaction. "So all we have to do is await official notification?"

"Yes."

An edge of uncertainty crept into Rafe's voice. "By Gad, Brockhampton, if you've made any mistake in all this—"

"I haven't. Damn it all, Warrender, as soon as I caught a whiff of who'd bought the St. Lawrence estate, I made a point of visiting Bath."

The St. Lawrence estate was a vast inheritance that had

come on the market when the last Earl of St. Lawrence died without heir. Its disposal had been the subject of much interest the length and breadth of the land, until a mystery purchaser had acquired it. The name of the buyer had never been made public.

Sir Quentin went on. "That fool of a lawyer didn't have a clue who I was, and left me alone in his room. I went through his files and saw the deeds. A few further inquiries here and there soon elicited the truth of the matter. The fellow in Bath handled the entire disposal of the St. Lawrence estate, and as you know, broadcast the sale as widely as he could. The asking price was very high, and the few prospective purchasers who showed an interest were soon discouraged. It seemed the executors were going to have to lower the price, but then Reynolds wrote from Caracas, where he'd just seen the notice of the sale. He bought it all at the full asking price. Like that." Sir Quentin snapped his fingers.

"And this information isn't widely known?"

"No. It was pure chance that brought it my way—an overheard confidence at my club. Relax, Warrender, for there is no doubt that Felix Reynolds is—was, if he's dead—an exceedingly wealthy man. There are no entails, other claimants, or any of the usual inconvenient legal obstacles, and we already know that Reynolds acknowledges being Emily Fairfield's father, for it is all there in the letter he left with me, along with the money. He wasn't wealthy then, of course, but certainly has been in later years. Precious stones from Brazil, and gold in Peru, or some such thing. So legitimate or not, your wife-to-be is a great heiress."

"And she is beautiful as well. Was there ever a more desirable bride?" Rafe murmured.

"I trust you have marriage arrangements well in hand? I'm keeping my side of the bargain. By now she will have received another letter from me. Seven hundred and fifty guineas this time. I forget to whom it is supposedly owed. Lord Fitchett, I think."

"Fitchett? He'll do as well as any, I suppose," Rafe replied. "As for the bargain, you may be sure I am doing my part. The official betrothal is to be the day after tomorrow, on Bonfire

Night. There is to be an assembly at the Royal Oak in the market square."

"I see. What of the marriage itself?"

"Christmas Eve."

"Hmmm. Can't you bring it forward?"

Rafe looked at him in puzzlement. "Bring it forward? Why? Christmas Eve is less than two months away."

"Because if Reynolds really was at death's door when the *Stralsund* left Peru, the very next ship might bring his death certificate, which will go straight to that fool in Bath, who will immediately implement the last will and testament, which I strongly suspect has been drawn up in readiness! Think about it, man. As soon as Emily Fairfield realizes she is wealthy, she isn't going to need *your* helpful purse, is she? And I should imagine she will call your bluff about her late husband's spying activities. It is one thing to face scandal in penury, quite another to do it from the vantage point of a vast fortune. If you want her and her inheritance, you had best get on with it posthaste."

Rafe gazed at him. "Maybe you're right," he murmured.

"I am. Look, there's more I have to tell you yet—"

"You said that was all Gustavus told you!" Rafe interrupted sharply.

"About Reynolds, yes." Sir Quentin looked at him. "While I was talking with Gustavus, he also mentioned a passenger who came to England on the *Stralsund*. A certain Jack Lincoln."

Rafe stared at him, then shook his head. "Not a common name, I grant you, but not all that *uncommon* either."

"I asked Gustavus to describe him. It's your cousin, all right. He boarded the *Stralsund* at Lima with two companions. I don't know who they were, but that's by and by, for it's Lincoln's presence in the Peruvian capital that makes me feel uneasy. Can it really be coincidence that he and Reynolds were there at the same time?"

"Lima is a capital city, damn it, and while it may not be the size of London, it's quite possible for two Englishmen to be there without bumping into each other! Anyway, I fail to see what difference it would make if they *were* acquainted. Reynolds didn't know about my designs upon his daughter, so

I can't see that knowing Lincoln's tale of self-pity and woe will have had an impact upon anything."

Sir Quentin pushed his food around the plate with his fork. "But they both know me, Warrender."

"So? That still doesn't affect the odds. Look, Lincoln's being back in England may not please me, but I hardly think he's going to toddle all the way here to confront me again. Nor can he possibly be aware of my thus far tenuous connection with Reynolds through Emily Fairfield. Relax about Lincoln, for his having been in Lima is the beginning and end of it. Mere coincidence, no more and no less."

Sir Quentin wasn't so sure. A feeling of apprehension nagged away at him. "Look, Warrender, I know you think I'm worrying about nothing, but I strongly advise you to do all you can to persuade your bride-to-be to bring the wedding forward. The sooner you are her husband, the better."

Rafe nodded. "I intend to, but I fear she is rather set on waiting until Christmas Eve. Because it's her birthday." The last words were uttered in imitation of a whining female tone.

"Right now she isn't in any position to set the terms. Damn it, man, she *needs* this match to keep herself out of the nearest Bridewell! Give her an ultimatum! An immediate wedding, or the whole thing is off."

"It's easy to see why you are the darling of the fair sex," Rafe murmured coolly.

Sir Quentin flushed. "I'm merely being practical."

"Yes, well, I think you can leave that side of things to me. I want to coax the lady into my bed, not send her screaming to the nearest sanctuary." Rafe smiled. "Relax, dear fellow, for I'm not without finesse when it comes to matters amatory."

"I hope you're right."

Rafe helped himself to another slice of toast, which he buttered liberally and spread thickly with marmalade. "You worry too much, Brockhampton. Everything is going to go splendidly, you mark my words. Now then, I suppose you wish to stay here awhile, on account of a certain lady?"

Sir Quentin flushed. "I would appreciate the opportunity to further my cause with her, yes."

"An odd situation, you must agree. You hanker after the mother, while I desire the daughter."

"Cora Preston has a rather low opinion of me, I fear. I could see the doubt in her eyes when I told her Felix Reynolds hadn't left any money in my safekeeping."

"Doubt, but not certainty, which means she wonders the same about Reynolds himself. So don't give up yet, my friend. Faint heart never won fair lady."

"Hmm."

"I'll see that a guest room is prepared for you." Rafe rose from his chair. "Well, I've finished now and must get ready to go over to Fairfield Hall. I sent word earlier that I would call this morning."

"I could do with a decent sleep. Even my bruises have bruises after that damned journey," grumbled Sir Quentin.

Rafe paused. "I have an idea. I mentioned the Bonfire Night assembly at the Royal Oak. Well, you must be my guest."

"I can't abide country assemblies!"

Rafe spread his hands. "Do you or do you not wish to insinuate yourself in Cora Preston's good graces?"

"I do."

"Then show some good grace of your own, for she adores socializing of any description."

18

Autumn leaves lay in abundance on the sloping, tree-clad slope as Emily and Jack rode away from the Hall after morning service. They made their way east across the open acres of the park toward the narrow, winding valley of the River Teme, into which the horses had to pick their way with care.

They moved upstream along a fern-edged path right beside the river. The sound of flowing water echoed pleasantly between the trees, and the air was good to breathe. The fiery colors of the season blazed across the landscape, and here and there the dark green of holly or other evergreens showed. There was a light breeze, and leafy shadows dappled the ground as the sun slanted through the branches. Birdsong was shrill in the valley, and occasionally the raucous cries of pheasants followed the horses from the edge of the park.

Emily could not help glancing at Jack as he rode beside her on her late husband's red bay hunter. He wore Geoffrey's purple coat and leather breeches as well, but in spite of this, somehow he did not put her in mind of the man she had lost. Perhaps it was his blue eyes and flowing blond locks, which were so opposite in every way to Geoffrey's dark eyes and cropped dark hair. Jack was a natural horseman too, at ease no matter what mount he rode.

She saw how his body flexed gracefully to the motion of the hunter, and then she thought again of last night and the way that lithe but muscular body had responded to her . . . No, she *mustn't* think like this! Jack Lincoln was here for the moment, but would soon be gone again, so she would be playing with fire if she allowed anything to happen. Rafe had to be her future now; the letter from Sir Quentin had reminded her of that!

Jack was aware of the change in her, a further withdrawal since the breakfast table. Then there had been shy embarrassment, but now there was almost a wall between them. What had happened? he wondered. He didn't know about the letter from Sir Quentin, so his unhappiness was considerable as they rode farther and farther into the winding valley, where the noise of the Teme became louder as the valley sides steepened.

The water wasn't wide, but neither was it shallow in the center. Certainly it was too deep and swift for horses to cross. Rocks and boulders were scattered everywhere, forcing the current to find a way, sometimes roaring over white rapids, sometimes sliding strongly through like a liquid mirror. Several fallen trees had been swept downstream in times of flood, and now, bleached by the sun of several summers, they were stranded high and dry on banks of pebbles.

Beech and oak overhung the path, with scattered clearings that in springtime would be clothed with bluebells. On the far side of the water, the valley slope suddenly became more gentle, opening to an area of flat sunlit rocks that looked very inviting—a perfect place to sit and rest.

Emily reined in her mare and glanced at Jack. "This paltry stream can hardly amount to anything in your much-traveled eyes, Mr. Lincoln, but it is the best we can offer." Her voice was almost lost in the racket of the water.

"I find it very pleasing, Mrs. Fairfield. The Andes can be a little too majestic at times."

"Well, majestic is hardly a word to describe Shropshire," she replied.

"Do not belittle your county, Mrs. Fairfield, for to my eyes this spot is charming."

The faintest of smiles made a fleeting appearance on her lips. "Geoffrey and I used to come here quite often, especially in the summer. We'd sit on a flat rock a little farther upstream, near a packhorse-bridge. I thought we might pause there awhile now, to rest the horses?"

"By all means."

She looked away. "The path crosses over at the bridge, then separates into two. One fork leads to an old ruined watermill, which is a few hundred yards farther upstream from here; the other leads to the disused gatehouse you probably noticed on your way from Temford. We'll take that route, and ride back through the boundary woods to the Hall. Will that be in order?"

"Of course it will, Mrs. Fairfield." He wished she would relax a little, for she was making him feel more uncomfortable by the moment. Last night, before those final moments in the long gallery, they had been easy in each other's company; now everything had changed. He felt as if he were going backward instead of forward with her, which made it impossible for him to know where to begin regarding his promise to Felix.

She moved her mare along the path, which was narrow and quite dangerous in places because the land on this side of the Teme was so steep. An electric-blue kingfisher darted before them, a silver fish in its beak, and there was a movement by the treeline on the far bank as a deer was caught unawares by the riders' approach.

The packhorse-bridge was a simple stone arch, low and without a parapet, and as Emily led the way across, Jack was very conscious of the water rushing by barely a foot below. On the far side the path divided in two as she had said, the one fork swinging away upstream toward the second mill, the other curving in the opposite direction toward the road, some half a mile distant.

Emily dismounted reluctantly on the grass where the path divided. She didn't want to prolong the time spent alone with Jack, but the horses needed to be rested awhile after the rigors of the riverside path. Jack dismounted as well. He noticed how swiftly she slipped down from the mare, without giving him any opportunity to be the gentleman and assist her. She was strengthening the wall between them; no, she had virtually placed battlements along it! But he said nothing as they tied the horses to a bush, then made their way down to the flat rocks by the water.

They sat down, and she removed her riding hat. The sun brought out the rich golden brown of her short hair and made her hazel eyes seem larger. She wore an older riding habit, sky blue wool trimmed with black braiding, and the color stood out charmingly amid the autumn tints all around.

He discarded his top hat and gloves, then leaned back against a rock. The sun beamed down, and the air was unexpectedly warm. He felt that his neckcloth was too tight. "Mrs. Fairfield, would you mind very much if I loosened my neckcloth? I am woefully unaccustomed to such things, and feel well nigh choked in this heat."

"Of course you may, Mr. Lincoln. I hardly see the point of standing on ceremony in a place like this." She forgot herself and smiled. He did not merely loosen the neckcloth, but untied it completely, so the ends lifted gently in the breeze that glanced off the water. He undid the throat of his shirt as well, and she saw again the Inca necklace gleaming rich gold against his skin. She wished she was not so very conscious of everything about him, but even though she was trying her best to be indifferent, that was the last thing she was succeeding in being.

He made himself comfortable against the rock, then glanced around. It really was an enchanting place, and he could well believe that she and her husband had come here often. Upstream, beyond the bridge, he could just make out the ruins of the water mill she had mentioned. It was just a few crumbling stone walls now, with the rotting, moss-covered remains of the wheel tilting precariously into the very race from which it had once drawn power.

The silence between them weighed a little, and he searched for something to say. "Did your husband paint only portraits, Mrs. Fairfield?" Dear God, he thought, how feeble the question sounded!

"Generally. Why do you ask?"

"Because I was thinking how very picturesque a scene the old mill makes."

She smiled, with a spark more warmth and naturalness than hitherto. "Geoffrey thought so too, and I admit that he did attempt to paint it. But he was dissatisfied with the result. He said he could not achieve the quality of the water, so he destroyed all the work he'd done. I was sad because I rather liked it."

Their eyes met again, and she looked away so quickly that this time it became too much for Jack. "Mrs. Fairfield, have I offended in some way?"

"Offended?" She tried to sound surprised, but her eyes admitted something different.

"You are quite clearly ill at ease in my company, more so now than even at the breakfast table. Please do not deny it, for I know this to be so. If it is because of last night—"

"Yes, in part it is, sir," she said quickly. "Those moments in the long gallery should not have happened, Mr. Lincoln, and I would regard it as a great courtesy on your part if you behaved as if they did not."

He knew he had to tread carefully. "But nothing *did* happen, Mrs. Fairfield. You were upset, and I offered a little comfort, that is all."

Her gaze became accusing. "That is not all, sir, and we both know it."

He could not deny it a second time, and so glanced away. "And if I admit it, what then? Nothing really took place, certainly nothing that I would ever speak of elsewhere, so if that is your concern . . ." He drew a deep breath. "No doubt you are thinking of your betrothal?"

"Of course I am, sir, for it is to take place the day after tomorrow. I should have kept it more in mind last night, but I was upset and . . . Well, I do not think I need to explain, do I? I wish to forget all about it, and now that I have told you how I feel, I trust that will be the end of it."

How stilted and self-conscious she was, he mused, and how unflatteringly doubtful of his status as a gentleman! "Mrs. Fairfield, you do me a grave injustice by doubting my honor in this. If it is your wish to forget all about this, then of *course* I will speak no more of it."

"Please don't be angry with me, sir," she said quietly. "If I have seemed to insult you, I apologize with all my heart. It isn't you that I doubt, but myself."

His eyes flew hopefully to meet hers. "If that is—"

"Please, don't say anything more!" she interrupted. "Please, I beg of you. Nothing has changed, I still wish to forget everything that happened last night." She was lying, for it wasn't what she wanted at all. She longed to be taken into his strong arms, to be kissed and made love to, here by the river . . . The truth flustered her, and she began to get up, but suddenly he prevented her.

"Please, don't go," he begged.

She tried to pull her arm away. "Mr. Lincoln, this is not . . ."

"You have asked me to forget what happened last night, and I have promised that I will, but first I have to tell you how I feel. There is no one else here, just the two of us, and I want you to know . . ." He gazed into her eyes, unable to say anything more. But surely she could see into his very soul? Surely she knew how deeply he felt about her, even though they had still not known each other for more than a day?

"This will do no good," she replied, again trying to pull away from him.

The sun on her hair and in her eyes, the slight parting of her lips, the fragrance of lavender that seemed to be part of her—all of these things combined to make him her jailer. He couldn't release her, wouldn't release her . . . "Mrs. Fairfield—Emily—exactly why are you at such pains to forget last night? I cannot and will not believe that it is solely on account of Warrender."

Her eyes were accusing. "Shame on you, sir, for you *know* why! I am no shrinking virgin, but a widow who enjoyed her married life to the full, so I am well aware of your thoughts and feelings last night!"

"As I am equally aware of yours," he countered. She had also given herself away during that brief embrace, and he wanted her to admit that she had been as aroused by him as he had been by her.

"You surely do not want me to say more than I already have?" she whispered.

He took her by the arms and leaned forward so that his lips were only inches from hers. "I don't think you understand how I feel about you, Emily. All you believe is that I lust after you, and that I would take advantage if I possibly could."

"No, I—"

"Yes, Emily, you *do* think that! But it isn't the truth. I feel much more for you than mere desire. I want to shield you, look after you, cherish you, spend my entire life at your side . . . I love you, Emily, *that* is the truth. Believe me, there is such a thing as love at first sight, for my heart was bought and sold from the moment I saw you . . ."

Her eyes brimmed with tears. "Please, don't . . ." she whispered.

"If I do not say it now, then I may never have another chance," he replied, his tone much more gentle. Her tears broke his heart, and broke his resolve as well. He had meant to stand by his promise to forget all that had passed between them in the long gallery, but it was impossible. Just as it was equally impossible to let her remain at arm's length. He pulled her toward him, found her lips, and crushed them with a kiss that was so filled with raw, undeniable emotion that it robbed him of finesse. It was a kiss that came from his heart—and his soul.

She tried to resist, to force him away and make him stop. But he didn't stop, and gradually her resistance began to dissolve into submission. Her lips parted, softened, responded. She sank against him and returned the kiss.

For a long, long moment they were locked in each other's arms, their lips joined. Neither of them wished to break the wonderful sexual spell that wound around them both, but end it they had to, and as he drew back to look into her desire-darkened eyes, he made a fatal error of judgment. "Please don't marry Warrender, Emily," he begged.

Cold reality returned to Emily, and with it the debts, the threat of jail, the prospect of shocking and shaming revelations about Geoffrey. It was too much! With a gasp she wrenched herself free and scrambled to her feet.

"Emily . . ." Jack stretched a hand toward her, but she stepped back.

"I . . . I think it is best if you leave the Hall immediately, Mr. Lincoln."

"Leave? But . . ."

"That is my last word on the matter! You will not spend another night under my roof!" With that she fled to the horses and remounted, then galloped off along the path that led toward the disused gatehouse.

Jack got up to stare helplessly after her. What an unspeakable fool he'd been! If ever a man wished he had held his tongue, it was he. Emily Fairfield might want him as much as he wanted her, but she was not an easy conquest at all.

19

Jack decided not to pursue Emily. She had made her wishes very plain, and this time he had to accept them. He'd muffed the situation, and had rightly been given his congé.

He tossed his hair back and raised his face to the sun, closing his eyes for a moment. "I've let you down, Felix," he murmured, then went to his horse and remounted. His spirits could not have been more low as he gathered the reins, then paused to decide which route to take back to the Hall. He followed in Emily's wake, riding slowly in order not to run the risk of catching up with her. The bay moved up the gentle incline into the trees, and the noise of the rapids faded away, soon to be heard no more as once again the trees folded over him.

The slow, gentle clip-clop of hooves upon the path seemed to be ticking away his remaining time at the Hall, and suddenly he could not bear it anymore and turned the horse into the ferns and long grass. He was so deep in thought—and self-recrimination—that he paid little attention to where he was going. It wasn't until he almost struck his head on a low-hanging branch and paused to look around that he realized he had lost all sense of direction. The sun had gone behind a cloud, and there were no shadows to indicate to which point of the compass he was moving. He was lost. He glanced around, but there just seemed to be trees wherever he looked. Trees, more trees, and not a sound of human activity, even in the distance.

He glanced above the branches, hoping to see a curl of smoke that would show him the way to the gatehouse, but there was nothing. He cupped his hands to his mouth. "Hello? Can anyone hear me?" The words reminded him of his search for Emily only the day before. He listened, but there was no response to his call. He shouted again, but still there was nothing. Which way should he go? With a sigh he turned the horse to the right and rode on again.

The square in Temford was still quiet as Cristoval's chaise arrived from London. Tomorrow, Monday, the market would be in full swing, but today all was quiet. The horses' hooves clattered and the wheels rattled as the tired postboy urged the team along the final yards to the yawning archway into the inn's yard, where he reined them in for the last time. Ostlers and grooms emerged reluctantly to attend to the newcomers, but for whose presence the Sunday morning idleness would have continued.

The Royal Oak's fine new redbrick assembly room rose splendidly on the site of a former orchard. Its impressive main entrance was approached directly from the inn yard up a flight of three wide steps, and its windows were high on the walls to prevent outsiders from looking in. Beyond it, where the cleared orchard had yet to be developed, an immense bonfire was abuilding, in readiness for the fireworks display that would take place during the opening evening. The finishing touches were still being put to the interior of the ballroom, where three men were having difficulty hauling up one of the three chandeliers that had been delivered from London the day before.

As Cristoval and Manco alighted from the carriage, all eyes turned sharply toward the Indian as he once again commenced his display of thanksgiving for a safe journey's end. Everyone gaped as he swayed and turned in his stately way, and a buzz of astonished conversation broke out as he began to sing as well, spreading his arms and hands to the square of sky above the yard.

Cristoval tried to look normal and dignified as he waited by the entrance to the taproom. He always squirmed when Manco claimed so much attention, for it was a little like being a sideshow at a fair. The Indian was a novel enough sight even in great cities like London and Bristol, but in a small Shropshire market town he came as a very great shock indeed to the local populace.

The landlord, Mr. Porter, came out to see what was causing the stir. He was a tall, thin man, who wore a leather apron over his neat brown coat and fawn breeches, and a nosegay of Michaelmas daisies adorning his lapel buttonhole. He was wiping his hands on a towel, having just repaired the tap on an ale barrel, and he too halted in amazement as he saw the strange sight in the yard.

"By all the powers . . ." he breathed, tipping his low-crowned hat back.

Cristoval turned to him. "You must forgive Manco, sir, but it is his custom to give thanks to the gods for having seen him safely to journey's end."

"Journey's end?" the landlord repeated warily, preferring such noisy exhibitions to pass on through.

"Yes, indeed. We hope to stay here, for the time being at least." Cristoval inclined his head and introduced himself. "Don Cristoval de Soto, your servant, sir."

"Sir." The landlord nodded. "Well, Don Cristoval, what else might I expect your servant to do, *if* I let you both stay here?"

"I will see that he behaves," Cristoval said reassuringly, his fingers crossed in the pocket of his fine new greatcoat. "As to how long we may stay, well, that depends. Maybe only one night, maybe more."

"I see." Mr. Porter eyed Manco's antics again. "Right, Don Cristoval, you and your friend may stay, but only if he conducts himself in a proper manner."

"Yes, of course." *Proper manner? Manco? That would be the day*, Cristoval thought.

Half an hour later found Manco and his master in a suite of handsome third-floor rooms facing over the square. Their accommodation consisted of two bedrooms joined by a parlor in between, and in the parlor the newly lit fire had smoked considerably, obliging the maid to leave the window open to clear the air. Being on the third floor, it was possible to see over the yew hedge into the castle grounds.

As Cristoval and Manco looked out at the residence of Jack's villainous cousin, a groom wearing white breeches and a mustard-colored jacket led a glossy black thoroughbred around to the front of the barbican. The horse was a large animal, and willful, tossing its head and capering impatiently as it fought the groom's hold. Then two gentlemen emerged from the castle, one Cristoval did not know, but the other was Sir Quentin Brockhampton.

Cristoval pointed him out to Manco. "There is my informative lawyer friend, so I think the gentleman about to mount the horse must be Sir Rafe Warrender. Mark him well, my friend, for he is a devil. Definitely a Pizarro fellow," Cristóval advised.

The Indian gazed at Rafe, who took his leave of Sir Quentin and urged the horse toward the gates, which swung open in readiness. Manco's face didn't alter at all as he calmly took his sling and a pebble from his purse. Cristoval didn't notice, for he was too intent upon the rider who now emerged from the castle grounds into the square. Manco stepped back, whirled the sling, then expertly aimed and released the pebble through the open window. It flew through the air and struck Rafe's top hat, knocking it clean from his head.

Cristoval gave a start. "*Madre de dios!*" he gasped, only then realizing what the Indian had done. In a second he'd grabbed Manco and hauled him safely back out of sight, then he peeped around the edge of the curtain to see that Rafe had reined sharply in and was glancing furiously around for the culprit. There had been some boys standing outside a closed cobbler's shop, but they had fled the moment the hat went flying.

Rafe struggled to bring the restive horse under control, then quickly dismounted to retrieve the hat, but Manco was poised to strike again, although not with his sling this time. Instead, he thrust his hand into his purse, drew it out again, and flicked his fingers. Rafe's hat rolled from his outstretched hand. Rafe cursed and moved after it. Manco's fingers flicked yet again, and the hat rolled farther.

Cristoval shook the Indian's arm furiously. "Stop it! Do you hear me?"

"Manco teach devil lesson."

"Manco is supposed to be behaving!" Cristoval reminded him.

"Hmm." The Indian closed his purse and left the hat alone.

Rafe immediately grabbed it, then examined it closely, as if fearing it had acquired little wheels. Then, satisfied that it was indeed just a normal top hat, he dusted it with his glove and donned it again. He looked around suspiciously a last time before remounting and urging the horse away toward the broad street that led down to the bridge over the River Teme.

Only when he had vanished from sight did Cristoval release Manco, whom he immediately berated. "*Dios,* you fool, you might easily have been seen!"

The Inca was bewildered. "But Pizarro fellow did not see, Capac!" He was a little insulted, for he prided himself on remaining invisible to any prey, human, or animal.

"Maybe, but don't do anything like that again, do you hear? I am obliged to be responsible for you beneath this roof, so behave, damn you!"

"Manco be good," the Inca promised solemnly.

"Right." Cristoval exhaled slowly, wishing they were both safely back in Lima, where the likes of Manco were nothing out of the ordinary.

The Indian went into his bedroom to sling his hammock—made of netted vicuna wool—between the posts of the bed, for nothing would induce him to sleep on a mattress. "Manco not understand. A little magic, and devil die."

"That sort of magic counts as murder in England," Cristoval pointed out.

"All right. No magic. Use bow and arrow instead. One arrow, devil die," Manco said then.

"It would still be murder here," Cristoval said from the doorway behind him. "So not only would the devil die, but you would too—on a gallows tree." Cristoval drew an expressive finger across his throat.

The Indian was scornful. "Manco not caught," he said firmly.

"Just keep your magic, your arrows, and everything else, to yourself, my friend."

Manco knotted the hammock ropes deftly for a moment, then paused. "If devil die, we go home?" he inquired.

"That's enough. Is that clear?"

"Yes, Capac Cristoval," the Indian replied meekly. Too meekly. Cristoval looked suspiciously at him, but the Indian's face gave nothing away, and after a moment Cristoval changed the subject.

"I must get a message to Fairfield Hall, in the hope that Jack is there."

"Manco take message."

"No, thank you all the same, but I think I'll just send a local boy," Cristoval said quickly. "I'll write a note now, asking Jack to come here."

As the door closed behind him, Manco sniffed. "Magic work well. All over quickly," he muttered. "Then Manco go home."

20

Peter felt as if his grandmother's French lesson had been going on forever. He was tired of irregular verbs, and of contorting his throat in order to chant Gallic vowels over and over again, his face grimacing as he tried not to sound painfully English. He was tired too of trying to remember where certain cities were to be found on the blank map she had drawn on a piece of paper. Who cared where Nantes was, or Lyons? As for the towns along the Loire, he simply wasn't interested! Not when he was forced to learn about them, anyway. Left to his own devices, he'd have pored over a map for hours, committing as much to memory as he could, but when Grandmama was lecturing him like this, he hated it.

He was seated at the table in the long gallery, where his father's painting things still lay, and his pen scratched and blobbed as he struck some work through and began again. How on earth, he wondered, did the French say "he wouldn't have done even if he could?" Oh, what did it matter anyway? Britain and France had been at war nearly all his life, so he wasn't likely to go to France to find out how they said anything. His attention wandered, and he began to count the leads in one of the windows.

Cora strolled idly up and down, addressing him in French all the time. "Very well, sir, since you are more interested in the windows than your lessons, I will make you chant your vowels again. Begin."

"Please, not the vowels *again*!" he groaned.

"Begin," she repeated in her irritating way.

Peter's visage became mutinous, and he said his vowels, but in as exaggerated an English way as possible. "Ay, ee, eye, oh, yew."

Cora was cross, but as she was about to tick him off in no uncertain way, something outside caught her attention. "Good heavens, your mama is returning from the ride, and there is no sign of Mr. Lincoln! Oh dear, I hope nothing is wrong!"

Peter's chair scraped, and he hurried to join her. Sure enough, his mother was riding back toward the Hall on her own, but she didn't seem in all that much of a hurry. "She's only cantering, Grandmama, so I don't think anything can have befallen Mr. Lincoln."

"Then where is he?"

"I don't know." Then another movement caught Peter's attention, and he glanced along the drive to see Rafe riding toward the Hall as well. He pointed. "Look, Sir Rafe!"

Cora sighed. "This is most tiresome," she muttered.

Peter looked curiously at her. "Tiresome?"

"I was hoping Sir Rafe would have been and gone before she returned," Cora explained.

"You mean, you *knew* he was coming today?"

"Yes, I confess I did. That is why I bundled your mama off with Mr. Lincoln."

Peter grinned. "Well done, Grandmama!"

"Well, it would have been, if only it had worked," she pointed out with some accuracy.

Peter looked at Rafe again. "I don't want to see him at all, so please can I go out now, Grandmama?"

"Yes, I see no reason why not, but I expect you to be more helpful at your next lesson."

"Yes, Grandmama."

"I mean it, young man!"

Peter gave her a sudden hug. "So do I!" Then he ran toward the staircase and disappeared.

Cora watched the approaching riders again, especially her daughter. Why wasn't Jack Lincoln with her? she wondered. Clearly he hadn't met with an accident, or as Peter had pointed out, Emily would have been riding at a gallop to bring help. So why else would he not be accompanying her? A thoughtful look came over Cora's eyes. Well, it would be easy enough to find out, for Emily would arrive back at the Hall before Rafe, whom she had now seen. As Emily quickened her mount accordingly, Cora gathered up her skirts and left the long gallery.

Emily hastened into the hall just as Cora reached the bottom of the staircase. "Mama, Sir Rafe is coming here!"

"I know, dear," Cora replied, taking full shrewd note of her daughter's flushed face and bright eyes, which she could tell were not entirely due to the exercise of riding—*or* to the dubious thrill of Sir Rafe Warrender's imminent arrival.

"You do not seem surprised he's coming," Emily said then.

Confession was good for the soul, Cora thought, and gave an apologetic smile. "I'm afraid it slipped my mind earlier that this was delivered from the castle." She produced the note from her bodice.

Emily read it hastily, then looked accusingly at her mother. "It was addressed to me, yet I notice you have broken the seal and presumed to read it."

"It fell on the floor, and I trod on it by mistake," Cora fibbed.

"Really? I think I will take that with a pinch of salt. This is too bad of you, Mama. The note must have come well before Mr. Lincoln and I set out on our ride."

"Yes, it did. Before breakfast, actually. My memory is so unreliable these days. No doubt it is my age."

"There isn't anything wrong with your memory. You deliberately omitted to mention it, then you contrived to send me out with Mr. Lincoln in order to be sure I was out of the house when Sir Rafe called!"

"Oh, Emily, my dear, do you really think I would stoop so ignobly?"

"Yes, I do," Emily replied crushingly. "Well, you have been hoist with your own scheming petard, for I am here anyway."

"More is the pity," Cora muttered.

Emily was incensed. "Mama, you *know* how important this match is if I am to keep the Hall, yet you seem intent upon undermining my efforts."

"This Warrender marriage is an abomination, Emily Fairfield, and the sooner you realize it the better!" Cora quickly changed the subject. "Anyway, where is Mr. Lincoln?"

The color on Emily's cheeks deepened. "Somewhere in the park. I neither know nor care exactly where."

"My dear, how can you speak in such a way?"

"Because Mr. Lincoln is not a gentleman after all!"

Cora's lips parted. "Emily, are you saying that he . . . ?"

"Made improper advances? Yes, Mama, I am." But Emily had to avoid her mother's eyes, for that had not been quite how it happened.

But Cora was too wily a bird to be so easily taken in. "Forgive me, my dear, but I find it hard to believe that he would act so without any encouragement."

Emily's breath caught indignantly. "Mama, are you suggesting that I led him on?"

"Did you?"

"Certainly not!" But Emily's eyes slid away again, and the bloom on her cheeks told another tale.

"Methinks this lady doth protest too much, and that if anything it was six of one and half a dozen of the other," Cora murmured.

Emily searched her mother's eyes. "Why are you so prepared to think leniently of him?"

"Leniently? My dear, I don't know what you mean . . ."

"Yes, you do. What's going on, Mama? I can tell when you are up to something."

Cora spread her hands in a gesture of angelic innocence. "I have no idea what you mean," she said in an infuriatingly bland tone.

Emily would have quizzed her more, but Rafe's horse was heard in the courtyard. She glanced uneasily back, then whispered urgently to Cora, "Please, Mama, right now it doesn't matter who was to blame. I have informed Mr. Lincoln that he is to leave the Hall without further ado, and that is the end of it."

"Oh, Emily, you surely do not mean it!" Cora cried.

"I most certainly do mean it. In the meantime, I would prefer it if Sir Rafe knew nothing about him, and to that end I shall see that we walk in the topiary garden, so there is no chance at all of us encountering Mr. Lincoln before he leaves."

"Emily—"

"Mama, I wish to wipe this particular slate clean, do you understand? So let it seem that I went out to ride alone. What Sir Rafe doesn't know will not cause him concern."

"I will observe your wishes regarding not saying anything to your odious future lord, my dear, but as to Mr. Lincoln being thrown out in such a summary way, I'm afraid I cannot allow it."

"Mama!"

"No, my dear. He came here to see me, and he is therefore *my* guest. I will not hear of him being sent away."

"Even though he behaved monstrously toward me?" Emily was outraged.

Cora's expression was wry. "My dear Emily, that monstrous behavior has made you glow! Don't try to gull me with your talk of unwelcome advances, for I know you. Mr. Lincoln has brought you to life again, so I intend to keep him here come rain or shine."

Emily was nonplussed, for it had never crossed her mind that her mother would not back her. But there was no time to say anything more because Rafe strode through the open door behind them.

"Ah, ladies," he declared, and bowed dashingly over their hands.

Emily was still a little rattled by her mother's attitude, and only managed a weak smile of greeting. "Why, Rafe, how good it is to see you again," she said untruthfully, for right now she wished to have it out with dear Mama!

"You sound as if you were not expecting me." His brows drew together slightly.

Cora gave a tinkle of laughter. "Oh, la, Sir Rafe, it is just that you have caught her before she was quite ready. She meant to have returned from her ride and changed into a pretty gown before you arrived."

His brows resumed their customary level, and he smiled at Emily. "You are beautiful enough in your riding habit, my dear," he said.

She lowered her eyes. "You are too kind, sir. Er, shall we walk in the topiary garden?"

"Walk? Why, yes, that would be most agreeable," he replied, for it suited him to get her alone. "But first, I must beg a favor of Mrs. Preston."

"Of me?" Cora said in surprise, for as a rule he would rather be strung up by his thumbs than ask anything of her.

"Yes. You see, I have an unexpected guest at the castle at

the moment, and I rather think you know him. Sir Quentin Brockhampton?"

Cora paused, her eyes suddenly wary. "Yes, I am acquainted with Sir Quentin."

"I understand that there may be some, er, awkwardness between you?"

"Awkwardness? Now how on earth would you imagine that? You must know that we *delight* in receiving the fellow's legal but nevertheless threatening letters!" Cora's tone verged on the frigid.

"Mama!" Emily wished the ground would open up and swallow her.

But Cora merely tossed her head and looked at Rafe again. "What of Sir Quentin, sir?"

"Well, he, er . . ." Rafe cleared his throat. "He feels most culpable about a certain matter of business. He has not confided in me as to the nature of the business, of course, but—"

"Sir, the fellow should feel culpable about *all* the business he has dealt with concerning this house." Cora was even more cool than before.

"That's as may be, Mrs. Preston, but the matter I refer to in particular concerns his lack of knowledge about something you clearly thought was in his possession."

Cora looked at him. "Sir, I trust I am not expected to reassure Sir Quentin that I hold him blameless in this?"

Emily was appalled. "Please, Mama!"

But Rafe held up a hand. "No, no, my dear, Mrs. Preston is entitled to her point of view. However, I trust I can stand up for my friend and say that I am certain he is indeed blameless. His distress over the whole thing is all the proof necessary."

Cora fell into a silence that was almost more eloquent than her spoken words.

Rafe cleared his throat again. "Mrs. Preston, all of this brings me to the matter of Tuesday's assembly. It was my intention, my, er, most earnest hope, that I could pour oil on any troubled water that might linger over this unfortunate matter, whatever it is."

"Sir Rafe, there is not sufficient oil in all the world—" Cora began, but Emily interrupted.

"Mama, I am sure you do not wish to make any difficulty.

May I remind you that Sir Rafe and I are to announce our betrothal at the assembly? Therefore it will not be in the least desirable for you to demonstrate your true feelings with regard to Sir Quentin. I therefore beg you to be at least civil toward him."

Cora gave her an arch look. "I am always civil when the occasion calls for it, my dear."

"This occasion most certainly calls for it," Emily replied, only too aware of the ambiguity of her mother's observation.

"Of course, my dear. Sir Rafe, you may be sure that my conduct will be above reproach."

Rafe inclined his head to her, then offered his arm to Emily. "The topiary garden, my dear?" he murmured.

Emily slipped her hand over his sleeve, and they walked out into the courtyard.

Cora gazed after them. "If either of you thinks I am going to bestow smiles upon that . . . that *toad* Brockhampton, you have another think coming!" she breathed, then turned on her heel and marched away through the house toward the low stone doorway that gave on to the knot garden at the rear.

She now knew from Felix's letter that there had indeed been a sum of money deposited with Sir Quentin all those years ago. She therefore also knew beyond all shadow of doubt that the lawyer had lied to her when she went to see him after Geoffrey's death. That Sir Quentin was now a guest at Temford Castle also served to confirm her growing belief that he and Sir Rafe Warrender were acting together against Fairfield Hall. They were hand in glove, and she wished she knew exactly why.

Surely it was too concerted a plot to be simply on account of Sir Rafe's desire for Emily? Did the marriage offer have a hidden price? If so, what could it be? Emily had nothing; she was even holding the Hall for Peter. So why would Sir Rafe Warrender and his cronies be at such pains to crush her with debt and force her into this match? Cora sighed. There was nothing for it but to join forces with Jack, whose purpose in coming to the Hall had also been revealed in Felix's letter. What point was there in working separately, when together they might be able to solve the Hall's difficulties *and* defeat Sir Rafe Warrender?

There was another important circumstance to deal with as

well. She had not intended to reveal to Jack her awareness of the attraction that had so swiftly sprung up between Emily and him; but if true love was to be guided onto the right path, Emily's precipitate action today in ordering him away made such a revelation necessary. Cora would much have preferred to let nature take its course. However, it was one thing to stand idly by, giving the odd assisting nudge if the lovers' reluctance threatened to get in the way, but it was quite another to be so idle as to let Emily toss aside her golden opportunity for true happiness.

There were some things that were too important to ignore, too important to turn one's back on because of inherited debts. Cora could see that Jack Lincoln was Emily's once-in-a-lifetime man. Felix could not have written more highly of him, or made his secret hopes more plain, and Cora took Felix's opinion as nothing less than gospel. Especially when she could sense there was much she had not been told in the letter.

Felix knew all about Emily's debts and Jack's lack of capital, yet he still expressed a strong desire that they would make a match of it. He would not say that unless he had reason to be sure all would be well that ended well. So, if that was what Felix wanted, it was what Cora wanted too, and to perdition with Sir Rafe Warrender, slippery lawyers, devious bankers, money owed, et cetera. On no account must Jack be permitted to leave. Oh no, she swore to herself, he had to be prevailed upon to stay on at Fairfield Hall, because if Cora Preston and Felix Reynolds had anything to do with it, he was going to marry Emily!

Tears pricked Cora's eyes as she emerged from the back of the house into the knot garden, which happened to be the place where she and Felix had last spoken. He had returned to England—oh, so briefly—and they had snatched half an hour together after dark.

"I won't fail you, my love," she whispered. "I'll see they come together as you and I should have done all that time ago. The same mistake won't be permitted to happen twice."

21

Peter had waited until Rafe's horse disappeared into the courtyard before he ran off across the park toward the woods. Soon, breathless and hot, he reached the pool in the clearing. After getting out his fishing line and hook, he took off his coat and left it over the fallen tree, then clambered up to his branch. Within moments he was once again sprawled along it, with the line lowered hopefully into the water.

To his amazement the line pulled, the water rippled, and for a split second he glimpsed a fish on the end. A fine fat tench! In his excitement he almost fell off the branch, but then the fish leapt, the hook was dislodged, and his catch darted cleanly down into the depths of the pool. Peter was speechless. Furious, he flung the line away across the pool and began to climb down again, but then he paused as he heard hooves approaching. Who could it be? Not Sir Rafe again, because he had only just called at the Hall. Curious to know the answer, the boy pulled himself back on to the branch and lay flat as he waited to see who came.

It was Jack who rode toward the clearing. He had his bearings a little now, having found his way to the disused gatehouse, and thus realized which direction to take for the Hall. Nevertheless he was immensely relieved to recognize the fallen tree and the pool, for until they came into view, he still feared he might somehow have gone around in a circle among so many trees.

As he passed slowly through the clearing, Jack's glance flickered toward the coat. Peter was here somewhere. He glanced surreptitiously around, and soon spied the boy lying so secretly on the branch. Smiling to himself, Jack rode straight through the clearing and on toward the drive as if he hadn't realized anyone was there. He heard the slight rustle of leaves as Peter dropped down to the ground, grabbed his coat, then began to stalk him.

Jack's smile increased. From Manco he had learned a thing or two about laying an ambush, so young Peter did not stand a chance. Quickening the horse just a little, Jack waited until a convenient holly bush offered a hiding place, and as soon as he was out of sight behind it, slipped down from the saddle and slapped the horse's rump to keep it going. Then, crouching low and quiet, he listened as Peter hurried stealthily toward him. The horse trotted on, rustling through the ferns, the rhythm of its hoofbeats unchanged.

Peter couldn't see his prey, but he could hear, so as he came around the holly bush he sensed nothing of the trap. Suddenly, he had been leapt upon and flattened. He gave a frightened yell and struggled for all he was worth, but his captor was too strong. Two iron hands grasped his shoulders, pinning him to the ground, and he heard Jack laughing.

"So, sir, you thought to creep after me unseen, did you?"

"I wasn't doing any harm!" Peter protested, spluttering into the moss and mud.

"I know, lad, I know." Jack released him and got up. "I just thought I would teach you a lesson. It doesn't do to stalk people, Peter. One day you'll choose the wrong man to do it to." He glanced after the horse, which had come to a halt now and was grazing upon a patch of grass.

Peter struggled to his feet, brushing the leaves and dirt from his clothes. "I wasn't doing anything wrong," he grumbled.

"But you *are* doing wrong. Look, I'll be honest with you. I've overheard your grandmother complaining about your antics, so I know you get up to this sort of thing as a matter of course."

Peter colored. "It's something to do."

Jack folded his arms and looked at the boy. "I'm sure you could find better and more satisfying things if you tried."

Peter put on his coat, then brushed his breeches. "You already know what I really want to do. I want to see the world, like Grandmama's cousin Felix."

"Ah."

"Well, *you've* seen the world, so you know what I mean.

It . . . it's like an itch I cannot scratch. I think about it all the time now. I just want to see everything there is to see. Egypt, Greece, Africa, maybe even Australia, but most of all I want to go to South America."

Jack gazed at him. This was what Felix must have been like as a boy, the same keen urge to explore the world, the same ardor, and need to know. One only had to hear Peter speak like this to know that Felix Reynolds was his grandfather.

Peter looked earnestly at him. "Will you tell me more about South America and the Incas, Mr. Lincoln? I . . . I mean, the things you couldn't say in front of Mama and Grandmama."

"And what things might that be?" Jack inquired, puzzled.

"You know, the ancient religious rites, the horrible sacrifices, the—"

"How bloodthirsty you are, to be sure," Jack murmured.

"I just want to know, sir."

"And I *would* tell you, truly I would, but I fear I will not be able to."

Peter's face fell. "Mama hasn't forbidden it, has she?"

"No, of course not. My reason is simply that I will not be here to tell you. When I return to the Hall, I intend to pack my things and leave."

Peter was dismayed. "Oh, no, please don't say that, sir. Why are you going?" He thought of something. "Have you and Mama had words? Is that it? She returned without you, and—"

"It's not that either," Jack interrupted hastily. "No, it's just that I have remembered something important that I have to attend to. It had slipped my mind completely, and now that I've remembered I have no choice but to get on with it. Business matters, you know," he added vaguely.

Peter hung his head. "I wish you were staying."

"So do I, Peter."

"But you can come back afterward, can't you?"

"Maybe. I don't know." Jack wished the boy would leave the subject alone.

But Peter was anxious to persuade him. "Please say that you will, Mr. Lincoln. I'm sure Mama would agree, and I *know* Grandmama would. She likes you very much because you can tell her all about her cousin Felix."

"If my business doesn't take too long, of course I'll return,"

Jack promised, feeling very much the rat because he knew he would never return.

"I think Grandmama hopes you will take Mama away from Sir Rafe," Peter said suddenly.

"I beg your pardon?" Jack was surprised by the boy's words.

Peter flushed a little. "Before breakfast Grandmama intercepted a message from Sir Rafe to Mama. It was to say he'd call at the Hall this morning. Grandmama didn't give it to Mama, and instead made certain that she rode out with you."

So *that* was Cora's purpose! Jack's eyes cleared. He had an ally in Emily's mother, which made it all the more a pity that Emily herself was now so alienated.

Peter touched some of the berries on the holly bush. "Sir Rafe is at the Hall now. He arrived just after Mama. Grandmama was most displeased."

"Yes, I can imagine she was. I'm not all that pleased myself." Jack met the boy's eyes. "Believe me, Peter, if I thought I could win your Mama, I would," he said candidly.

Peter's face brightened. "Really?"

"I fear so."

"Stay," Peter begged. "Forget your business and stay here."

"I must go, Peter. Come on, we'll return to the Hall together. We'll ride double, mm?"

"I suppose so." Peter's voice reflected his disappointment as they made their way to the waiting horse.

The drive was only a few yards away beyond the bushes as they reached the animal, and they both turned as they heard light running footsteps going in the direction of the Hall. It was the boy Jack had seen the day before, peering from the gatehouse window.

Peter craned his neck until the boy was out of sight. "That was Archie Bradwell; his father keeps the gatehouse. I wonder why he's going to the Hall?"

"Heaven alone knows," Jack answered, then mounted and leaned down to pull Peter up behind him.

They soon caught up with Archie, who turned on hearing the horse, then halted as if expecting to be spoken to. This smacked to Peter of typical Archie Bradwell presumptuousness, and he decided to take his hated rival down a peg or two.

He asked Jack to rein in, then leaned down in a very superior way. "What business do you have going to the Hall?" he demanded, as if they had happened upon a trespasser.

Archie looked up a little challengingly. "I'm 'ere with a message for Mr. Lincoln," he replied in a "So there!" tone of voice.

"Oh." Peter was annoyed. Specks of color flushed his cheeks, and he felt like flinging himself onto Archie and having it out fist to fist.

Jack was startled by Archie's announcement. "For me?" But only Cristoval and Manco knew he was here!

"Yes, sir," said Archie. "From Mr. Solo."

"Solo?" Jack repeated blankly, then smiled. "You mean Soto? Cristoval de Soto?"

"Yes, that's 'im. 'E says that 'im and Mr. Mango, or some such name, are staying at the Royal Oak, and they'd like you to go there as soon as you can. Mr. Solo says 'e 'as very important information for you."

Peter gave a sharp intake of breath. "Mr. Mango? Would that be Manco the Indian, Mr. Lincoln?" he asked, his eyes beginning to light up.

Jack nodded. "I believe so, Peter." Cristoval and Manco were in Temford? They were supposed to be in London! He dipped in his pocket for a coin and flicked it to Archie. "Tell Don Cristoval that I will come as soon as possible."

"Yes, sir." Archie looked at the coin in delight, then gave Peter a haughty look before running back along the drive the way he'd come.

Peter scowled after him. "You shouldn't have given him any money, Mr. Lincoln."

"Why not?"

"Because he's a lout."

Jack smiled. "A lout?"

"Yes. I hate him!" Peter continued to glower after the departing boy.

Jack had to laugh. "Well, the regard was clearly mutual. It's a shame, because if you and he got on better, he'd be company for you."

Peter was aghast. "Company? I would rather be friends with a lump of coal!"

Jack raised an eyebrow, but said nothing more as he moved the horse on.

Peter was silent for a while, then spoke again. "You . . . you won't forget me, will you? I mean, you won't let Mr. Manco leave again before I have had a chance to meet him?"

"Of course you can meet him, Peter, but only provided your Mama gives permission." Which right now, Jack knew, was rather doubtful.

22

As Jack and Peter drew nearer to the Hall, they glimpsed Emily and Rafe strolling in the topiary garden, so they took a rather circuitous route to the stables in order to avoid being seen. They crossed the moat on the other side of the house using a wooden plank that served as a footbridge for the servants, and entered from the knot garden. Then they went through into the courtyard, where Rafe's unamiable black thoroughbred was being walked up and down by one of the grooms, from the archway toward the topiary garden, where Emily and Rafe were now seated in the summerhouse.

Jack gazed coldly at the close kinsman who had wronged him so very greatly. Of all the men in England, why did cruel fate have to give Emily Fairfield to Rafe Warrender? he puzzled.

"Come on, let's spy on them," Peter breathed, and before Jack knew it, the boy had run across the stone bridge and down to the garden wall, where the entrance was almost hidden among climbing roses and honeysuckle.

Jack hesitated, but then something made him follow. Soon he too was gazing through the entrance toward the summerhouse, where Emily and Rafe seemed deep in conversation.

Emily had perceived both of them, but gave no intimation to Rafe as he remarked on how splendid the peacocks were this autumn, especially the white ones, of which the Hall possessed four pair. She smiled and murmured something in reply, she knew not really what.

Bees hummed among the asters that bloomed around the summerhouse, and the autumn sun shimmered on the little raised pool in the very center of the garden. It was the sort of magical moment that should have been shared with someone she loved, not with Sir Rafe Warrender, whom she would marry but would never love. Her glance moved toward Jack Lincoln's silhouette in the gateway. Then a wave of anger suddenly washed over her, not only because he and her son were so blatantly watching, but because she wished it were Jack who sat here with her now. But it wasn't Jack, and it never could be.

Rafe couldn't help studying her profile. She really was enchantingly lovely. He might almost have married her even if she hadn't been Felix Reynolds's daughter! He certainly looked forward to getting her between the sheets. Sooner, rather than later. Could she be persuaded to bring the marriage day forward? He slipped his hand into his right pocket to call upon the aid of his lucky quartz pebble. "You do know that my feelings for you grow deeper each time we meet, don't you, Emily?"

"Why, Rafe, I . . ." She gave a weak smile and forced herself to stop thinking about Jack.

Suddenly, he reached for her hand and raised her fingertips to his lips. After carefully kissing each one, he gazed ardently into her eyes. "I will cherish you, Emily. No bride will ever have been more cared for."

"You are too kind, Rafe."

"No, my dear, I merely state a fact. I look forward to the moment we are together as man and wife, when I may claim you in the fullest sense of the word."

Her cheeks became a little pink. "Your eagerness flatters me greatly, and . . . and I will do all in my power to be a dutiful wife."

"I know that you expressed a desire to marry on Christmas Eve, but that seems an unconscionable time away."

"Unconscionable? But it is less than two months." *Please don't ask me to change it to an earlier date . . .* Concealing her other hand, she crossed her fingers, a superstitious gesture that was worthy of Rafe himself.

"To me, even a month seems a lifetime," he declared passionately. "Please let us marry sooner. Much sooner."

She was so horrified that it was all she could do to hide her reaction. Somehow she managed a trill of teasing laughter. "Sir, you should know better than to expect a bride to hurry her wedding preparations! I have it all planned, and nothing must be permitted to spoil it. For it *will* be spoiled if things are rushed."

"But—"

"Please, Rafe. Indulge me. Let me be your perfect bride." She forced herself to give him a limpid look.

He knew that to press the point would raise her suspicions, so he decided to back down. But as he smiled understandingly, he really felt like shaking her. "If that is your true wish, my dear, then of course we will leave matters as they are." He kissed her fingertips again.

Her eyes were drawn to his signet ring—the famous Agincourt ring that Henry V had bestowed upon Rafe's ancestor in 1415. Something about it puzzled her, but she couldn't quite think what it was. Suddenly, she realized. The stem of the rose had five thorns, yet there were only four on the ring Geoffrey had sketched! She remembered particularly because the four had balanced the design quite perfectly; the addition of a fifth robbed it of symmetry. And now she came to really study the ring; it did not seem old enough to have been worn in 1415. The engraving was too clearly defined, and the gold itself too shining and unblemished. It couldn't possibly be the treasured medieval heirloom. "You have a new ring?" she asked, unable to help herself even though the abrupt change of subject must have seemed rather pointed.

He was taken unawares. "Why do you ask?"

She thought an odd glint entered his eyes, a sharpening almost. "I notice that it isn't the one you wore for the portrait Geoffrey was painting. That had four thorns, this has five."

He stared at her, then let go of her hand in order to look at the ring. "I, er . . ." He recovered a little. "How observant you are, my dear, more observant than Geoffrey, as it happens. You see, I lost the original ring at a St. James's Palace reception two years ago, and was obliged to have this copy made. The fool of a jeweler bungled things at the last moment and had to add the extra thorn to hide his clumsiness. He charged me much less, of course, so I accepted it as it was."

"Oh, I see. How very unfortunate to have lost the original."

"Most unfortunate," he murmured. "However, Geoffrey

cannot have noticed when he painted it. Maybe the light was wrong."

"Yes, that must be it," she replied, but she knew he was lying. The light in the long gallery was always good, and if there was one thing upon which Geoffrey prided himself, it was his complete accuracy! If he drew four thorns, then four thorns were there, which meant that Rafe had not lost the Agincourt ring two years before in London. In fact, she recalled that Geoffrey had sketched the hand and ring on the very day of his death. She remembered watching his pencil skim deftly over the canvas; and the thorns, one, two, three, four . . . Geoffrey had counted them under his breath, then smiled at her.

Rafe watched her face intently, but her manner soothed him. Damn Geoffrey Fairfield for his slavish attention to detail, he thought, and damn that jeweler to perdition and back for making such an elementary mistake! But the error had been observed now; it was too late to rectify matters. He would have to trust to luck, which, after all, had been on his side for some time now. So he smiled again. "You are making me the happiest man on earth, Emily."

"Now I *know* you flatter me," she replied lightly, wishing he would stop pretending an affection he did not feel. The ring ceased to matter as her glance stole back to the entrance to the garden, and Jack. *Oh, Jack . . .*

"But it isn't mere flattery, for I mean every word," Rafe protested. He *definitely* meant every word, for he had his sights upon Felix Reynolds's fortune! He put a hand to her cheek and made her look at him. "We have not sealed our bargain with a kiss," he whispered.

She wanted to say no, and to get up to continue the walk, but knew she could not. Just as she also knew she could not have the man she really wanted. With a huge effort she resisted the need to look toward Jack again, and instead gave Rafe a too-bright smile. "A kiss, sir? Yes, of course," she said softly and leaned toward him.

His hand slid from her cheek into her hair, which felt so warm and seductive against his fingers that he could almost have forgotten himself. But he didn't forget himself; he was very careful to kiss her offered lips as gently and lovingly as if she had been a virgin on her first tryst. He felt her allure reaching out to him, arousing the passion he knew he must keep in check for the time being. All in good time. He'd have her as often as he liked once she was his wife. And he'd use her for his pleasure, oh, how he'd use her . . . So he drew back, a tender smile warming his face, his eyes alight with something she could not read.

As she gazed at him, she had no idea at all that what he really wanted to do was thrust her against one of the columns and take her as if she were a whore lying against a tree in St. James's Park.

Peering through the wrought iron door, Peter was appalled at what he saw. "How can she kiss him? How can she bear to let him . . . ?" He bit his lip and had to take a huge breath to keep tears at bay.

Jack put a comforting hand on the boy's shoulder, although he himself was scarcely less upset. "You have to accept it, Peter, for that is the way it is going to be," he murmured.

Another voice spoke, startling them both. "We cannot permit this nonsense to continue, gentlemen. Are we agreed?"

They turned to see Cora standing there. She had observed them from an upper window, and had come down to commence her stratagems. She nodded toward the summerhouse. "It galls me to think of that scoundrel becoming my son-in-law, and I do not think that either of you find it to your liking either. Am I right?"

Jack did not think it was his place to express an opinion, but Peter made his feelings plain. "I don't want Mama to marry him. She's far too good for him."

Cora's glance encompassed Jack's silent lips, then returned to her grandson. "Now then, Peter, I wish to have words in private with Mr. Lincoln, so you must leave us."

"Oh, but—"

"Do as I ask, there's a good boy."

Peter looked rebellious for a moment, then gave in, but before hurrying away, he gave Jack an imploring look. "You do promise not to leave without saying good-bye, don't you?"

"I wouldn't dream of going without taking a proper farewell, Peter."

Reassured, the boy hastened away.

Cora then confronted Jack. "Have you no opinion of Emily's dealings with Sir Rafe?"

"It is hardly my business to pronounce on such a matter, Mrs. Preston, especially as I am about to leave Fairfield Hall. Er, urgent business, you understand . . ."

"Urgent business? Come sir, we both know why you are expected to leave."

"Do we?" He felt his cheeks heat up a little with embarrassment, for he had not expected Emily to confide this particular matter.

Cora read his thoughts. "Oh, nothing was actually said, sir, but then it wasn't necessary. A mother can read her daughter like a book, believe me."

"Then you will understand why I must go."

"Sir, it will be over my dead body that you leave this house," she answered, then added, "especially when I strongly suspect the blame in the matter to be equally apportioned! She doesn't want Sir Rafe to know anything about you. In fact, she was at great pains to extract my silence on the matter. What do you make of that?"

"I don't know," he replied truthfully.

"Then I shall tell you. She has a guilty conscience, sir. She knows she was at fault, and she would prefer to draw a discreet curtain over the whole business."

"Mrs. Preston—"

"Enough, sir! You did not come here to meekly slip away again, like a cur with its tail between its legs. You came to save us from your cousin, and save us you will!"

Jack stared at her, shaken to the core that she knew he and Rafe were related.

Cora took a step closer. "You do not think Felix wrote a long letter to me without explaining exactly what he wished, do you?"

Jack recovered a little. "If he has told you everything, Mrs. Preston, then you know full well that I gave him my word I would come here and do everything in my power to make you all secure again, secure from debt and from Rafe Warrender. I have already proved a failure, for in a single day I have managed to get myself ordered off the estate. So much for being your secret guardian!"

"Being ordered off the estate and actually going are two very different matters, sir." Cora's voice broke slightly, and she blinked back tears. "Felix's wishes are everything to me, Mr. Lincoln. His letter told me more than I have said, for he confided that he thinks you are the perfect man for Emily. I agree with him, so I *beg* you not leave, sir. You can still rescue us from the Warrender dragon, and carry Emily off in your manly arms. She does not know it, but she has been waiting all her life for you."

Neither of them had heard a stealthy step among the bushes that shaded the entrance to the garden; and neither of them had seen Peter part the leaves to listen to all they said. His eyes had widened with each word.

23

Cora pursed her lips a little. "We have both been drawn into Felix's web, Mr. Lincoln, and I for one am determined to see his wishes come to fruition. If you leave the Hall, you will be failing Felix most signally. And you will be failing yourself, to say nothing of Emily, who needs you very much indeed."

"Mrs. Preston, I do not think your daughter would agree at all; indeed, things between us could hardly be worse."

"If that is what you think, you clearly do not understand women as well as I imagined from the look of you," Cora said a little wryly.

"Maybe women have not mattered as much to me until now."

"I'm very glad to hear it."

"My cousin is the most abhorrent man on this earth, and I believe I would rather die than permit him to marry Emily," Jack said frankly, then hastily corrected himself. "I, er, mean Mrs. Fairfield."

"No, you don't, sir, you mean Emily." Cora smiled knowingly. "As to your sentiments regarding Sir Rafe, well, I can well understand. He and Sir Quentin Brockhampton laid false evidence in order to take what was yours, didn't they? *You* are the rightful bearer of the blue rose badge he wears with such swagger." She smiled again. "Oh, yes, Felix's letter was most informative."

Among the bushes, Peter's lips parted.

Jack felt the need to explain his reticence about Rafe. "Mrs. Preston, when I first arrived here, it didn't seem appropriate to mention the blood tie because of Emily's imminent betrothal to him. I could hardly say, 'Oh, apropos of Rafe Warrender, he is the cousin who cheated me of my birthright, and I despise him.' "

"I quite accept your reason, Mr. Lincoln, but I think you should tell Emily."

"And blacken myself still more in her eyes?" Jack raised an eyebrow.

"She ought to be made aware."

"You may think so, Mrs. Preston, but what if I were to say to you that I thought Emily should also know Felix is her father?"

The revelation made Peter gasp.

Cora heard the sound, but did not know what it was or exactly where it came from. "Did you hear that?" she asked uneasily, glancing around, but at that moment a cat slipped out of the garden and ran belly-low up the slope toward the house. Cora immediately relaxed again and returned her attention to Jack. "I know Emily has to learn my rather shocking secret, Mr. Lincoln, especially when I see daily how much like his grandfather Peter is becoming. They are peas from the same pod, are they not?"

"Yes."

"So I will tell her soon, and I expect you to do the same."

He nodded reluctantly. "If that is your advice, then I will act upon it, but I cannot help thinking—"

"I know what I'm talking about in this, sir. Just tell her everything." Cora inhaled. "Now then, we digress a little by speaking of my secret, for we were discussing the problem of Sir Rafe Warrender. You cannot be aware yet, but Sir Quentin Brockhampton is his guest at the castle."

"Birds of a feather," Jack murmured.

"Oh, indeed so. Vultures, I fancy." Cora drew a long breath. "We must do something about all of this, sir, and to that end we need to pool all our knowledge."

"There are more of us with knowledge to pool than perhaps you realize," Jack said, and told her about the message from Cristoval.

"Cristoval? Ah, yes, Felix mentions him, and you spoke of him at dinner last night. Don Cristoval de Soto is his full name, I believe? There is an Indian too, I believe. Er, Minco, or some such name?"

"Manco."

"That's it. Well, no doubt the presence of a real Peruvian Indian in Temford will make Peter smile for a change. What do you think Don Cristoval has to tell you, Mr. Lincoln?"

"I don't know, but it must be of importance for them to abandon their stay in London in order to come to Temford. I intend to go to the Royal Oak when I leave here."

"But you are *not* leaving here, sir," Cora pointed out firmly.

"Mrs. Preston—"

"Forget Emily's wishes in this, sir, for you are *my* guest, not hers. And I will not hear of Don Cristoval and Manco staying at an inn when there are rooms aplenty at the Hall. No, do not protest anymore, for my mind is made up. You stay here, and so do your friends . . . *Felix's* friends," she added pointedly, as if that would put a stop to the nonsense once and for all.

In his leafy hiding place, Peter hugged himself with delight. Manco was going to actually come to the hall? *Oh, joy!*

But Jack could not leave the matter at that. "Mrs. Preston, in spite of what you say, neither I nor my friends can—"

"Heavens above, Mr. Lincoln, how many times must I make myself clear on this point? You came here ostensibly to see me, and you are therefore *my* guest, not Emily's. I will deal with her directly, for I can argue with some justification that she has no right to send my guest away."

"But she does have the right, Mrs. Preston, because I transgressed in a very grave way."

"Did you? I rather fancy that you are assuming too much of the blame. Can you state quite categorically that she did not at any point welcome your attentions?"

Peter's jaw dropped. *Attentions? What did Grandmama mean? What had Mr. Lincoln done?*

Jack looked away. Could he say it? No, of course he couldn't. Damn it, he *knew* Emily had welcomed him.

Cora smiled triumphantly. "You see? You know you have to stay—for everyone's sake. I am so opposed to Sir Rafe that I can hardly bear even to look at the fellow. I never thought I would stoop to such things as hiding people's notes, but I even did that today. I would do *anything* to prevent this marriage, anything at all." Her glance moved to the pair in the summerhouse. "So let us go over the facts as we know them and see if two heads can make the business more clear."

So they did just that, listing and discussing until they were sure they had considered everything. But at the end, Cora shook her head in bewilderment. "Why is he so determined to marry her, Mr. Lincoln? Oh, she is beautiful, but I have the strongest instinct that there is much more to this than meets the eye. He is going to inordinate lengths to see that the match comes off. I'm sure it is no coincidence that so many letters of demand come from clients of Sir Quentin Brockhampton! I sometimes think our only friend in all the world is Mr. Mackay, who has put himself out most considerably on our behalf. It is not his fault that all his efforts have been in vain. Apart from him, everyone else has done all they can to make things more difficult and pressing for Emily."

"I am as mystified as you what reason may lie behind it all," Jack replied. "If Emily were a great heiress, I could understand it, but we both know she isn't."

"Yes, I fear we do. However, mysteries beg to be solved, sir, and you and I appear to be cast in the role of investigators."

Jack smiled. "We do indeed."

"So I take it you will not argue anymore about staying on?"

"I will not argue anymore."

Peter beamed among the leaves.

Barely an hour later, Emily confronted Jack in the grand parlor. Her hazel eyes sparked with mixed emotions as she closed the door, then leaned back against it to meet his gaze across the room. "How *dare* you stay on here when I expressly asked you to leave!" she breathed.

Rafe had gone now, and Cora and Peter had wisely made themselves very scarce after Cora had endured an exceedingly difficult meeting with her daughter. Their raised voices had been heard all over the house, and then Emily had come for this next confrontation. She had changed into her heather pink gown, and her short hair was a little wayward because she had worn her riding hat for so long earlier on. He could see by the quick rise and fall of her breast that her anger was very real. But her eyes reflected other feelings too. Or was he simply hoping that he detected more in their bright depths? He struggled for something to say.

"Mrs. Fairfield . . . Emily, I—"

"I gave you no leave to address me in so familiar a fashion!" she cried, straightening from the door and advancing a few steps.

"I don't mean to insult you in any way, I just want there to be no ill feeling."

"Then you should leave the Hall immediately!"

He met her eyes. "I would have done, believe me, but I have been prevailed upon to stay."

"So my wishes mean nothing to you?"

"You know that isn't so," he replied reproachfully.

"I know nothing of the sort! You broke every rule when we were by the river, and if you had an ounce of honor, you would leave, whether or not my foolish mother begs you to stay."

His anger began to rise too. "Maybe I did break the rules, but I don't think you were as entirely opposed to my actions as you would now have me believe!"

Heat rushed into her cheeks. "That you should say so is yet another mark of your dishonor," she replied.

"There is no dishonor in this particular truth," he said.

"I want you to leave this house, Mr. Lincoln," she repeated levelly without looking at him.

"Please don't ask this of me, for I have given my word to Mrs. Preston," he said quietly. *And I gave my word to your father before that* . . .

"You were pleased to bestow your promise to her *after* I had already ordered you to leave."

He was now equally as incensed. "An order that was issued in the heat of the moment!"

Her lips parted on a gasp of outrage. "The heat of the moment!"

"Are you going to tell me that *isn't* how it was?"

Her chin came up. "Yes."

"So I misinterpreted events immediately before your attack of conscience? I *imagined* you were in my arms, returning my kiss?" His voice and manner defied her to deny the truth.

"I . . . I was carried away. I used to go there with Geoffrey . . ."

"Don't make excuses, Emily! This has nothing to do with the past, it is to do with now! You *wanted* to be in my arms, you *wanted* that kiss, and you would have continued if I hadn't said what I did. I reminded you of your debts, and so you overreacted. Now we have come to this, bandying angry words like spiteful children. Well, you will have to forgive my refusal to leave, because this particular cuckoo remains in the nest at your mother's behest." And remains, he vowed to himself, because he promised his help to Felix!

She stared at him, unable to credit that she was being defied beneath her own roof. But deep within, hidden but not completely denied, there was a part of her that was glad he was staying. She looked away. "I find you quite detestable," she breathed.

"No, you don't. You like me as much as I like you. And don't pretend otherwise, for it will not wash!"

Her eyes flew furiously back to him. "Why are you doing this, sir? Is it my seduction you have in mind? Do you imagine I will after all prove an easy conquest who will swoon into your masculine arms when next you beckon? Well, you are going to be disappointed, Mr. Lincoln, because I would rather marry a thousand Sir Rafes than surrender another kiss to you!"

"Then you would rather marry a devious, thieving scoundrel who bends the law in order to take what does not belong to him!" Jack cried.

Emily flinched. "What do you mean by that?"

"Simply that Warrender is my cousin, and had records forged in order to appear legally justified when he challenged me through the courts for my birthright! He won, thanks to Sir Quentin Brockhampton, and I lost everything that was dear to me. Warrender is the reason I left England, the reason I have spent years in exile. He is a disgrace to his title, a disgrace to the rank of gentleman, and a disgrace to England itself. So, my dear Mrs. Fairfield, if you would rather marry him a thousand times over than accept a kiss from me, I wish you well!"

With that, he pushed past her and flung the door open. As he walked away, he did not look back, but his heart felt as if it would burst. "Oh, Emily, Emily, what have you done to me?" he whispered.

24

Emily was shaken as she went downstairs after the recriminative encounter with Jack. She could hardly believe what he had just told her, and her thoughts were still in turmoil as she found her mother waiting for her in the hall.

"Emily, I have something important to discuss with you . . ." Cora began, having steeled herself to confess about her affair with Felix.

Emily pulled herself together, determined to have a few things out with her troublesome parent. "Well, better late than never," she replied shortly, her gaze accusing.

Cora drew back. "I . . . I beg your pardon?"

"Presumably you are about to tell me that Sir Rafe and Mr. Lincoln are cousins?"

Cora blinked. "I, er . . ."

"Mama, did it not occur to you to tell me?" Reproach rang in the question.

"Well, I . . ." Cora didn't know what to say. She cleared her throat and managed to meet Emily's eyes. "What is to happen now that Mr. Lincoln has told you?"

"Happen? Well, he still flatly refuses to leave, but then you already know that, don't you? In spite of everything, and in the face of his being the enemy of the man I am to marry, your guest is arrogantly determined to stay."

"Yes, my dear, because I have made it impossible for him to go," Cora said quietly.

"Why? Why is it so important to *you* that he stays?" Emily demanded. "Does it simply amuse you to have Sir Rafe's foe beneath this roof?"

"That was unworthy, Emily. I want Mr. Lincoln here because he brings Felix a little closer."

"And that is the only reason?"

"Isn't it enough?"

"I suppose it will have to be, since I apparently have no say in what happens in this house."

"Oh, come now, Emily, don't be so theatrical. You really are making a mountain out of a molehill."

"A mountain out of a—? Mama, Mr. Lincoln *despises* Sir Rafe!"

"I know how he feels," Cora observed wryly.

"Don't try to turn this into something amusing, because I will not have it!" Emily cried.

"Amusing? Oh, my dear, that is the last thing I think it is, for Sir Rafe cheated Mr. Lincoln out of all that was his."

"So it pleases you to believe."

Cora's eyes flickered. "It also pleases Felix to think it. Sir Rafe—with the legal sleight of hand of Sir Quentin Brockhampton—conspired to forge an entry of birth that seemed to prove that his ancestress, not Mr. Lincoln's, was born first. Mr. Lincoln said nothing to us because he did not know if you loved Sir Rafe." Cora paused. "This disgraceful history gives me yet another reason to oppose this match, for how can I possibly support your alliance with such an unmitigated villain?"

"I still say that we only have Mr. Lincoln's side of the story, which, I may point out, is all Felix has too." Emily's chin came up in that mulish way that conveyed a determination not to be reasonable in any way, shape, or form.

"Be honest with yourself, Emily Fairfield, admit that in your heart of hearts you know the truth to be on Mr. Lincoln's side."

"I will not stoop to answer that."

"Which is answer in itself," Cora observed smoothly. "Well, my dear, you now have another problem to contend with as well, because Peter and I not only wish Mr. Lincoln to remain here, but we also wish to invite his Peruvian friends to stay as well. May I proceed with the invitation?"

Emily struggled to regain her aplomb. "Mama, I do not know why you bother to ask, for you will do as you please anyway," she said, not a little resentfully.

"Only because you indulge me, my dear." Cora smiled infuriatingly.

"I wish *you* would indulge *me* occasionally."

"I do, my dear, and you know it."

"Do I? Mama, you are obstructing this match at every turn—at least, you are attempting to. It hurts me very much that you cannot accept that in spite of everything, I have very good reason for wishing to become Lady Warrender."

"I know you do, Emily. You have debts, but surely Felix's purse has alleviated matters a little?"

"A little, and only temporarily." Emily felt she had to overlook part of her promise to Rafe. She would tell her mother about Geoffrey's IOUs; his possible French sympathies were a different matter, however. "Mama, the situation is far worse than you realize. Far worse."

Cora gazed at her. "What are you saying, my dear?" she asked quietly.

"That Geoffrey left many extra gaming debts—outstanding IOUs—than originally seemed the case, and Rafe's assistance is now more essential than ever."

Cora breathed out slowly. "How did you hear about these extra debts?"

"Rafe told me."

"Oh, Emily! And you believe him?"

Emily's eyes darkened resentfully. "Yes, Mama, I believe him. He showed me one of them. It was made out to Sir Lumsley Carrowby, and Rafe settled it. It was Geoffrey's writing, there is no mistake."

"So dear Sir Rafe has produced a new lever to use upon you, has he?" Cora observed with cool anger.

"I admit that I now feel under more pressure than before to comply with his wishes, but he says he holds me in high regard, and I believe him."

"Oh, don't make me shudder, for we are talking of the scapegrace who had evidence fabricated in order to rob his cousin of what was rightfully his!"

"Mama, I cannot stop you from opposing the match, but one thing I *do* ask of you. Please don't mention these extra debts to anyone else. It is Rafe's wish—and mine—that Geoffrey's reputation should not be harmed, which it certainly would be if it became generally known that he left behind a sheaf of IOUs as well as the other debts."

"A *sheaf*?"

"Yes. And maybe you should know that it was Rafe himself who expressed a desire to shield Peter by preventing any stigma attaching to his father's name."

"So he's the Archangel Rafe now, is he?" Cora murmured.

Emily ignored the acid remark. "Do I have your promise of silence about what I have just told you, Mama?"

"Yes."

"Thank you." Emily caught up her skirts and hurried away, her shoes tapping on the echoing floor, but Cora called desperately after her. She *had* to make her confession now . . . !

"Emily, there is something else I must say to you."

Emily halted and turned. "Something else?"

Cora gazed at her, suddenly unable to put it all into words. Tears sprang to her eyes, her lips trembled, and she bowed her head. Greatly concerned, Emily hurried back to her. "Mama? What is it? What's wrong?"

"I . . . I have a confession," Cora whispered.

Emily led her to the window seat that looked out at the knot garden. It was a particularly poignant view, reminding Cora once again of the last time she and Felix had been together. Emily took her hand. "Tell me what is upsetting you, Mama. I know we have just had words, but you realize it has not altered my regard for you, don't you?"

Cora exhaled very slowly. "Yes, my dear, but what I am about to tell you may make all the difference. You see, I . . . I have a past . . ."

Emily's lips parted. "A past? Mama, you make it sound as if you were a . . . well, a scarlet woman."

"Mayhap that is what you will think of me when you know."

"Know what?" Felix's name slid unbidden into Emily's mind.

Cora swallowed. "My dear, you know I did not love your father . . ."

"Yes."

"And that I *did* love Felix?"

The truth began to dawn on Emily. "Yes," she said slowly.

"And have you never wondered about Peter's adventurous spirit? His desire to travel the world?"

"Felix is my father, isn't he?" Emily said quietly.

Cora closed her eyes. "Yes," she whispered.

Emily rose slowly to her feet. She supposed she had known it ever since she first realized there had been something between Felix and her mother; she just hadn't acknowledged the secret thought.

Cora watched her anxiously, uncertain of how she was reacting. "Felix is a thousand times finer than the man you have always thought of as your father. He is to me what Jack Lincoln should—" She broke off.

Again Emily finished the sentence for her. "What Jack Lincoln should be to me? Is that what you were going to say, Mama?"

Cora looked out of the window. "Yes," she said softly. "Yes, that's exactly what I'm saying, my dear. I loved and lost, and that pain still cuts through me every day of my life. Please don't let the same thing happen to you."

Emily couldn't bear it a moment longer. She caught up her skirts and ran from the hall.

Cora hid her face in her hands.

25

Not long after his painful meeting with Emily, Jack drove to the Royal Oak to see Cristoval and Manco. He took Cora's chariot, at that lady's absolute insistence, for she was quite determined that Cristoval and Manco should stay at the Hall.

The winter afternoon was drawing in, and there were lights in window as the chariot drove into the inn yard. Jack alighted, then turned as his attention was drawn by the noise issuing from the handsome new assembly room. Preparations for Bonfire Night were now moving swiftly toward completion. Hammering, voices, and general noise carried into the yard, and more shouting came from the gloom by the bonfire beyond the new building, where more men were piling it with the remains of a rotten old cart.

The air was very cold, and Jack's breath was visible as he removed his top hat and lowered his head to enter the inn, where the landlord, Mr. Porter, soon directed him to the rooms occupied by his friends. The innkeeper did not look best pleased when Manco's name was mentioned, and muttered something about "damned heathen music at all hours."

"Heathen music?" Jack repeated curiously. Not flute playing in the middle of Shropshire!

"Mr. Manco started playing his pennywhistle, or whatever it is, at three o'clock last night, and woke everyone up with his stamping. He said he was preparing for some woman named Vera Cotcher to come in the morning. I had the devil's own job telling him he couldn't cause such a disturbance here in Temford. I also warned him not to entertain any women in his room. The Royal Oak is a respectable house. Don Cristoval prevailed upon him in the end."

"Ah."

"If it happens again tonight, I shall have no alternative but to request them to leave."

"I don't think it will come to that, sir."

"I trust not, sir, I trust not, for it does a hostelry's reputation no good at all to have to eject guests."

Manco was running true to form, Jack thought as he hastened upstairs.

Cristoval was delighted to see him. "Ah, my dear friend! Come in, come in."

"I thought you were in London," Jack said, closing the door behind him.

"And so we would be, but for a certain development," Cristoval replied, going through to the hammock and prodding Manco, who had fallen into a deep sleep.

The Indian awoke up with a start, then his face broke into a glad smile when he saw their visitor. "Capac Jack!" he cried, and slipped lithely from the swaying hammock to hurry over to pump Jack's arm.

Jack grinned at him. "I hear you've been serenading the unserenadable again. Manco, you old reprobate."

Manco scowled. "Flute good. Please Viracocha."

Cristoval gave Jack a long-suffering look. "I do not think I can endure it here much longer, Jack. Trouble seems to follow Manco around, and it has become quite intolerable."

Manco continued to scowl. "England very silly place," he said, sitting down on the floor and crossing his legs.

Cristoval produced a glass from one of the portmanteaux, then took it to a table where stood an open bottle of *aguardiente* and two other glasses. He poured a lavish measure into all three, and a friendship toast was warmly shared. Jack then leaned back against the windowsill and looked at Cristoval. "What is this important news you have for me?"

Cristoval sat in an armchair. "Well, the laws of coincidence being what they are, I happened to take refreshment at a London coffeehouse where a certain Sir Quentin Brockhampton was obliged to share my table. Ah, I see you recall Sir Quentin's name."

"I do. Coincidence indeed, Cristoval."

"And a rewarding one to boot. Sir Quentin is a very busy

man who is also clumsy with the sheaves of papers he carries with him. He spilled some to the floor, and I helped to retrieve them." Cristoval drew the stolen letter from his pocket and held it out to Jack. "This rather caught my eye, so I saw fit to keep it. It may or may not refer to the disappearance of the money Felix lodged with Sir Quentin all those years ago, but the date—December 14th—made me rather suspicious."

Jack cast his eyes swiftly over it. "Suspicious with some justification," he murmured. "'The lady' must be Emily Fairfield, for it fits too well with the date. And GF must be her late husband, Geoffrey."

"Brockhampton is here in Temford," Cristoval said then.

"I know."

"Did you also know that the unfortunate Mrs. Preston has kindled a flame in his unlovable heart?"

"Really?"

"So he informed me."

"Did he say anything else?" Jack inquired, sipping the *aguardiente* and savoring the taste. He'd forgotten how much he liked it.

"Well, he said he had to see Warrender as a matter of some urgency because he had heard something from a third party."

"Something?"

Cristoval nodded. "Unfortunately, he did not say what this news was, simply that it was information he felt he had to pass on quickly." He smiled. "Rather like my reason for coming to Temford, eh, my friend?"

Jack smiled. "True." Then the smile faded as he thought about what Cristoval had just said. "Still, although we are sure this letter refers to Fairfield Hall, we cannot be equally certain about the reason for Brockhampton's visit. This 'matter of urgency' might be in connection with any number of things. Men like these have fingers in all manner of pies."

Cristoval nodded again. "That is true, although a feeling in my gut tells me there is a connection."

"Probably. My dear cousin pays his toad well for his tricky services, mm? I have no doubt that Brockhampton received similar sums when he successfully conducted Warrender's case against me." Jack glanced back out of the window toward the castle and the flag bearing the blue rose badge that fluttered from one of the towers. *His* rose! His eyes grew cold. "You have no idea how much I detest Rafe Warrender, or how it tears my very heart out to think of him marrying Emily Fairfield," he murmured.

Manco got to his feet and joined him at the window. "One arrow or one magic, devil die, finish," he muttered, bestowing a dark look upon the castle, then going to help himself to some more *aguardiente,* for there were many times when it pleased him to forget he was Cristoval's servant.

Jack turned inquiringly to Cristoval, who rolled his eyes, then related the story of Rafe's top hat. "Manco believes we could bring this whole matter to a satisfactory conclusion by slaying Warrender on the spot," he finished.

Jack grinned. "An excellent notion, but I for one have no desire to swing for murder."

Manco wasn't impressed. "Hmm," he said as he resumed his place on the floor.

"Have you encountered Warrender yet?" Cristoval asked Jack.

"No. Actually, he doesn't even know I am here. He soon will though, because Emily has learned that I am his cousin."

Silence fell on the room for a while, then Cristoval spoke again. "Jack, from what you have said, can we take it that your feelings toward Mrs. Fairfield are somewhat warmer than anticipated?"

Jack nodded. "Yes, damn it, although Felix anticipated it well enough. But things have not gone well in that respect, or indeed in respect of my whole purpose in coming here. I promised Felix I would do all in my power to save his secret family from Warrender, but I have not advanced one inch in the matter of prizing the villain's claws out of Fairfield Hall."

Cristoval looked sympathetically at him. "Tell us all that has happened since you arrived."

Jack did as he was asked, finishing, "So there you have it. Emily Fairfield is drawn to me and certainly doesn't love Warrender, but she seems to think she has no choice except to marry him. Nothing anyone says makes any difference; she doesn't waver from her decision. And I cling to my welcome at the Hall because her mother and son wish it, not because the lady herself wishes it."

Manco gave a rare bark of laughter. "You are fool, Capac Jack. If woman wish you go, then you go. She say one thing, mean another. All women same."

Cristoval nodded. "He's right, Jack, my friend."

"Maybe . . . probably . . . oh, I don't know."

Manco went so far as to laugh again. "Capac Jack in love!" he declared. "Is air here. Pizarro air."

"It wasn't the air that went too far by the river, it was me. I inadvertently reminded her of her problems, and she took fright."

Manco nodded. "Took fright, maybe, but not until kiss over," he pointed out sagely.

Jack gave a long sigh. "Well, I live to fight another day—just—although what difference it will make I cannot think. She is absolutely set upon becoming Lady Warrender."

Cristoval looked at him. "Is that the root of it? She simply desires a title?"

Jack shook his head. "No, it's because she thinks she must."

Manco was curious. "But why Warrender devil do all this? Why he so keen to marry woman with nothing? You have answer, Capac Jack?"

"No," Jack admitted. "Actually, that is what Cora Preston and I have been wondering too. Warrender isn't the sort of man to do anything for nothing, and I for one do not think he would regard desire for Emily Fairfield as sufficient reason to go to all these astonishing lengths. If she were a great heiress, I could understand it. But she isn't. She doesn't even have Fairfield Hall, but merely holds it during Peter's minority."

Silence fell again, then Cristoval glanced curiously at Jack. "What is Cora Preston like, my friend? Is she worthy of Felix?"

"Oh, yes, Cristoval, more than worthy."

"I wish I could meet her."

"You will meet her, for she insists that you and Manco stay at the Hall."

Manco groaned. "But Manco want go home!"

Cristoval frowned at him. "Well, you can't go home. Not yet, anyway. Shame on you, Manco, would you leave our friend here with his problems unresolved?"

Manco shifted uncomfortably on the floor. "No. That not fair, Capac Cristoval."

"Maybe, but I want you to stop moaning. You've been nothing but trouble since we set foot in England."

"Manco good, say nothing even when we go Bath."

"That's enough," Cristoval said sharply, giving the Indian a warning look.

As Manco fell into an immediate sulk, Jack looked curiously at them both. "Bath? You went there?"

Cristoval cleared his throat. "Er, yes, as it is on the way to London from Bristol. But we stayed only briefly, for it was disagreeably crowded. The season, you know, so we went quickly on to London."

Manco gave him a look, but said nothing. Jack observed the look, and also said nothing, but he thought very much. Clearly there was a little mystery here, and he could not help wondering what on earth it was. The silence hung a little heavily, so Jack roused himself to speak to Manco again. "You won't have time to be homesick once you reach the Hall, because Emily's son, Peter, will be dogging your tracks all the time. He is already your ardent fan."

"Fan?" The Indian didn't understand.

"Admirer. He is very much Felix's grandson, even to longing to explore the world, and he is utterly fascinated by everything to do with the Incas."

Manco smiled approvingly. "Boy good," he declared.

"No doubt, but if you have him at your heels all day every day, do not be surprised. And maybe I should also warn you that he is inclined to stalk anything that moves." Jack smiled at them both. "Well, if you're coming to the Hall, you had better get ready, because the carriage is waiting. And, by the way, please don't forget that although Cora Preston knows everything because Felix was very thorough in his letter, Emily and her son do not yet know about their relationship to him—at least, they may by now, for Cora was going to speak to Emily about it. But I'm not sure whether or not it has been done, so a guarded tongue would be wise."

They promised to be careful.

Cora and Emily were seated in the great parlor with Peter, waiting for Jack to conduct his friends in to introduce them. It was early evening, and the candles had been lit. Peter was in a lather of excitement, having glimpsed Manco arriving. The two women did not know quite what to expect, for they had no experience whatsoever of either Peruvian noblemen or Indians.

The atmosphere between Cora and her daughter was a little strained because Emily felt as if she did not really know her mother as well as she had always thought. Cora almost seemed more of an opponent than an ally, and the revelation about Felix had been one too many for the time being. There wasn't a chill between them, just a slight awkwardness, as if both felt they had to relearn a closeness they had hitherto been able to take for granted. By now they also realized that Peter somehow knew about it already. Emily had discovered this when she took her son aside to tell him what she herself had only just learned. Cora denied having told him, but admitted telling Jack; which left Emily to draw what seemed the obvious conclusion.

The thought that Jack had taken it upon himself to tell such a secret to her son incensed her all over again, to such an extent that as she now awaited his arrival with his two friends, her whole body quivered with suppressed anger. But she was determined not to make a scene of any kind; indeed she had set herself the task of being the perfect hostess. She had to give herself something difficult to do, something that would take a great deal of effort, or all her rage and bitterness would boil over.

So she sat neatly in her royal blue velvet dinner gown, a silver silk shawl around her shoulders, toying with the fan resting in her lap. Diamonds sparkled at her ears and throat, and there was no need for any rouge to warm her cheeks, for the glow Cora had mentioned earlier in the day was upon her still, although its cause was no longer quite as straightforward as it had been then.

At last, footsteps approached, the door swung open, and Peter leapt politely to his feet as the three men came in. The boy's eyes flew to Manco, Cora's to Cristoval, and Emily's to both—then lingered reluctantly upon Jack. With a shock she found he was already looking at her. For a moment both their hearts missed secret beats, then they looked hastily away again.

Cristoval observed Cora with complete approval. How excellently her mauve satin gown became her, and how charmingly she had dressed her silvery hair. Felix Reynolds was clearly a man of great discernment. Cristoval crossed the room to draw her hand to his lips. Admiration shone in his dark Spanish eyes. "Ah, Señora Preston, how very charmed I am to make your acquaintance."

Cora smiled up at him. "And I yours, Don Cristoval."

Next came Emily, and both Cristoval and Manco could see why Jack's heart had been lost to her. The bloom on her skin, the quick glance of her lovely hazel eyes, the slight uncertainty in her smile, all these features served to meet with their approval because they were aware that she could not possibly want them here.

Peter stumbled over his words when addressing Cristoval, and was completely tongue-tied when it was at last time to address Manco. The Indian had given Cora and Emily polite but perfunctory greetings; Peter he honored with a beaming smile. "Ah, Capac Peter. You and I friends, I think?"

"Oh, yes, please," breathed the boy, almost transported with delight at such a prospect.

26

The Hall was in darkness, except for a night candle on the landing. The faint glow crept along the passage, lengthening Jack's shadow almost grotesquely as he made his way toward Emily's rooms. He was still fully dressed, for he had not retired to his room with any intention of sleeping. What he was about to do was wrong, but he had to speak to her, alone and without danger of interruption, and this seemed the only way. He paused to glance back as he reached her door. For a split second he felt as if he were being watched, but then the sensation passed, and slowly, gently, he turned the handle and slipped inside.

Behind him eyes had indeed been watching. Two pairs of eyes, to be precise. Peter's and Manco's. The boy and the Indian had been about to go out, so that the Indian, ever ready to show off his skills, could show Peter how to fish by moonlight. They both wore ponchos, Peter having received his as promised, and on seeing Jack they had drawn hastily out of sight behind the same curtain where the cat had watched the mouse hole the night before. As Jack disappeared into Emily's rooms, they looked at each other. Peter's lips parted to speak, but Manco shook his head.

"Not boy's business," he whispered.

"But—"

"Boy want fish from sacred pool?"

"Sacred . . . ? Er, yes." Peter wanted to be able to show Archie Bradwell a thing or two!

"Then boy hold tongue," the Indian said, taking Peter by the arm and propelling him toward the landing.

Jack had no idea he had been seen. He stood just inside Emily's door, and gazed at her as she slept. A shaft of moonlight pierced the badly drawn curtains at the window, and lay across her face. She looked like an alabaster statue, pale, ghostly almost, and so beautiful that just to look at her made his heart squeeze tight with emotion.

She stirred a little, and he was filled with sudden alarm at his own foolishness. What in God's own name had possessed him to come here like this? Was he quite mad? He turned to leave again, but she awakened and saw him. He heard her breathe in sharply, so he quickly faced her again. "Please don't be afraid, for I mean you no harm," he said urgently.

She struggled to sit up, staring at him. "How *dare* you come in here!" she cried.

Fearing that she would scream and disturb the rest of the house, he moved swiftly to the bedside and clamped a firm hand over her parted lips. "If you raise the alarm, you will have to explain how I am in here with you. Believe me, I am capable of claiming to have been invited!" He wasn't, but it seemed an excellent way of making her think again. He was right, for she ceased to struggle. "Can I remove my hand without your making a noise?" he inquired.

She nodded, and slowly he took his hand away. Her eyes glinted with fury in the moonlight as she addressed him in a harsh whisper. "This is monstrous, sirrah! How you have the gall to—"

"To wish to speak sensibly with you in private?" he interrupted.

"You call this 'sensibly?' "

"Yes, for we are not likely to be disturbed, are we?" Without asking, he sat on the edge of the bed.

She edged away. "We have nothing to say to each other, Mr. Lincoln."

"That isn't true, and you know it." His glance dropped to the throat of her nightgown. The ribbon fastening had come undone, and he could see the curve of her breast in the moonlight.

Quickly, she tied the ribbons again. "Just who do you think you are to treat me in this cavalier fashion?" She was frightened, but not of him. It was her own treacherous heart that unnerved her now . . .

"Cavalier fashion? Oh, Emily, if you think that, you wrong

me greatly. I am driven to this because you will not speak to me any other way. You have made it abundantly clear that you are determined to pretend nothing has arisen between us, but I am equally determined to confront the truth."

"The truth, sir, is not only that you are Sir Rafe's cousin and sworn enemy, but that you saw fit to tell Peter that Felix was his grandfather!"

Jack stared at her. "I haven't said anything to Peter! I admit that I knew about Felix and your mother, because Felix himself told me before I left Peru, but I have *not* spoken to Peter about it."

"Then how does he know? My mother certainly hasn't told him."

"I have no idea, but given his propensity for creeping around and eavesdropping, I can quite believe he found out all by himself."

The explanation had a ring of truth about it, and she looked away. "I admit that could be so," she conceded.

"Then admit too that there are other things between us that must be addressed."

"Please go, Jack." It was the first time she had used his given name, and she knew she shouldn't have done it even now, but it seemed so very foolish to insist upon formality when he was right. Something *had* arisen between them; it shouldn't have done, but it had, and it was breaking her heart.

"I love you, Emily."

She closed her eyes. *Please leave me*, she thought, *please leave me so that I can at least try to adhere to the path I know I must take . . .*

"Emily?"

"This will do no good, Jack. I am going to marry Sir Rafe, and nothing, *nothing* will change that fact."

"Even though you love me and I love you?" he pressed.

She was silent for a moment. "Can you settle the debts Geoffrey left behind? Do you have funds enough to satisfy all the duns crowding at my door? No, you can't, because Rafe has your inheritance, or so you say."

"All I say of him is the truth, Emily. I swear it is."

She was silent for a moment. "I believe you," she whispered.

"You do?" Joy leapt through him, and he stretched a hand toward her, but she drew away.

"Yes, but it makes no difference. I must still marry him." She swallowed. "I would have to marry him even if Geoffrey had left me well provided for."

Jack stared at her. "What do you mean? Why would you have to marry Rafe anyway? For God's own sake, tell me everything, Emily."

"I . . . I can't . . ."

He seized her by the arms and made her look fully into his eyes. "The truth, Emily."

She wrestled with her conscience, but knew it was no good. She had to tell him everything, "Jack, it is for Peter's sake, not just to provide for him, but to protect him from . . . from—" She broke off, then pressed on determinedly. "From the shame of the world knowing his father attempted to steal secret cabinet papers in order to give them to the French."

Jack stared at her, so taken aback that for a moment his mind became blank. But then he recovered. "Geoffrey was a French sympathizer?"

"So it seems. I knew nothing of it, although I confess he was an admirer of Bonaparte. There is French blood in the Fairfield family, and he was always torn by this war, but I never for a moment imagined his loyalty to Britain was in question."

"And how do you know of these, er, spying activities?"

"From Rafe. Oh, don't *you* look at me like that as well, for I have already endured it from Mama, and she only knows about the IOUs."

"IOUs? Forgive me, Emily, but you are going a little fast here. Whose IOUs? Geoffrey's?"

"Yes. Rafe holds gaming parties at Temford Castle, and some of the gentlemen who are his guests are in the government, cabinet ministers included. It seems that Geoffrey plunged far too deeply into play, and left a veritable paper trail of IOUs behind him. It seems that he had also started pilfering cabinet secrets at the same time."

Jack got up, his mind racing. "And Warrender can prove all this?"

"Well, he says he has some of the IOUs, and—"

Jack gave a cynical laugh. "Never trust any document that has been touched by my dear cousin. I know the importance of *that* advice!"

"You mean, the IOUs may not be genuine?"

He shrugged. "I don't know, Emily, but when Rafe Warrender is involved, nothing is simply black and white, but very gray indeed."

She thought for a moment. "I was sure the one he showed me was in Geoffrey's hand. His writing was very distinctive, you see. This one was made out to Sir Lumsley Carrowby. Rafe said he himself had settled it, so I should no longer worry. But he went on to say there were many more, which he would settle once I was his wife."

Jack paced slowly up and down the moonlit bedroom. "So all you know for certain is that there is one IOU that purports to be Geoffrey's?"

"Yes."

He drew a deep breath. "It's my guess that it is a forgery. Counterfeit papers are Rafe's specialty."

"But what of the spying?" Emily asked.

"Do you believe, in your heart of hearts, that Geoffrey was a traitor to England?" Jack asked quietly.

She stared at him, then lowered her eyes slowly and shook her head. "No," she whispered.

"Nor do I. It is just a very neat way of forcing you to do Rafe's bidding." A nerve fluttered at Jack's temple. Never had he held his cousin in more contempt than he did at that moment.

Emily spoke again. "Whether or not it is true, the threat of such a charge would do irreparable harm to Peter's future. There would always be a question mark over his head because of whispers about his traitor of a father. I could weather such shame, and so too could Mama, but Peter would suffer greatly. That is why I have agreed to this marriage. I will be betrothed to Rafe at the Royal Oak the day after tomorrow, and I will marry him on Christmas Eve."

She closed her eyes. *The day after tomorrow?* Why did it suddenly seem only minutes away? It was as if the hours she was due had sneaked away somewhere, closing the gates of freedom behind them. Soon Rafe's betrothal ring would be on her finger, like a key in the lock that defended her liberty; and at Christmas the key would be turned . . .

Jack saw tears shining on her lashes in the moonlight. In a moment he had returned to the bed and reached out to take her hand. Her fingers curled in his, clasping as longingly as they were clasped.

He wrenched her into his arms, his lips seeking hers as if his very life depended upon it. She didn't resist, nor did she pretend that propriety mattered. It was a moment that transcended everything else, a moment of declaration, of facing the facts. They were in love, and for these few seconds she acknowledged it. She conceded a truth that had existed from the first moment she saw him, after her fall in the clearing, and this exciting man, this golden Viking, had come to her rescue. When he'd touched her then, she'd known she desired him. She longed now to lie back between the sheets and welcome him to invade her whole being.

He was the once-in-a-lifetime man of whom her mother had spoken, the man who would always mean more to her than any other, even Geoffrey. She wanted Jack Lincoln with a ferocity she had not even imagined before. That she was even capable of such emotion shocked her, but as his kiss beguiled her more and more, she knew that her resistance became less and less. If he were to take her now, she would welcome it, as a lost soul would welcome the portals of paradise. She lay back and drew him seductively down with her. She had no shame now, and made no nod in the direction of right or wrong.

He yearned to possess her, and for a sweet, sweet moment he considered consummating the desire that seared through them both. How simple it would be to be one with her, and seal their love in the only true way. But come the morning they might—would—both regret it. "No . . ." He got up from the bed and turned away, willing his barely controlled passion to subside.

She lay there in confusion. Never before had she been so swept away by forbidden desires that all her inhibitions had been washed away into the shadows. She would have given herself to him, gladly, eagerly, longingly, but it would have been wrong.

He looked at her again. "If we were to do this now . . ."

"I know."

He reached out to put trembling fingertips to her tousled hair. "I'm going to save you from Rafe Warrender and see that this sword of Damocles no longer hangs over your head," he said softly. Then almost before she knew it, he had turned on his heel and left the room.

Emily lay there, alone and suddenly very lonely. She wished she had seduced him beyond the point of no return. If she had held him more tightly, bewitched him more fully with her body, banished his control, they would both be warm and satisfied now. Guilty, but thirsty no more—for a while. Such passion as this was not easily slaked; maybe it could never be slaked, but would conjure desire between them forever. Yes, she thought, that was what it would do. She belonged to Jack Lincoln now, and even if she still had to marry his hated cousin, she would remain Jack's.

All the tangled emotions of the day suddenly overwhelmed her, and she began to cry. Huge sobs racked her as she turned to bury her face in the pillows. She didn't hear the door open behind her as Cora hurried in, drawn by the sound of her child's unhappiness.

"Oh, Emily, my dearest girl, my darling baby," she whispered, tears leaping to her own eyes. She sat on the bed and gathered Emily into her arms.

Mother and daughter clung to each other, the wounds healing as they wept together.

27

When Jack left Emily, he returned to his room only to collect his outdoor clothes and his pistol. His emotions were in chaos too, swinging from the joy of knowing Emily returned his love, to the disgust and outrage of discovering that Rafe had added blackmail to his already long list of crimes.

Anger throbbed through him, firing his blood and burning away his restraint to the point that it barely existed. He had to confront Rafe, have it out with him, both for now *and* the past! Suddenly, Jack knew how to honor his promise to Felix; how to save Fairfield Hall from debt, and from the serpent that threatened its Eden. It was all so clear. So simple. By the time he had finished with his cousin, not only would all Emily's debts be settled, but Rafe would know the folly of blackmailing Emily with threats about her husband's supposed activities! It didn't matter whether or not Geoffrey Fairfield had been a spy for the French, only that his innocent widow was being coerced into becoming Lady Warrender in order to protect her son.

Jack changed swiftly into his day clothes, tucked the pistol inside his coat, and left the house. The recklessness of his present course did not matter; indeed, the possible hazards did not exist for him at all as he walked swiftly around to the stables. The night air was cold, and the temperature was dropping almost tangibly. Stars sprinkled the black velvet sky, the moon was just rising, and a low mist drifted knee-high, swirling aside in the draft Jack made as he walked. The first frost was inevitable, he thought as he saddled the same horse he had ridden earlier in the day.

Within a quarter of an hour of leaving Emily, he was riding across the moonlit park. He followed the route he and Emily had taken to the rapids, and crossed the packhorse bridge, where the river reflected the moon. He intended to leave the estate by way of the disputed gatehouse because he knew no one would be any the wiser if he did that. To go by the main drive would mean arousing Bradwell to open the gates. These other deserted gates were closed only by a rusty padlock that would not offer much resistance to anyone determined.

He remembered the way through the mist-twined woods, for his years in the Andes had trained him to remember places he had been before. A tree of a certain shape, a rock, a drift of ferns, all had been consigned to his memory when he had been lost earlier in the day. The dilapidated gatehouse loomed dark and silent, and a fox slunk across the way as Jack rode the final yards out of the trees. The mist was still no more than thigh high, billowing aimlessly over the ground, as if undecided whether to materialize in full, or slide away into obscurity again. He dismounted by the gates and searched for a stone to break the old padlock. It was then that he noticed the door of the gatehouse. The ivy growing over it had been recently torn, and even in the moonlight he could see that someone had shoved the door open and then closed it again. Curiosity got the better of him, and with his pistol at the ready he pushed the door open once again and went inside.

The low room beyond was deserted. It smelled of damp and mildew, and had such an air of decay that Jack marveled the building was still standing. He opened a door to a staircase, and a waft of chill air swept down over him. Cobwebs laced the way in the moonlight, and he knew no one had gone up there in a long time. Nor was there anyone in the small kitchen or scullery that led off the first room. The gatehouse was deserted, except for himself.

But someone had been there recently, for there was a very old copy of the *Gentleman's Magazine* lying open on the window shelf, together with a grubby sheet of paper and a pencil stub. The paper was slightly damp, but only just, which suggested it had not been there for more than a day or so. Someone illiterate had been attempting to copy words from the open page of the magazine. An article about new farming methods in Norfolk, of all things! Who was it? he wondered. Well, he could muse upon the mystery until the proverbial cows came home, and still not find the right name, so there was no point in bothering.

Leaving the things as they were on the sill, he went outside again to find a stone for the padlock. He found one almost immediately. After three blows the padlock clattered broken to the ground, and he was able to push the gates open. He coaxed the horse through, closed the gates again, then rode swiftly toward Temford.

Of course, Jack was not the only person abroad on the Fairfield Hall estate that starry night, for Manco and Peter had preceded him from the house. They had gone to the clearing where Geoffrey Fairfield had died, but Peter was not thinking about his father, or indeed about Jack's nocturnal activities in Emily's room; it was Manco's amazing talent for fishing with only his bare hands that completely absorbed the boy's interest.

Peter crouched in the mist at the end of the pool. He was snug in the poncho Jack had given him after dinner, feeling warmer than he would have done in his greatcoat. He was watching Manco, who lay on the bank, an arm plunged shoulder-deep into the ice-cold water. The Indian's knitted hat had slipped sideways, and the golden discs in his earlobes glinted in the moonlight. Already two fat tench lay twitching on the grass, having been scooped from the depths as if with a ladle. The water splashed a little, and with a deft movement Manco drew another fish from its haven and tossed it on the bank. Then he scrambled to his feet, making the mist recoil as if stung. He grinned at Peter.

"See? Viracocha make Manco fine fisherman," he said. "Viracocha, great god of sun, of everything, and all creatures in universe." Manco waved an arm to indicate the earth and the sky.

Peter hoped the Indian wasn't about to launch into another hymn of praise in his guttural, almost explosive native tongue. He had shouted to the heavens when they arrived in the clearing. *Aticsi Uiracochan caylla Uiracochan tocapu acnupu Uiracochan . . . !* Oh Creator! Oh conquering Viracocha! Ever present Viracocha . . . !

Manco glanced up as an owl called. "Bird of bewitching eyes," he murmured. Then pointed to his own eyes and smiled at Peter. "Manco have owl eyes too. Cast magic with eyes. Conquer evil spirits and make enemy obey will."

"Really?" Peter was impressed.

"Manco is weaver of spells." The Indian put a hand in his purse, then flicked his fingers toward the pool. The surface of the water quivered, then concentric circles surged strongly toward the banks, where they washed audibly by Peter's feet.

"How did you do that?" the boy gasped.

"Inca magic. Boy not Inca, so boy cannot be told."

"Oh, please," Peter begged, but Manco was not to be moved. Instead, he bent to toss all the landed fish back into the pool.

"Catch fish easy when Viracocha give help," he said.

"You might think so," Peter answered, his breath as silver as the mist. He wasn't quite able to keep a peevish note out of his voice, because Archie Bradwell was in his way as clever a fisherman as Manco, albeit taking longer and having to use a line.

"Tomorrow you show Manco all estate?"

"If that is what you want, then certainly I'll show you," Peter agreed.

"Manco want to know every granny."

"Granny?" Peter looked blankly at him.

"Every granny and book."

Peter laughed. "You mean every nook and cranny."

"Yes, that what I say."

Peter didn't argue. "If you want to see everything, you can."

"Yes, everything. Including House of Viracocha?"

"Where?"

"House of the Viracocha, House of the Sun. On road. Place that guard locked gates that are never opened," Manco explained.

Peter's eyes cleared. "Oh, you mean the old gatehouse." He frowned a little. "Why on earth do you call it the House of Viracocha?"

"Because it where sun live. Windows shine brightly because Viracocha take rest inside. He open door to go in. Leave open."

Peter was bemused. "I . . . I suppose you mean something about the sun reflecting on the window, but the door can't have been open. The place is locked up and no one goes there now."

"Is abode of Viracocha. Manco see. Nothing wrong Manco's eyes." The Indian's tone indicated a miff.

Peter shifted awkwardly. "No, of course there isn't. Well, if you want to go there, then we'll go."

Mollified, Manco smiled again. "Now Manco teach boy catch fish."

"Oh, yes! I want to show Archie Bradwell a thing or two!" Peter flicked his poncho back and rolled up his sleeve.

"Archie Bradwell?"

"The gatekeeper's obnoxious son," Peter explained.

Manco's brows drew into an uncomprehending frown. "Ob-nock—? Manco not know word."

"Horrid, mean, sneering. Anything like that as far as Archie is concerned."

"Ah. Archie boy is Pizarro boy." Manco understood now.

"Yes." Peter had become accustomed to the adjective by now. He lay down on the bank as Manco had shortly before, and plunged his arm into the bitterly cold pool.

Manco leaned over him, instructing him carefully, and in what seemed like no time at all a tench seemed to place itself in Peter's palm! The boy's fingers closed and with an excited whoop he scooped the fish out of the water. Cold droplets scattered, and then the tench lay flapping and slapping on the damp ground.

Peter leapt to his feet and danced excitedly around. "I caught one with my bare hand! I actually caught one!"

"Only with help of Viracocha," Manco reminded him.

"Yes, of course," Peter said quickly. Then, as Manco returned the tench to the pool, the boy's glance moved to the Indian's bow and arrow, sling, and knife, which had been temporarily discarded on the grass. "Will you show me how to use these as well, Manco?"

The Indian straightened and looked inquiringly at him. "You shoot Pizarro boy?"

"Shoot? Oh, Lord, no!" Peter gaped at him in the moonlight.

"Hmm." Manco watched the tench dart away to safety. "Capac Jack and Capac Miguel say shoot not good thing in England."

"Definitely not good."

Manco sniffed. "Then find other way. Magic way."

"Look, Manco, I know I don't like Archie Bradwell, but I

don't want him dead or anything like that! I just want to teach him a lesson. He's always so good at things, whether it's fishing or riding, or setting traps. He can even run faster than me! Everything I want to do well but find difficult, *he* can manage as easy as wink."

"Wink?"

"Oh, it doesn't matter," Peter said quickly, not wanting to embark upon another explanation.

Manco thought for a moment. "We make bargain? I help you with Pizarro boy, you help me with devil."

"Devil?"

"Man who want marry your mother. Man who keep Manco in England!"

Peter's eyes cleared. "Oh, Sir Rafe, you mean?"

Manco nodded. "Yes. That him. Manco want go home to Peru, but Capac Cristoval not leave until all good here. All good when devil out of way and Capac Jack take Palla Emily as wife."

"Wife?" Peter rather liked the thought of Jack Lincoln as a stepfather. Things had certainly been much more exciting at the Hall since he arrived!

"Capac Jack love her, and she love him. Manco know."

Peter nodded then, remembering what he had overheard by the entrance to the topiary garden. "And Grandmama loves Mr. Reynolds," he said.

Manco looked at him. "How boy know this?"

"I overheard her talking to Mr. Lincoln today. She said Mr. Reynolds is my grandfather."

Manco nodded. "It true. Boy lucky. Capac Felix great man."

"Do you really think so, Manco?"

"Manco know so."

Peter smiled, for in his eyes Felix Reynolds could have no better recommendation than to be praised by the Indian.

Manco smiled too. "So, Capac Peter, we have bargain? I show you things, you take me House of Viracocha? Manco make offerings, make magic. Then together we teach Sir Devil Rafe and Pizarro Archie a lesson."

"Yes."

28

When Jack reached Temford, he dismounted again and led the horse into a wide covered alley off the market square. There was no mist up here on the hill, and the moonlight bathed everything with a clarity that did not reach into the valleys.

He'd noticed the alley earlier from the window of the Royal Oak opposite. There were lights at the inn, and the occasional burst of laughter and fiddle music as someone left through the front entrance. But the alley was silent, for it led only into a yard behind one of the stores that Cora frequented so earnestly in her endeavors to keep up with all the changing fashions that came north from London.

He soothed the horse until it was quiet and relaxed, then went to the mouth of the alley to look toward the castle gates set in the yew hedge. They were closed for the night, and the windows of the little mock medieval lodge just inside them were aglow with candlelight behind drawn curtains. The gatekeeper was still awake, Jack noted with dismay, for at this hour he had expected all to be in darkness. He slipped past the shop frontages in the square toward the hedge, which was all of twenty feet high, and close-clipped in a way that must take several days and several ladders whenever trimming became necessary.

He paused in the shadows to glance around the square. There were lights at some upper-story windows, but for the moment there was no one actually out and about. Even the Royal Oak was temporarily quiet, the door firmly closed. The moment was perfect. In a trice he'd swarmed up the wrought iron gates, lifted himself lightly over the top, and then dropped down into the castle grounds. He immediately drew back against the hedge again, pressing warily out of sight with his gaze upon the lodge. But there was no sound of stirring within, no suggestion that his intrusion had been detected.

Several minutes passed, and all remained quiet, so Jack relaxed and turned his attention toward the castle, the battlements of which seemed to move against the sky, where clouds now dotted the starlit heavens. A peacock called, and he heard an owl, but of humans there was no sign at all. Except, perhaps . . .

His gaze was drawn to a light in the barbican, and the room above the now defunct portcullis. The original windows would have been small, little more than arrow slits, but in recent years much larger ones had been installed, latticed and set with colored glass, as if in a church. A casement was ajar, and from time to time he could just hear the chink of ivory balls as someone played billiards. Then Rafe stepped past the window, pausing to twist the leather tip of his cue against the uneven stonework of the wall before bending out of a sight again to play a shot. A cold glitter settled over Jack's eyes, and he began to make his way stealthily toward the castle entrance.

Gaining entry to the castle was almost ridiculously easy. The iron-studded main door was bolted on the inside, but the little postern beside it had been overlooked. It opened easily on hinges that had recently been greased, and in a moment he found himself inside his cousin's lair.

He entered the baronial hall, where the guardian suits of armor were barely discernible in the faint light of the flames in the wide stone fireplace, and the four lighted candles of an iron cartwheel-shaped chandelier were suspended from the loft roof far above. It was not warm inside, but felt so after the bitterness of the November night, and there was a definite smell of curry in the air. Clearly, Rafe and his bird-of-a-feather guest had enjoyed a dinner laced with hot oriental spices.

Hidden behind a heavy damask curtain, immediately beside the postern, was a spiral stone staircase that ascended steeply into the upper barbican. The dark red of the damask was deepened almost to black in the gloomy, indistinct light, but when Jack held the curtain aside to look up, he could see a much brighter light at the top. The chink of billiard balls was louder now. Of voices there was no sound, however, which made

Jack begin to hope Rafe might be on his own. Oh, how provident if that were so, for they could enjoy a cousin-to-cousin chat, in convenient privacy . . .

Unaware of approaching danger, Rafe was indeed playing alone. The room was so well heated by a small fireplace that he had discarded his coat and wore just his shirt and breeches as he leaned down to play a long shot against the felt cushion. The table had been built actually in the barbican room, all its parts having been hauled up the outside wall on ropes when the windows had been enlarged. It was a fine, bold piece of furniture, with green cloth laid upon slabs of marble, and it was illuminated by a patent oil lamp that hung from the ceiling to within three feet of the table top.

The cue jabbed forward, and the white ball rolled toward the cushion, where a red ball rested in a most difficult position. Ivory struck ivory, but the red ball did not run toward the corner pocket. Instead, it paused at the very lip, almost as if mocking him. Rafe straightened, his expression sour as he reached for the glass of cognac that he had placed on the cushion. It was as well he wasn't playing Brockhampton tonight, or he'd be trounced, he thought.

A voice spoke. "Ill met by lamplight, eh, Coz?"

"Lincoln—" Rafe began to whip around, but a pistol muzzle pressed icily to the nape of his neck, and the sound of it being cocked froze him where he stood. The glass fell from his fingers, bounced off the table and crashed to the floor. Rafe swallowed, for his tongue felt as if it had stuck to the roof of his mouth. "So . . . so Brockhampton was right, it *was* you of whom Gustavus spoke."

"Gustavus?"

"He told Brockhampton you were on the *Stralsund*."

"There is no secret about my return to England. Or about my desire to crush you vengefully beneath my heel, like the dung beetle you are." Jack twisted the pistol against his cousin's perspiring skin.

Rafe was terrified. His tongue passed over lips that were suddenly desert-dry. "What do you want?" he whispered.

"Want? Apart from the return of my inheritance, you mean?"

"It was proved to be *my* inheritance, and—" Rafe's voice broke off as the pistol drove into his flesh.

"Your dishonesty is proving tiresome, Coz. First you and your creature Brockhampton forge an entry of birth in order to deprive me of my rights, then you see to the disappearance of the purse that Felix Reynolds left behind for Cora Preston. Now you are busy with IOUs and talk of French spies. My, my, I could almost take my hat off to your industry."

Rafe was stunned by Jack's knowledge. "Who has told you all this?" he demanded, wording the question carefully so that he admitted nothing. His thoughts were racing. *Brockhampton! Had the lawyer been less than discreet?* It did not occur to him that Emily might have confided any of the facts.

"Ah, now wouldn't you like to know?" breathed Jack, again pressing the pistol into the other's neck.

"Yes, I would, because it is all lies." Rafe began to turn, but the pistol jabbed again.

"Face the front, Coz. If I wanted to see a weasel, I would have gone to the nearest wood," Jack said softly. "Now then, if you wish to play games and pretend you don't know what I'm talking about, allow me to make it a little more clear. The forged entry of birth is definitely known to you, or have you forgotten those days you spent telling monstrous lies in court? As for the purse Felix Reynolds left with Brockhampton, I rather think you know about that as well."

"What have you to do with Felix Reynolds?" Rafe demanded.

"I am honored to name him among my closest friends. But surely it is more to the point to ask what *you* have to do with Felix Reynolds? Eh, Coz? Why have you been dipping your dirty paws into his affairs?"

"I don't know what you're talking about."

"Oh? So I am mistaken to think you wrote a letter to Brockhampton, thanking him for his assistance in the matter of the disappearing purse?"

Rafe's lips parted, and his thoughts raced. So Brockhampton *was* the source!

"You haven't answered my question, Coz. Why have you made Felix Reynolds's business your business too?"

"I haven't."

"Forgive me if I call you liar, Rafe dearest," Jack said softly. "Which brings us to the matter of IOUs and French spies. I rather think we both know that Geoffrey Fairfield had nothing to do with either of these, don't we? Admit it now, Coz. Geoffrey was a good boy, but *you* have always been a very bad boy indeed. Quite the blot on the family escutcheon, eh?"

Beads of perspiration now stood out on Rafe's forehead. "I . . . I can understand your wanting your inheritance back, Lincoln, but of what possible interest to you is Fairfield Hall?"

"I happen to be the guest of Fairfield's mother-in-law."

"Cora Preston?"

"Unless he was bigamously married, yes, of course, Cora Preston," Jack replied.

Rafe's thoughts turned in all directions at once. It must surely mean that he knew all about Felix and Cora Preston; therefore about Emily Fairfield's parentage. But did he also know how wealthy Reynolds had become? Was that why he was involved in all this? Maybe there was more than one fortune hunter in the family!

"Where's Brockhampton?" Jack asked suddenly.

"Asleep."

"Dreaming sweet dreams of lost innocence, no doubt."

"We have indulged enough in small talk, Lincoln. What do you want of me?" Rafe cried.

"An end to your loathsome grip upon Emily Fairfield."

"Loathsome grip? Damn it, I'm going to *marry* her!"

"I think not, Coz. The lady is too good for the likes of you, too good by far."

Rafe's eyes cleared. "Do you want her yourself? Yes, I think you do. Which makes you no better than I, Lincoln. You may give yourself airs and graces, but inside you are my black-hearted, scheming twin!"

The pistol stabbed sharply. "Don't presume to compare me with you, Coz! I may not have anything to offer Emily, but even so I am a thousand times better than you will ever be. I love her, and intend to save her from you."

Rafe began to realize that the secret about Felix Reynolds's fortune was safe. "I'll see you in Hades first, Lincoln," he breathed.

A nerve twitched at Jack's temple. "I've been in Hades

since our day in court, Coz, so the prospect no longer frightens me. Now then, one of the reasons I've come here tonight is to warn you that if you ever utter one single unflattering word about Geoffrey Fairfield, I will personally rip the hide from your miserable body. Then I will hang it out to dry from the tallest tower of this heap of stones you call home. Do I make myself clear?"

Rafe didn't reply.

The pistol prodded warningly. "Another reason for my visit is to see that you protect Emily from her husband's debts without imposing your odoriferous self upon her at the same time. I want you to settle all her outstanding bills, as a fond gesture from a fiancé who must regretfully withdraw from the match."

"Eh? Are you mad?"

"No, Coz, I'm just the man with his finger on the trigger," Jack replied smoothly. "Now, either you're a sensible fellow and agree to my demand, or I'll drop you here and now. It's up to you."

29

"You wouldn't dare!" But Rafe's words were false bravado, for in truth he didn't know what his disaffected cousin might do.

Jack smiled. "Think again, Coz, for you have given me sufficient incentive to exterminate you ten times over."

Rafe swallowed. "And . . . and what makes you think I'll do as you want? I could agree to anything while you're here with the upper hand, then go back on it all afterward."

"That would be most unwise, for I am not known for my forgiving nature."

"Devil take you, Lincoln."

"From now on he's more likely to roast your backside in Hades than mine, unless I roast it first, of course. Or my good friend Manco."

"Manco?"

"A Peruvian Indian of Inca descent. He is also a guest at the Hall, and happens to hold Inca values. He has magical powers—courtesy of the great sun god, Viracocha—and uses them to take Inca revenge. Your top hat suffered at his hands when you rode across the square. He is rather keen to eliminate you properly, but so far has been dissuaded. It would not take much for a sling-stone to be replaced by a much more deadly arrow, or even a poisoned dart. Or mayhap something *much* more fearsome and supernatural," Jack added softly.

Rafe was rigid with fright. All his superstitious dread surged to the fore, and his glance fled to his coat, which lay over a chair. His quartz pebble! He needed it . . . !

His terror was tangible to Jack, who smiled coolly. "Retribution comes from nowhere, does it not? So beware of taking the Peruvian wolf by the ears, Coz, for you will not win, and I would as soon have you dead as alive. You will also be dead if you are ever foolish enough to implement your threats about exposing Geoffrey Fairfield as a French agent." Jack softened his voice warningly. "One word out of place, Rafe, and you won't hear Manco as he treads behind you, or feel his magic as it folds over you."

Rafe felt faint. His whole body shook, and he had to grip the billiard table to give himself strength.

Jack realized that by pure chance he had happened on the one threat that reduced Rafe to terror. So he pressed his advantage home. "You will know nothing until it is too late, Coz, so my advice is that you do as I tell you now."

"Yes! All . . . all right, I'll do anything you ask!" Rafe cried cravenly.

"I want you to write some letters, Coz. But be warned, if you try to overturn anything that I have made you do tonight, it will be the end of you. Do you understand?"

Rafe nodded. "Yes," he whispered. "Whom am I to write to?"

"We'll start off with Emily, and then the Fairfield Hall banker in Shrewsbury—Mackay, isn't that his name?—instructing him to transfer funds to Emily. There, is that not a clever thing?"

For the space of two heartbeats Rafe did not respond, but then he gave in. "Very well, I will do as you wish."

The surrender was a little too willing, Jack thought suspiciously. "If you imagine you can get up to something, Coz, I warn you—"

"Look, Lincoln, I've agreed to your terms. That *is* what you want, isn't it? I'm not fool enough to argue long with a man who threatens me with a pistol!" Rafe began to turn toward Jack, who once again forced him to face the front.

"I don't want to look at your miserable visage, Coz, so just look the other way." Jack's suspicions weren't allayed by Rafe's words, for it never did to trust this man, but getting the letter out of him was the prime consideration. "Lead the way, and remember, one false move and I'll put an end to you." The pistol jabbed. "Off we toddle."

"My coat . . ." Being careful to avert his face, Rafe took the garment and put it on, then slipped his hand over the comforting pebble of quartz in the pocket.

Jack saw the action and swiftly caught Rafe's wrist. "Not so fast, Coz," he breathed. But when he examined the contents of the pocket, he found only the pebble. "What's this?"

"A memento."

"From where?"

"Naples." It was the truth.

Jack hesitated, being of half a mind to toss it out of the window, but instead he replaced it in the pocket. "Don't make any more sudden movements, Coz."

"I won't." Rafe slowly put his hand into the pocket again, and breathed out steadily as his fingers closed over the quartz. Almost immediately he felt better, stronger, more able to deal with his fears. He led the way from the room, and as they descended the twisting staircase, he was aware of the pistol only inches from the back of his head.

They made their way to the former chapel that was now his study. A fireplace had been built against an outer wall of the chancel, where a mullioned window, pointed and leaded, allowed the moon to shine palely through. The fire had burned low, adding little to the dull silver light, but there was sufficient light for Jack to see that the whole room was furnished in the Gothic style. There were bookcases with trefoil carving and leaded doors that matched the window, and an immense oak desk and chair that might have come from an abbey.

Rafe sat at the desk and met Jack's eyes for the first time. Cousin looked at cousin, with that peculiar bitterness and loathing that only shared blood can bring, then Rafe reached for a sheet of paper. He dipped a gold-nibbed pen in the inkwell and looked inquiringly at Jack, who stood on the other side of the desk, the pistol still leveled. "Well?"

"The sum of forty thousand guineas has been mentioned, as have various IOUs. Now then, Coz, do those IOUs exist or not?"

Rafe looked at him. "Geoffrey Fairfield was a fool, but not that much of one."

"So they are a figment of your imagination?"

"I fear so."

"This had better be the truth."

"It is." Rafe met Jack's eyes, and the latter knew that for once his slippery kinsman was not lying.

"Right, I think fifty thousand should do it," Jack said calmly.

Rafe's lips parted. *"Fifty?"*

"I thought you'd like to be gallant and allow his widow a sum for her own comfort," Jack said smoothly, taking the candle from the desk and lighting it at the fire in readiness for the sealing wax. The swaying light of the new flame advanced and retreated as he returned to the desk and put the candle down. "Come on now, Coz, I know you have funds enough, because you have *my* funds, and I know how much income you receive each year from that alone. So pay up, there's a good lad."

At Jack's dictation, Rafe wrote the necessary letter to the banker, and another to Emily. Then he sanded and folded them both, and removed his signet ring in readiness to seal it. Jack immediately picked it up to examine. "What's this?"

"You don't recognize it?"

"No, I don't, and you know I don't. Where's the original?"

"Lost, unfortunately."

Jack looked at him with utter contempt. "You've *lost* the ring our ancestor was given by Henry V at Agincourt?"

"These things happen."

"Do they? Somehow I think even you would have preferred to keep a tight grip upon such an heirloom. What happened? Where did you lose it?"

Rafe spread his hands. "I have no idea. I just realized it was missing. Look, is it important? The damned ring has gone, and I use this one now, so do you or do you not want me to seal the letters?"

"Yes, I do." But Jack's suspicions were still strong. This was far too easy. Rafe was hiding something—but what? He returned the signet ring, but then realized there was no sealing wax on the desk. Rafe realized it as well, and hesitated, his glance sliding toward a drawer near his right hand.

Jack followed the glance. "What do you keep in there, Coz?"

"Nothing. Just the sealing wax."

"Then get it out," Jack ordered, waving the pistol.

Rafe's reluctance to open the drawer was almost palpable.

He searched in his pocket for the key, almost dropped it, then hesitated again.

In exasperation Jack came around the desk, snatched the key from him, and unlocked the drawer. Inside lay the block of yellow sealing wax, but it wasn't the only thing, for a leather-bound book lay there too, with a folded sheet of paper as a bookmark.

Curious, Jack transferred the pistol to his left hand, with which he was almost as adept as the right, and pressed it to Rafe's neck once more. Then with his right hand he flipped through the book, which was a volume of seventeenth-century French poems. "Poems? You do surprise me," he murmured as he briefly examined the sheet of paper. On it were written sequences of numbers, apparently random. It was meaningless. From the corner of his eye he saw Rafe's gaze upon the book, and the way his tongue passed nervously over his lower lip.

"What are these numbers, Rafe?" Jack demanded.

"I don't know. The paper was in the book when I purchased it."

Jack didn't believe him. The sheet of paper had some importance, and it might do to keep it. So he secretly pushed it in his pocket, then returned the pistol to his right hand and moved around the desk to face Rafe. "Seal the letter," he said shortly.

Rafe did as he was told, holding the sealing wax in one hand and the lighted candle in the other and bringing them together so that several blobs of molten yellow fell upon one letter and then the other. Then he pressed his ring into the setting wax, leaving perfect imprints of Jack's rose.

Jack waited a second or so for the sealing wax to harden, then he pushed the letters into his coat next to the sheet of numbers. "Right, that's one exercise over and done with. Now we come to the next."

"Next?"

"I want what's mine, Coz, and while I hold this pistol, you dance to my tune."

"If you think I'm going to hand over—"

"I don't *think* that's what you're going to do, I *know* it." Jack leaned forward over the desk and aimed the pistol directly between Rafe's eyes. "Remember Manco," he breathed. "Now, take a fresh sheet of paper."

But as Warrender reluctantly began to obey, they both heard footsteps approaching the door, which had been left slightly ajar. "Are you in there, Warrender?" called Sir Quentin's voice.

Jack's reaction was like lightning. He brought his left fist to Rafe's jaw, knocking him unconscious so that he slumped forward onto the desk, the new sheet of paper still clutched in his hand. Then Jack darted behind the door and waited for the lawyer to enter.

"Warrender?" Sir Quentin peered into the room, his chin obligingly within reach, and in a trice he too was on the receiving end of Jack's fist. He fell in a crumpled heap of white nightshirt and floral brocade dressing gown, and the long golden tassel of his nightcap settled neatly over his nose.

Jack looked angrily down at him. "Damn your timing, Brockhampton!" he breathed. He glanced back at Rafe, who was absolutely still. They were both out for the count. "Best get out of here while you can, Jack, my laddo," he breathed, and slipped from the room like a shadow.

He hurried through the castle, out through the postern gate, then over the lawns toward the gates. Peering cautiously through them, he saw the square was still empty, so he scrambled up and over the wrought iron, then ran swiftly past the shops to the alley, where his horse still waited. There was no hint of the alarm being raised at the castle as he rode out of the square and down toward the bridge over the Teme, down into the mist that now cloaked everything.

Within half an hour he was back at the stables at the Hall. Within five minutes of that he was on his way up to his room. But as he ascended the staircase, he found Emily waiting for him at the top. She had gone to his room and found it empty. He paused in concern. "Emily?" he said softly, seeing the stain of tears on her face.

She flung her arms around his neck, clinging to him so tightly that he could feel her heartbeats. He enveloped her in his embrace, resting his cheek against her hair. "What is it, my darling? Has something else happened?" he whispered.

"No, I . . . I just need to be with you," she answered, her

voice choked with fresh tears. She thought she had wept away all her tears with her mother, but seeing him made them flow again.

His cheek moved against her hair. "Soon everything will be all right again, and we will be able to be together," he said quietly.

She drew back to look into his eyes. "What do you mean?"

He heard a sound from Cora's room and caught Emily's hand to draw her swiftly to his own room. Once inside, he quickly lighted a candle at the fire, then faced her in the gentle light. "I have something for you," he said, and handed her Rafe's letter.

She recognized the writing and the seal, and looked inquiringly at him. "But how—?"

"Ask no questions, and be told no lies. Suffice it that the letters are genuine. Yes, there are two. The second is for Mr. Mackay. You can give it to him when he calls here in response to your mother's message. But before you read the one addressed to you . . ."

"Yes?"

"All I ask is that you do not say anything about receiving either of them from my hand tonight. In the morning you can 'find' them among the daily mail."

She searched his eyes and nodded. "Of course, if that is what you want." She broke the seal and what she read left her dumbfounded. "Rafe is withdrawing from the match *and* settling my debts?"

"Is that not noble of him?"

She was afraid to be joyful. "You haven't done anything . . . anything awful, have you?"

"Well, I put a pistol to his head and frightened him half to death with threats involving Manco and his Inca magic, but that is all. I managed to restrain myself from actually squeezing the trigger. The fifty thousand guineas are yours, Emily. You no longer have to become Lady Warrender, and Geoffrey's reputation will remain intact. Peter can return to Harrow if that is still his wish, and everything will be as it should again."

"You . . . you are sure?"

"Upon my own life," he said gently, and placed his hand

over his heart. "There will be no betrothal on Bonfire Night. You do not even have to go to the Royal Oak if you do not wish to. You are your own mistress again, Emily."

She covered her mouth with her hands, as if she feared that only the wrong words would come out. Salt tears stung her eyes again, and her heart had begun to beat so swiftly that she was sure he would hear it. At last she took her hands away. "It's over? It's really over?"

"Yes."

"Oh, how can I thank you enough?" Joy rushed in, and the letter slipped from her fingers as she again flung her arms around his neck.

Jack smiled wryly as he held her. "Oh, I can think of any number of ways, but I fear I am a gentleman."

She raised her lips to his, but as they kissed, a tiny sliver of doubt crept back into Jack's heart. Not about her, never about her. But about Rafe, who had given in just that little too easily. Even taking into account that he had been in fear—both physically and supernaturally—for his life, there had been too little protest. The gnawing suspicion crept over Jack that his cousin might yet have a trump up his sleeve.

30

Sir Quentin began to slowly regain consciousness on the floor at Temford Castle. His jaw felt hellish painful, and for a moment he couldn't think where he was or what had happened. He managed to sit up, and then tentatively felt his swollen jaw. Memory returned. He hadn't been able to sleep and had gone to see if Rafe was still in the billiard room. On finding no one there, and Rafe's apartments open and unoccupied, he decided to look for him.

Using the door, he pulled himself to his feet. Then he saw Rafe slumped over the desk. "Warrender!" He stumbled over to him and shook his shoulders. "Warrender?"

Rafe moved a little and groaned.

Sir Quentin cast around for the cognac he knew Rafe kept somewhere in the room. He saw it in one of the bookcases, and hastened to pour two large glasses, which he slammed down on the desk. Then he shook Rafe again, more imperatively this time. "Wake up, Warrender!" he ordered.

Rafe's eyes opened and gazed blankly for a moment, then he sat up with a start as he recalled being with Jack. "Lincoln!" he gasped, wincing because of his cut and swollen lip.

"Lincoln?"

"He was here, damn it! My confounded cousin was here!" Thoughts hurtled through Rafe's recovering mind, and he snatched one of the glasses Sir Quentin had placed on the desk. The fiery liquid stung his damaged lip, but he hardly noticed.

The lawyer gaped. "Jack Lincoln? Damn it all, we must have the felon arrested! He can't come here and attack us without—!"

"I don't want attention drawn here," Rafe interrupted sharply.

"But—"

"Leave it, I say! I'll deal with this in my own way."

"All right, all right." Sir Quentin leaned back against the desk, rubbing his throbbing jaw. "What did he want?"

"Apart from putting thumb screws on me to return his inheritance? At a guess, I'd say it was Emily Fairfield," Rafe murmured thoughtfully.

Sir Quentin straightened. "Eh? Emily Fairfield? Does he know about—"

"Felix Reynolds's brimming coffers? I don't think so. Close friend or not, it's my guess that for some reason Reynolds held his tongue about his fortune—and about his forthcoming demise, if indeed Gustavus's information about that is correct. Lincoln's purpose tonight was to, er, *persuade* me to withdraw from the match with Emily Fairfield, and to settle her debts for her in the process. I don't somehow think he'd be concerned about her present financial straits, which are a drop in the ocean compared with how much she will eventually be worth. Any bank would sustain her on such expectations."

"You're probably right." Sir Quentin thought for a moment, then looked curiously at Rafe. "And did Lincoln make you do his bidding?"

"I had begun to, with a little prodding from his loaded pistol." *And the threat of the supernatural!* Rafe swallowed as this latter thought crept insidiously into his head. Once again his hand slid nervously into his pocket to seek reassurance from the pebble. Once again that reassurance was forthcoming. With the pebble safe in his palm, his fear of Manco began to diminish. It had all been lies about the Indian's powers. Somehow Lincoln had found out about his hated cousin's superstitious fears, and was playing upon them. Yes, that was surely it . . .

"A loaded pistol is rather persuasive," Sir Quentin conceded.

"It is, so I accommodated him in every way where Fairfield Hall is concerned. Thanks to your nocturnal wanderings, he did not have time to force his birthright out of me as well. For that I'm much obliged to you, dear fellow." Rafe raised his glass.

Sir Quentin was confused, for Rafe seemed altogether too calm about this complete demolition of his plans.

Rafe smiled. "Don't look at me like that, dear fellow, for all is not lost. You see, the instructions about transferring the money are addressed to Mackay."

Sir Quentin's eyes cleared. "Ah."

"Ah, indeed. I can't believe those fools at Fairfield Hall still think he is their friend, but it seems they do. However, you and I both know he is *my* friend, my lapdog in every way. Not a penny will be transferred from my account into Emily Fairfield's, and the lady will once again be obliged to accept me. Only this time there will be no kid gloves."

"And you think Lincoln will stand idly by while all this goes on?" Sir Quentin could not quite suppress the deriding tone in his voice, for if Jack Lincoln had come boldly to Temford Castle to force his cousin to do his bidding, he was hardly likely to let Rafe overturn it all at will.

"Lincoln will be dealt with," Rafe replied quietly.

"Dealt with?" A cold finger ran down Sir Quentin's spine.

Rafe smiled. "He does not fit into my requirements, dear boy, so I shall have him removed." *And his so-called Inca magician!*

Sir Quentin swallowed, for although he had been guilty of legal sleight of hand, he had no desire to be involved in murder; for what else but murder could be in question now?

Rafe's eyes glittered coldly. "And if I discover that dear Emily has been less then faithful to me in her dealings with him, I will make her rue it!" Suddenly, something occurred to him, and his eyes flew to the desk drawer, which was still open. *The paper!* His breath caught and he leapt to his feet. It was an instinctive action, like that of a cornered animal.

Sir Quentin looked curiously at him. "What is it?

"He's taken the code!" Rafe cried without thinking. In an instant he regretted the words, but it was too late.

"What code?" Sir Quentin demanded.

"Oh, nothing of import," Rafe replied, but he quickly took the book of poems and went to the fireplace. After poking some life into the embers, he began to tear the pages out of the book, crumpling them into balls, and dropping them on the glowing coals, where they ignited and soon burned to nothing but cinders.

Sir Quentin watched with growing concern. "What's all this

about, Warrender? What code? And why are you burning that book?"

Rafe didn't reply, but continued to destroy the volume. Only when he had tossed the leather-bound covers onto the fire, did he answer the lawyer. "You aren't that naïve, so don't pretend you haven't guessed," he muttered, seizing his glass of cognac again and downing what remained in a single gulp. Then he went to pour another.

Sir Quentin stared at him. "Guessed what? Damn it all, Warrender, I cannot read minds!"

"That much is obvious." Rafe flung himself in his chair again and leaned his head back. "Oh, you may as well know, since you are in too deep anyway. You don't imagine I have cultivated Carrowby and his friends because I *like* them, do you? I never do anything unless it brings reward."

"What are you saying?" Sir Quentin asked uneasily.

"Exactly what you begin to fear I mean," Sir Rafe said, giving him a cold smile.

Sir Quentin's horrified gaze swung to the fire, where the title of the burned book was still legible on the cover. The French title of a book of French poems . . .

"That's right, dear boy," Rafe murmured. "I have been indulging in exactly the crime of which I pretend Fairfield was guilty; to wit, the exceedingly lucrative pastime of selling cabinet secrets to our enemy."

An appalled gasp escaped Sir Quentin, who took an involuntary step backward. "I want nothing to do with this! I will do many a thing, but not betray my country!"

"I don't expect you to do anything, except hold your tongue."

"And thus become your *accomplice*?"

Rafe smiled. "You already are my accomplice, Brockhampton."

"Never!" Sir Quentin's face was ashen.

"If you imagine I will die a traitor's death on my own, you had better think again. You are my right hand, Brockhampton, and one telltale word from you about me will ensure a veritable diatribe about you from me. You may count upon it that I will drag you to execution with me."

Sir Quentin felt—and looked—sick. He knew Rafe meant

what he said; and also knew that few were likely to disbelieve such a claim. Many enemies had been made during the course of a legal career that had flourished on chicanery, and some of those enemies were in a position to grind their axes to the sharpest of blades.

Rafe's thin smile was cool. "Well, you can relax, Brockhampton, for Lincoln may have taken the paper, but without the book it is useless, just a jumble of figures. In actual fact, the figures refer to words and letters in the book, which when written down together make a readable message."

"Are you quite sure nothing can be deduced from the figures on their own?"

"Certain beyond all shadow of doubt," Rafe murmured, swirling his cognac and savoring the bouquet.

Sir Quentin went to the only other chair in the room, a leather armchair next to the fireplace. He flung himself into it, then exhaled slowly and tried to collect himself. When he had thrown in his lot with Rafe, it had been solely in order to benefit financially from Felix Reynolds's fortune. This was something very different; this was high treason!

Rafe chuckled. "It is interesting how close one can come to the truth, and yet manage to twist it beyond all recognition."

"What do you mean?"

"I managed to convince Emily Fairfield that her husband was a French spy. I told her I caught him sifting through Carrowby's papers. The truth was the other way around; *he* caught *me*."

A look of complete distaste descended over Sir Quentin's face. "Are there no depths to which you will not sink, Warrender?"

"Very few. I disposed of Fairfield because he was a threat to me, so be warned, Brockhampton, that I am quite prepared to also consign you to the hereafter if I think it necessary."

Sir Quentin stared at him. "You . . . killed Geoffrey Fairfield?" Agitatedly, he got up to refill his glass. His hand trembled so much as he poured the cognac that the crystal decanter rattled against the glass.

Rafe smiled smoothly. "Yes, I'm afraid I did. The morning after he caught me in the act, I went to the Hall to reason with him, but Emily was close by all the time, so we went through the charade of a horse race in order to have it out somewhere suitably isolated and private. The pool in the woods seemed ideal. But once there I could not prevail upon him to hold his tongue about me, so he had to die, d'you see? I was base enough to blame my poor, innocent horse for the calamity. I told everyone I had lost track of Fairfield in the woods, and that I went back to the house without seeing him." Rafe stretched across the desk for the signet ring, which still lay by the block of sealing wax. "This is a copy. I lost the actual Henry V signet ring during the struggle with Fairfield. He wrenched it from my finger and tossed it aside. I've searched, but it seems to have vanished. Yet I *know* it's there somewhere."

Sir Quentin sensed that the loss of the ring was of more significance than simply its value as a family heirloom.

Rafe went on. "Emily Fairfield has noticed that this ring is a copy because the idiot of a jeweler who made it added an extra thorn. I told her I'd lost the original two years ago in London, but it seems dear Fairfield only drew four thorns on my portrait on the day of his death, which is rather inconvenient."

"Why on earth did you invent a tale about London two years ago? You're sometimes too glib for your own good."

"Well, no matter. With luck the real ring will remain lost forever. A pity, for it is valuable, but then I value my neck somewhat more."

"So what happens now?" Sir Quentin took a gulp of cognac.

"Regarding the ring? Nothing."

"Then what about Lincoln and the paper he took?"

"I've already told you he cannot know what it means. It is useless without the accompanying book, and as the book is no longer with us . . ." Rafe gestured elegantly toward the remains on the fire.

"So we say and do nothing?"

Rafe glanced at him. "*You* say and do nothing, Brockhampton, but I have much to say and do. Not the least being to reacquaint Mackay with my true wishes regarding Emily Fairfield's account. No matter what is contained in the letter forced out of me tonight, I wish her purse to remain as empty as possible. So the letter is to be destroyed. There will not be another because I don't intend Lincoln to be around for long enough to extract a replacement." *Nor do I intent his Indian sorcerer to be around either.*

Sir Quentin's tongue passed nervously over his dry lips. Warrender spoke of murder as easily as if he discussed the price of wheat!

Rafe smiled. "As it happens, I am seeing Mackay in the morning anyway. He has sent me word that Cora Preston has summoned him to Fairfield Hall. Every time he is in communication with the Hall he notifies me, and we meet to discuss matters. He is always most anxious to carry out my wishes to the 'T.'"

I'll bet *he is*, Sir Quentin thought, *for he values his neck too!*

Rafe got up. "Well, I need to sleep now. If I can when my head thumps like an anvil." Rubbing his aching jaw, he left the room to go to his apartments.

Sir Quentin put his glass down slowly. *Sleep?* He doubted if he would ever sleep again. His fists clenched into balls, whitening his knuckles so that the bone almost seemed to show through. He was being sucked into something far more dangerous and wide-reaching than any mere tweaking of the law, and he didn't like it one small bit. His glance moved to the desk, and he went to it. Making himself comfortable in Rafe's chair, he took paper and pen, then began to write.

31

Seldom had a foggy Monday morning in November been happier than the one that now dawned over Fairfield Hall. The rising sun tried in vain to pierce the vapor that swirled eerily between the trees in the topiary garden and enveloped the park so completely that all was a ghostly silver-gray.

Because of Rafe's letters, which Emily claimed to have "found" among the rest of the mail, the atmosphere around the breakfast table had been almost jolly. No one could understand why Rafe had undergone such a generous change of heart, except Manco, of course, but then he always seemed to know things without being privy to events. But no one really cared what Rafe's reasons were, just that he had acted upon them. All that mattered was that he had decided not to proceed with the match, that there were no IOUs, and that he was sweetening Emily's imagined disappointment by donating sufficient funds to cover all the debts that so weighed down her existence. Manco made it plain that he hoped a speedy return to Peru would soon follow.

Cora guessed that Jack's hand lay behind it, for she noticed him exchange several rather odd glances with Emily. There was something going on there, she thought, and it wasn't simply to do with them being in love with each other, which patently they were, much to her satisfaction. But what did anything matter now? The Hall's difficulties were at an end, and Mr. Mackay was expected at any time. Soon the fifty thousand guineas would be transferred, and the business of disposing of the debts could begin. Hey, ho, this November 4th was the very best red-letter day anyone could wish for!

Manco was still determined to visit the old disused gatehouse, which he was convinced was the abode of Viracocha, so after breakfast he and Peter set off through the mist. They wore their ponchos and hardly noticed the clammy cold as they ran over the cold, wet grass.

Cora and Cristoval went out as well, but only for a brief stroll in the topiary garden. Cora often indulged in a morning constitutional before settling to her music practice, and Cristoval was disposed to accompany her. He wore his greatcoat and top hat, but was so used to the thick, drizzling *garúa* of his homeland that the light fog of an English autumn was of very little consequence. Beside him, Cora wore a hooded cloak over her cinnamon-colored morning gown, and the lace lappets of her day bonnet peeped prettily from beneath her hood.

It was of Peru that they talked, and she again displayed such an avid interest that at last Cristoval halted and faced her. "Manco and I will return there soon. Why do you not come with us?" he invited, his breath clearly visible in the cold.

She stared at him. "Come with you?" she repeated.

"See Felix again." He spread his hands. "My hacienda has all the comforts, and has missed a woman's touch. Come with us, Cora."

She hardly noticed the use of her first name. "Do . . . do you really think I could?"

"Could? Of course. But whether you *will* . . ."

She smiled. "Sir, I have spent most of the last thirty years wishing I had shown the courage to go when Felix asked me. If you imagine I intend to spend the *next* thirty years doing the same, you are mistaken. Now that Emily's debts have been so miraculously disposed of, the next thing I want most in all the world is to see Felix again. So I accept your invitation."

Emily and Jack stood at an upper window, watching the two figures in the garden, and after a moment Jack smiled. "I do believe your mother will go to Peru as well when Cristoval and Manco return," he said.

Emily's lips parted. "You really think so?"

"It will be the perfect opportunity for her. She is clearly still in love with Felix, and he certainly is with her."

Emily gazed at the misty, indistinct figures in the garden. "If you are right, Jack, then I fear . . ."

"That Peter will wish to go as well?" he finished for her.

"Yes."

Jack turned her to face him. "If he wishes to go, my advice is that you let him."

"Oh, but—"

He put a finger to her lips. "Let him go, but give him a time limit. Tell him he must return to finish his education, and that he must also follow an education while he is there. Lima has many wonders to teach him, and he is a boy who hungers to learn."

Emily's eyes filled with tears. "But he may not wish to return! He may want to stay there."

"Look, we are only speculating anyway, but I still advise you to let him go. That way he will be with your mother if she goes, and he will certainly be with Felix, Cristoval, and Manco. I could not wish for any finer guardians if he were my own son. Emily, if you refuse should these circumstances arise, there is a very grave risk of his running away."

She stared at him. "Peter would never . . ."

"Peter is Felix's grandson," he reminded her. "The lust to see the world is in his blood, and if he thinks you are blocking his path, he is headstrong enough to go anyway. Who knows what might befall him then? A boy alone? A handsome boy, innocent, unused to the baser ways of the human race? At least if he accompanies the others, he will be protected. So, if any of this *should* arise, agree to it."

"All right," she whispered, but the tears were wet on her cheeks.

He tilted her chin and smiled at her. "Good, for this way you will bind him to you more surely than any other. A mother who allows her son to follow his heart can be sure that heart will eventually bring him back to her again."

In spite of herself she laughed a little. "That sounded like a quotation!"

"Actually, it's an Inca proverb . . . well, it is according to Manco." He gazed down at her. She wore a pale green gown made of the softest wool. It was old-fashioned because of the train that whispered on the floorboards behind her when she walked, but its high-throated, long-sleeved simplicity became her quite perfectly, and its color brought out the lovely hazel shades in her eyes. Those eyes were upon him now, dark with love yet alight with laughter too. And her lips were upturned at the corners, so sweetly inviting that he could not—and did not—resist kissing them.

Then they stood in each other's arms, oblivious to the giggling maids who scurried past them. Nothing but Emily mattered to him. He knew how much he adored her, how much he worshipped everything about her. *Please don't let anything go wrong now*, he thought. *Let Rafe accept defeat, lick his wounds, and never again darken the threshold of Fairfield Hall.*

Please.

Manco and Peter had run all the way from the Hall to the abandoned gatehouse. Peter was exhausted and out of breath by the time the dilapidated building and rusty gates appeared through the mist ahead, but Manco was still fleet of foot and hardly seemed affected by the run. Peter was astonished and admiring, and the vain Indian did not have the grace to admit that he had chewed upon a little coca before leaving the house. It was because of the magical leaf that his Inca ancestors had been able to run fifty or more miles in a day along the steep and dangerous paths of the Andes, so the relatively short distance from Fairfield Hall to the House of Viracocha was nothing!

But as they drew closer to the gatehouse, Manco suddenly came to a wary halt. He put a restraining hand on Peter's shoulder. "Boy wait," he whispered.

"Why? What's—?" Peter's voice was smothered by Manco's hand.

"Boy quiet! Someone inside, but it not Viracocha. See, his light not shine." Manco nodded toward the gatehouse. "Maybe demon there, evil spirit that lie in wait."

Peter's eyes widened, and he stood quite still. Manco again urged him to stay where he was, then searched in his purse. When he drew out his hand, Peter saw that his fingers were tipped with blue dye. The Indian put marks on both his own and the boy's forehead. "Manco and boy now guarded by Viracocha," Manco whispered, then slipped silently away toward the building, which outwardly seemed totally deserted.

Peter hesitated, then disobeyed by following. He was under Viracocha's protection; nothing could befall him now . . .

Manco reached the door and paused. His acute hearing had detected a sound inaudible to Peter, a shuffling movement that was made by a human, not an animal, and certainly not a demon! He jerked angrily around as Peter appeared at his side, but he did not dare to say anything now they were so close. The fog exaggerated every little sound, from the dripping of moisture from the trees, to the alarm call of a blackbird somewhere in the hedge on the other side of the empty road.

The shuffling sound came from within again, and this time Peter heard it too. A shiver passed down his spine. *Who was it?* A demon, as Manco feared? What if it knew they were out here, and was only waiting to gobble them up? His faith in Viracocha's power wavered a little.

Suddenly, Manco kicked the door open and rushed in. There was a startled cry, a scuffle, then silence. Peter stepped nervously closer, and peered around the open door. To his astonishment he saw Archie Bradwell sprawled on the floor, with Manco standing threateningly over him. A copy of the *Gentleman's Magazine* lay nearby, together with some dirty sheets of paper. Archie was clutching a stubby pencil in his hand, which he waved at Manco.

"'Tisn't a weapon! Honest! 'Tis only a pencil!" he cried.

Peter hurried in. "He's telling the truth, Manco!"

The Indian gave him a look. "Manco know pencil when see one," he replied, and stepped back from Archie, who scrambled fearfully to his feet. His left wrist was tightly bandaged, Peter noticed.

Manco noticed as well, and pointed at the bandages. "Boy hurt?"

"I . . . I fell." His glance moved toward Peter. He'd stolen an apple from the same tree as Peter, but instead of dropping down agilely from the garden wall, he'd slithered down and twisted his wrist. *And* had a leathering for his trouble, because his father caught him! Peter Fairfield hadn't had a leathering for doing the same thing. Oh, no, he was a gentleman, so nothing bad ever happened to *him*!

Peter retrieved the magazine from the floor. "What are you doing here, Archie?"

"Learnin' my letters."

"Your letters?"

Archie gathered the sheets of paper and showed them to him, all the while keeping a very wary eye on Manco. "See? I copies the words."

Peter read the painstaking writing. Archie had managed a sentence all about a new type of plow someone had invented in Norfolk. Every letter was so laboriously formed that even this single sentence must have taken an age. Peter looked curiously at his arch rival. "Do you know what you've written?" he asked.

Archie flushed, then hung his head without replying.

A huge weight lifted from Peter. For the first time in his life, he felt infinitely superior to the gatehouse keeper's burly son. At last there was something he, Peter Fairfield, could do, that Archie couldn't! The realization almost made him like Archie!

Manco looked at him. "This Pizarro boy?"

"Yes," Peter replied.

Archie raised his head again, realizing they were talking about him. "Eh? What's that?"

"Oh, it doesn't matter," Peter replied, shoving the papers and magazine back into the other's hands. "I didn't know you couldn't read or write, Archie."

"There ent much call for it in our 'ouse," Archie replied.

"No, I don't suppose there is." Peter smiled a little sheepishly. "And in *my* house there's not much call for all the things you do well."

Archie nodded. "Well, reckon fish just appear on your table, Master Peter. We 'ave to catch 'em first. I get a leatherin' if I don't bring back some tench for supper, so I make sure I catch 'em."

Manco looked at them both. "Boys friends, teach each other," he observed.

Peter grinned. "Yes, that's just what I was thinking, Manco."

Archie's face lightened. "You . . . you mean you'll show me 'ow to read and write, proper like?"

"Yes, but only if you teach me things too."

"What things?" Archie couldn't imagine what a gentleman's son like Peter would want to learn from him! Aside from fishing, of course.

As the boys fell to talking, Manco glanced disappointedly around the gatehouse. There was no gold or finery of any kind, nothing to indicate it was the abode of Viracocha. Whatever it now was, the House of the Sun it was *not.* "Pizarro house," he muttered under his breath, but then he heard something and swiftly gestured to the boys to be quiet. "Someone come!" he breathed, and they all listened.

Gradually, there came the rattle of a pony and trap coming from the direction of Temford. They all three moved to the window to look out and saw the little vehicle emerge from the mist. But instead of driving on by, the man in the trap maneuvered the pony to a halt right by the gates. Then he settled more comfortably on the seat, hunched his shoulders, and turned up his greatcoat collar. He was short and stocky, with unexpectedly small hands and feet. For a moment he raised his jowled face toward the sky, as if hoping to see the sun about to break through.

Peter recognized him. "It's Mr. Mackay, the banker," he whispered.

Manco was about to reply when his sharp ears picked up another sound, this time the hooves of a ridden horse. He put a finger to his lips, and they watched again to see who came. A minute later, Rafe rode out of the swirling vapor and reined in alongside the trap. He had trouble with his black thoroughbred, which danced and shied, too full of energy to stand meekly while its rider indulged in conversation.

"Well, Mackay? What news is there?" Rafe demanded.

"Nothing of import, at least I don't think so," the banker replied in his distinctively Scottish voice, then he sat forward curiously. "Have you hurt your chin?"

"It's nothing. Well, get on with it, man."

"Eh? Oh, yes. Mrs. Preston wants me at the Hall. Something about a purse of coins from Felix Reynolds in Peru."

Peter stared. Mr. Mackay was nothing but a snake in the grass!

"A purse?" Rafe's tone was sharp.

"Oh, don't worry, it isn't a fortune. Just sufficient to settle some of the more immediate bills." Mackay kept a wary eye on the thoroughbred, which was making his pony stir uneasily.

"Are you sure?"

"Well, I haven't seen it yet, but that's what she says in her note. Do you want to read it?" The banker reached inside his coat, but Rafe shook his head.

"No, I'll take your word for it. Now look, I have something important for you to do. When you get to the Hall, you are almost certainly going to be given a letter. It is in my hand, and concerns the sum of fifty thousand guineas."

Mackay sat back in surprise. "Fifty thousand?"

"Yes. The letter instructs you to remove that amount from my account and see that it is given to Mrs. Fairfield. You are to pretend that you will comply with these instructions, but as soon as you are able I want you to destroy the letter. Is that clear?" Rafe's horse capered slightly and tossed its head so unexpectedly that it almost jerked the reins from his hands.

Mackay leaned away as the animal swung around, its jaws close to his face. "Destroy it? But—"

"I don't care how you do it, or what story you invent to explain its disappearance."

The Scotsman nodded. "As you wish, Sir Rafe."

"Don't fail me, or it will be the worst for you." Rafe regained mastery of his mount.

"When have I ever failed you, Sir Rafe? Reliability is my middle name. Besides, you pay me well for my, er, services."

"And I expect value for my money." Rafe leaned forward in the saddle. "There is something else I want you to do when you are at the Hall."

"Yes?" The banker was all attention.

"There is a man there, my cousin, Jack Lincoln. I want you to tell him there is something vital you must communicate to him concerning Felix Reynolds. Tell him his Indian friend is concerned as well. You are to say that it is too delicate to discuss in front of the others. Arrange to meet them both here—both, mind you—then leave. Be as quick as you can about all this because I don't want to kick my heels in this damp and cold for a moment longer than necessary. Do you understand?"

Mackay nodded again. "Yes, I understand. But what am I to say to him when he arrives here?"

"You won't be here. I will," Rafe said quietly, and took a pistol from inside his coat.

The onlookers in the gatehouse saw the barrel glint in the dull morning light. The banker's eyes widened. "So I am just to see that he comes here. That's all?"

"Yes. Now get going."

Without further ado the Scotsman flicked the reins and urged the pony away. The mist swirled after his departure, and the sound of the trap seemed audible for quite a long time until at last it dwindled into silence.

Rafe didn't ride off as well. Instead, he slowly dismounted and opened the gates, at which the watchers in the gatehouse drew back from the window in dismay. The gates groaned, then came the sound of snorting and hooves as the fractious horse was led through.

Peter stole a nervous glance outside and saw Rafe taking the horse around to the rear of the gatehouse. The animal was impatient and kept tossing its head, and now and then it tried to pull away from Rafe's grip. He managed to lead it behind the gatehouse and must have secured it somehow, because a minute later he returned to the door and pushed it open.

32

There was hardly any time to think. Manco stepped swiftly behind the door, leaving Peter and Archie in full view as Rafe entered. Rafe halted, taken completely by surprise to see them. Then the breath was knocked from him as Manco launched himself from behind the door.

Without seeing his assailant, Rafe went sprawling facedown on the floor, and in a moment Manco was seated astride him, dragging his hands behind his back and tying his wrists with a length of twine that had traveled all the way from Peru in the Inca's capacious purse. Rafe's mouth opened to threaten them with vile fates, but Manco silenced him by stuffing one of Archie's sheets of paper into his mouth. Within another few moments Rafe's ankles were tied together as well, and he lay there like a trussed turkey. He had yet to see the face of his assailant.

Peter and Archie stood rigid with dismay and shock. The consequences of such an assault were only too clear to them, for the master of Temford Castle was not a man to suffer such indignities without exacting the maximum revenge. But Manco was quite unruffled. He stood over his victim. "Devil die if give trouble," he warned.

Rafe writhed and managed to twist and look up at his attacker. His face drained of color, and his eyes widened in utter terror. A strangulated noise issued from his throat, and he tried to free his wrists in order to seek solace from his pebble, but Manco's knots were tight.

The Indian prodded him with a sandaled toe. "Devil not do harm now," he declared, then gave a cold smile. "Devil have business with Manco?" He bent to take the paper out of Rafe's mouth. "Speak. Manco all ears," he invited.

Rafe looked utterly sick, and made not a sound.

"Cat got devil's tongue?" Manco shoved the paper back into place, then straightened to speak to the two frightened boys. "Boys stay here. Manco go warn Hall about this devil and banker devil too."

Neither of them wished to stay with Rafe, but Archie spoke first. "I'll go! I can tek the 'orse and—"

Manco shook his head. "Boy have hurt wrist."

Peter piped up swiftly. "Then I'll go!"

The Indian looked at him. "Boy manage horse?"

"Yes," Peter replied bravely.

Manco nodded. "Then go, but take care. Horse not easy."

"I know." Peter turned on his heel and ran out of the gatehouse. Moments later, the thoroughbred was being urged away in the direction of the Hall.

Manco beamed at Archie. "All well now, you see," he said, and reached into his purse. He drew out a dried leaf, which he crumbled into dust between his fingers, muttering beneath his breath as he did so.

Rafe's eyes almost bulged from his head.

Archie watched curiously. "What was all that about?"

"Banker devil not burn letter now, letter cannot burn," Manco explained.

Archie didn't give a darn about any letter; he was more concerned about his own well-being if all this went wrong and Sir Rafe got his own back! He could feel Rafe's gaze upon him now, bright, dangerous, and full of warning. Steeling himself, Archie looked away from that compelling stare. He'd witnessed Rafe's meeting with the banker and knew him to have murder in mind. Archie Bradwell knew right from wrong, and Sir Rafe Warrender was definitely in the wrong!

Manco saw Rafe's look as well and nodded at Archie. "Boy wait outside," he said softly.

Archie was glad to get out. He hurried to the edge of the trees and waited there, wondering what was going on in the gatehouse. If he had but known it, Sir Rafe Warrender was at that moment almost fainting with terror, for Manco had taken out his knife and was crouching beside him. The tip of the sharp blade moved slowly toward the prisoner's throat . . .

* * *

Meanwhile, Sir Quentin was fleeing the coop. He had spent the rest of the night composing a long letter detailing all he knew of Rafe's many sins—and whitewashing his own, of course. The letter was addressed to the commanding officer of a barracks he knew to be on the road to Shrewsbury. As soon as Rafe had set off to meet Mackay, Sir Quentin ordered his traveling carriage to be made ready.

Rafe had hardly crossed the bridge over the Teme, than the carriage rattled out through the castle gates and set off north toward Shrewsbury, ultimately making for Liverpool. Sir Quentin had a sister in America—Philadelphia—whom he suddenly desired to see very much indeed, and Liverpool was the nearest port from which vessels sailed the Atlantic. America was a secure refuge, and comfortingly far away from any repercussions in Britain when Rafe's treasonous activities were exposed!

The letter was entrusted to an ostler at a wayside inn, who was paid handsomely to deliver it promptly at the barracks, then the chariot drove off again, en route for Holyhead, or so the ostler was told. By the time the scandal broke in full, Sir Quentin Brockhampton hoped to be safely away on the high seas.

Jack and Emily were standing at the bay window of the grand parlor. Behind them, Cora was playing the harpsichord while Cristoval turned the music sheets for her. The delicate strains of a Mozart minuet drifted prettily over the room, where hot chocolate and nutmeg-flavored Shrewsbury cakes had just been served on a silver tray that had been placed on a table near the fireplace. The silver reflected the light of the flames, and the scent of the warm cakes drifted on the air.

There was no sign now of Cora's tears; indeed she seemed quite composed, almost as if a weight had been lifted from her shoulders. She looked up at Cristoval from time to time and smiled. He smiled back. The rapport between them was almost tangible.

Emily turned to Jack, smiling too, and after a quick glance to see that the others were preoccupied, she slipped her arms around his waist. "This time yesterday I did not imagine I could be so very happy today."

"Nor I." He gazed deeply into her eyes, hardly able to believe that such a perfect creature, such an angel, was as much in love with him as he was with her. "Emily, I know we only met the day before yesterday, but I feel as if we have been together for a lot longer than that."

She smiled. "I trust you do not imply a variation on familiarity breeding contempt?" she teased.

"I imply nothing of the sort," he replied softly, putting his arms around her waist as well.

"I am relieved to hear it, sir," she replied playfully. Her lightheartedness took her by surprise. She hadn't felt like this for so long that it was almost like being reborn. Truth to tell, she had not felt like this for a number of years now . . . She pulled from his arms, her lips parting as she looked back on her marriage and realized how much light had gone out of it. She had not known it at the time, for it had been a gradual thing, a steady chipping away of the trust that had been there in the beginning. It had begun when she begged him not to go to Rafe's gaming parties because the Hall was short of money. He said he wouldn't, but he still had. Oh, he gave excuses to explain away his absences, but she knew the truth. The flame of love burned more dimly after that.

"Emily?" Jack looked at her in concern as he saw a tear trail down her cheek.

"It's nothing," she whispered.

"Tears are never there without reason," he said gently.

"I . . . I was just thinking—accepting—that I had begun to fall out of love with Geoffrey."

"Out of love?"

She met his eyes, unable to betray Geoffrey even more. It had been said, and that was sufficient.

Jack put his hand to her cheek and gently wiped the tear away with his thumb.

Then they both turned as a pony and trap rattled into the courtyard below. Emily composed herself, then glanced back at Cora. "Mama, Mr. Mackay is here," she said.

The music broke off.

The banker was shown up straightaway, and was all beaming smiles as he hastened over to Cora. "Ah, my dear Mrs.

Preston," he declared, and bowed chivalrously over her proffered hand.

She smiled. "Mr. Mackay, how prompt you are, to be sure."

"I am always at your beck and call, dear lady." He straightened then and put his fingertips together as he glanced around at the others. "Mrs. Fairfield," he said warmly, greeting Emily with another of his seemingly genuine smiles, but the two men were acknowledged with a very civil bow. "Sirs." They inclined their heads.

Cora got up from the harpsichord, gathered her cinnamon skirts, and went to the table drawer where she had placed the purse of coins in readiness. "Mr. Mackay, I have received this purse as a gift, and wish you to exchange the coins for sterling, then place the balance in the Hall's account. I understand from Mr. Lincoln that there should be approximately five hundred pounds." She smiled apologetically. "Oh, I am forgetting my manners. Allow me to present Mr. Lincoln and Don Cristoval de Soto. Gentlemen, this is our banker, Mr. Mackay."

The three men bowed to one another. Jack watched the Scotsman's face. It was a shifty visage, he thought, all smiles but no sincerity. Disquiet passed through Jack as the banker's fingers closed over the purse. He would not trust Mr. Mackay with a clay pipe, let alone five hundred pounds! He glanced at Cristoval and saw the same doubts written in his eyes.

But Emily was speaking now. "Mr. Mackay, I also have something for you." She took Rafe's letter from her reticule, which lay on the table beside the tray of chocolate and spiced cakes. She gave it to him.

The banker was all surprise on seeing the writing. "Is this not Sir Rafe Warrender's hand?"

"Indeed so," Cora replied. "Oh, do sit down, everyone, for I vow we make the room untidy. Do you care for chocolate, Mr. Mackay? If so, I will have another cup brought for you."

"Er, no, I fear it makes me bilious, but a Shrewsbury cake would not go amiss," the Scotsman replied, waiting until Emily was seated, then taking a chair himself. He broke the yellow seal on the letter and began to read.

Jack had taken a seat opposite him and was able to see his face quite clearly. The fellow did not seem surprised at the letter's contents; indeed it was almost as if he knew what to expect!

Cristoval caught Jack's eye and pursed his lips. Jack cleared his throat. "Er, Mr. Mackay, I am rather surprised you should so easily recognize Sir Rafe's writing, for it is a very ordinary hand."

Emily turned to him in surprise, and Cora paused with the dish of cakes half extended to Cristoval.

Mr. Mackay was caught off guard, but then recovered to give a light, vaguely dismissive laugh. "Oh, Sir Rafe's hand is well known to me, Mr. er, Lincoln. He has many dealings with my bank."

"Dealings enough for you to know what his letter contains before you have even read it?"

Emily's lips parted, and Cora dropped the dish of cakes.

The banker stared at Jack. "Oh, come, sir, what foolishness is this? Of course I did not know what the letter contained!"

"I think you did."

Cristoval sat forward. "So do I."

Mr. Mackay swallowed, the color seeping from his face. "I, er, don't know why you should think such a thing of me, gentlemen, but I assure you that you are both wrong." He folded the letter and pushed it inside his coat. The purse he had already consigned to his pocket.

Hoofbeats thundered into the courtyard, and a maid screamed. "Oh, Master Peter!"

Emily was on her feet in a moment, catching up her blue-and-white skirts to rush to the window. Then she gasped, her hands flying fearfully to her mouth, for she saw Rafe's big black horse, its flanks foam-flecked as it reared and capered, trying to dislodge Peter, who was clinging to its neck and mane for all he was worth. Her thoughts raced. What was he doing with Rafe's horse, that horse of *all* animals!

Cora watched her anxiously. "What is it, my dear? What's happening?"

"It's Peter, he's on Rafe's horse . . . !"

Jack and Cristoval hurried to the window, closely followed by Cora. But just as Jack was about to run downstairs, a manservant hurried out of the kitchens and grabbed the horse's reins. A moment later, he had it by the bridle, and Peter was able to slip from the saddle. Emily watched her son run into the house.

They all turned as the boy's running footsteps approached the door of the grand parlor. Then he burst in, breathless and overwrought. "Don't let Mr. Mackay have the letter. He's going to destroy it! He's Sir Rafe's man!" he cried, pointing an accusing finger toward the banker.

All eyes swung toward the Scotsman, who was no longer in his chair, but standing by the fire. He tossed Rafe's letter onto the flames, but it recoiled and floated safely onto the hearth. Again the banker snatched it, this time crumpling it to fling it onto the fire. Again it leapt out again, uncrumpling itself as it did so, then settling tidily on the hearth.

The Scotsman stared down at it, then his knees sagged and he fell in a swoon.

33

Jack rushed to the fallen banker, whose clothes were in danger from the fire. As he dragged him away, Mr. Mackay began to come around. He saw Jack looming over him, grasping his coat lapels, and gave a guilty squeak of alarm. "Don't hurt me! I *had* to do it!"

"Hurt you? Damn it all, man, I'm making you safe, although why I should bother with such a maggot as you, I really don't know!" Jack released the lapels so disgustedly that the Scotsman slumped onto the carpet like a sack. Jack then stood over him, fists clenched. "You can count yourself fortunate that I am more of a gentleman than you give me credit, otherwise right now I'd . . ." His voice died away, leaving unsaid whatever punishment he had in mind.

"I am in fear of my life! Sir Rafe will kill me if I don't assist him!"

Peter's voice rang out scornfully. "Liar! You're doing it for money! Sir Rafe pays you! You've come here now to tell Mr. Lincoln to go to the old gatehouse so he'll walk into Sir Rafe's ambush!"

"That's not true!" Mackay cried.

"It is, but the plan won't work now because Manco has already caught Sir Rafe and tied him up like a Christmas capon! Manco and Archie are there with him now."

Jack looked at the boy in astonishment. "Manco and Archie are there? Archie Bradwell? What's been going on, Peter?"

The boy swallowed. "Manco and I decided yesterday to go to the old gatehouse this morning. Manco was convinced that Viracocha, the sun god, was there. Oh, it's a long story. Anyway, when we arrived, we found Archie Bradwell. Huh, some Viracocha! It seems he goes there to teach himself to write."

Peter grinned at Emily. "I'm going to show him how to read and write, and he's going to show me things in return!" Then he realized he'd wandered from the subject in hand, and hastily returned his attention to Jack. "Anyway, Manco and I had hardly begun to talk to Archie when we heard a pony and trap. Mr. Mackay arrived and waited by the gates for Sir Rafe. We listened to all they said. Mr. Mackay has been helping Sir Rafe all along. He's no friend to us here!"

The banker's face was waxen with guilt. His lips moved, but no sound came out.

Jack glanced at Cristoval. "Find a rope. We'd best bind this maggot and lock him up somewhere while we decide what to do with him." Then he cast a dark glance down at the terrified banker. "You aren't going to go unpunished, my friend, and as for Warrender, well, my dear cousin is about to rue the day he was born!"

Emily feared his intentions and darted desperately forward to fling her arms around his neck. "No! Don't go! Leave it to the law to punish him!"

He held her close, resting his cheek against her hair for a moment, but then he put her gently but firmly from him. "I must go, Emily. It's time Rafe and I faced it out properly. Besides, it's best not to leave him to Manco's tender mercies." Jack knew that the Indian's fierce desire to kick his heels of England might prompt precipitate and—for Rafe—rather final action.

Cristoval looked at him, knowing what he was thinking. "Perhaps we had better get there as quickly as possible," he said quietly.

Rafe was still lying bound and gagged on the gatehouse floor with Manco's knife at his throat. The Inca had been motionless for minutes on end, except for the slow, relentless turning of the knifepoint against his victim's skin. Manco's face lacked all emotion and his eyes were empty, making it impossible to know what he was thinking or what he meant to do. His lips didn't move, but a strange sound emanated from his throat, an eerie chanting of magical words. It was as if the Indian were a ventriloquist.

Suddenly, the sound stopped, and Manco reached toward

his prisoner's pale chestnut hair. Rafe cringed in dread as the Indian carefully cut a lock, then held it in front of him. "Devil see this? Now Manco have part of devil, Manco have power over him. If Manco want, Manco make devil die. Watch."

The Indian swung around and pointed to a sheet of Archie's paper. Before Rafe's eyes it withered at the edges, becoming damp and moldy, and disintegrating until it became little more than just another grimy mark on the floor. A process that ought to have taken months, mayhap years, was over within seconds.

Manco leaned over the bound man, fixing him with dark, unfathomable Inca eyes. "Manco do that to paper because Manco in room with paper, but Manco can do that to devil from wherever Manco is. Hair part of body, part of soul, and while Manco have devil's hair, Manco have devil too. Understand?"

Rafe stared up at him, eyes bulging. He did not doubt that the Indian had the power to carry out his threat.

"Devil understand?" Manco repeated.

Rafe's head nodded up and down, as if upon a spring.

"If devil want save hide, devil do what Manco tell him."

Rafe goggled at him, still nodding. He'd do anything, anything at all!

"Devil give back to Capac Jack what belong to Capac Jack. And if banker destroy letter, then devil write another. Devil undo all wickedness, then devil go far away." Manco waved an arm to indicate the farthest corners of the earth. "But not Peru," he added quickly.

Rafe continued to stare up at him. *Go into exile?* He'd be damned if—! But then his glance crept back to the remains of the paper. Maybe exile would be wise after all . . .

"Devil agree?" Manco pressed conversationally.

Rafe swallowed and nodded.

The Indian straightened again and pushed the knife back into his belt, but for good measure he pointed a finger at the *Gentleman's Magazine.* Slowly it began to wither at the edges. "Monday is Pizarro day for all devils," he murmured.

Jack and Cristoval rode to the gatehouse at speed, and found Archie still hanging around nervously at the edge of the trees. There hadn't been a sound from the building, and the boy was too nervous to investigate. Anything might have happened inside, anything at all . . .

The two men dismounted, and Jack would have gone straight inside, but Cristoval held him back and called out, "Is all well, Manco?"

The door opened, and the Indian came out, a broad grin on his lips. "All excellent, Capac Cristoval. Devil not problem now."

Jack's heart sank. *Oh, dear God, no . . . !* He ran into the gatehouse with Cristoval at his heels, and immediately halted in relief as he saw Rafe on the floor—only too alive and squirming!

Manco came in behind them, a little put out. "Manco not kill. No need for that."

"What do you mean?" Jack demanded.

Manco spread his hands, the picture of saintly innocence. "Devil repent sins. That not what your church want?"

"Well, yes, but—"

Cristoval eyed the Indian. "What have you done, Manco?"

"Manco not do anything. Except show magic."

"Ah." Cristoval's eyes cleared.

Jack took the ball of paper from Rafe's mouth. "What have you to say for yourself, Coz?" he asked softly.

Rafe stared mutely up at him, then his eyes slid fearfully to Manco, who merely looked back. His face gave nothing away, yet at the same time it revealed a great deal. It certainly spoke volumes to the bound man.

"Well?" Jack prompted.

"Lincoln, I . . . I . . ." Rafe's voice died away. His mouth was dry, and his tongue felt as if it were too big for his mouth. His jaw ached too, and so did his head. In fact, he had never felt worse.

Manco searched in his purse and drew out the lock of hair, which he pretended to study with great concentration. Rafe immediately gave a squeak of dread, and words tumbled from his lips in a torrent.

"Lincoln, I deeply regret all I have done. I mean to put it all right, believe me. You can have your inheritance back. I will make it over to you as soon as I can. And I am going to name you my heir as well, so Temford Castle will be yours if anything should happen to me."

Jack was taken aback. "*Your* heir?" he repeated.

Rafe's head nodded up and down. "Yes, and if Mackay managed to destroy the first letter I wrote for you, I'll write another. I will never again do anything to harm Fairfield Hall, nor will I attempt to even approach Emily Fairfield."

"See that you don't," Jack said softly.

Rafe looked up at him. "So you will get everything, Lincoln. Your own fortune, mine, and Felix Reynolds's."

"Felix's? What do you mean?"

"You don't know? He's as rich as Croesus! At least, he was."

Jack glanced at Cristoval and saw an odd look on his face. And on Manco's. "What's he talking about? Come on, you clearly know something . . ."

Cristoval shifted uncomfortably, and it was Manco who answered. "Yes, we know. Capac Felix have much money. Make rich in Venezuela, or some Pizarro place. Know he old and not have much longer, so—"

"He's probably dead already!" Rafe cried. "Gustavus spoke to Reynolds's doctor in Lima and was told he was not going to recover from that ague, or whatever it was he had. Gustavus told Brockhampton all about it in London. Emily Fairfield is about to inherit a huge sum, from which it seems *you* will benefit as well, Lincoln! Oh, believe me, she is going to be far more rich than you or I have ever been." He gave a cold laugh. "There, that has put a question mark above your so-called honor, has it not? Will she ever be sure you did not know about her inheritance *before* you arrived at the Hall?"

Cristoval stepped over and leaned down to seize Rafe and shake him. "Don't you *ever* learn? Gustavus's information was wrong. Felix Reynolds was recovering when we left. I would lay odds that he is hale and hearty again now."

Manco nodded. "Yes, Capac Felix well again. Manco know."

Cristoval's eyes lightened. "There, you see? That is all the confirmation I need." He continued to gaze down at Rafe. "Besides, you may as well know that when Manco and I return to Peru, Mrs. Preston will be coming with us. She will see Felix and will hear from his lips that Jack knew nothing about his wealth. She will write to her daughter, and Emily will know beyond all doubt that Jack is true. Not that she will not know it anyway, Sir Rafe, for there is a great difference between you and your cousin. Jack is a noble spirit, but you are no better than the scum upon a filthy puddle."

Manco nodded, then grinned at Jack. "Capc Felix think you best man in world for Palla Emily. He right about that."

Jack ran a bewildered hand through his hair. "You two have known this about Felix and said nothing to me?"

Cristoval spread his hands. "Of course we said nothing. That was the whole point. Felix did not wish you to be deterred by any fear of being branded a fortune hunter."

"And so, even though he has all this wealth, he was going to leave his daughter defenseless, and at the mercy of this . . . this . . ." Jack waved a furious hand toward Rafe on the floor.

Cristoval shook his head. "No, my friend, if it had come to that, I am empowered to tell Emily her true situation. I was to stay my hand until the last moment, however, so that true love could take its course. As it has. Should it all have gone wrong, Felix gave me a letter granting me power of attorney, which I was instructed to take to his lawyer in Bath."

"So that's why you went to Bath?"

"Yes. Of course, what Felix—nor any of us—did not know was that your cousin would blackmail Emily with stories of Geoffrey's treasonous activities." In disgust, Cristoval shoved the prisoner with his foot. This particular aspect of Rafe's blackmail was no longer a secret at the Hall because Emily had decided it was best to tell everyone when they adjourned to the grand parlor for chocolate and to listen to Cora playing the harpsichord.

Manco took in the expressions flitting over Jack's face. "Capac Jack not need worry now, for he rich, and Emily rich. That very good."

Jack's attention returned to Rafe. "So Felix's fortune was your real reason for pursuing Emily?"

"Yes."

"But how in perdition did you find out?"

"Chance." Rafe told him of Sir Quentin's discovery of the sale of the St. Lawrence estate to Felix, and how he had gone to the Bath lawyer and been left alone for long enough to go through the files.

Jack could easily have reached down to put his hands to Rafe's throat for all he had done; indeed the urge was so fierce that he had to move away for fear of succumbing. "You had better abide by your decision to leave England, Rafe, because if you do not, I swear I will kill you."

"I'm going. I know I cannot stay here." *Not least because I have been spying for the French, a fact of which you as yet know nothing . . .*

"Just not go Peru," Manco reminded him.

"I won't, I swear it!"

Manco had already replaced the hair in his purse. "If devil good, Manco not harm him," he said. "But remember, if devil bad, Manco will know, no matter where in world Manco is."

Cristoval leaned over Rafe. "Believe him, sir, for he does not speak lightly. I have seen strong men die from Inca magic."

"I believe him! I believe him!" Rafe cried.

Manco turned to Jack and Cristoval. "What now?" he asked.

Cristoval answered before Jack had the chance. "Jack, you return to Emily and tell her all is well. Leave Sir Rafe to Manco and me."

"No! Don't leave me, Lincoln!" Rafe cried.

But Manco put his fingertips together and smiled, for all the world like a benevolent vicar. "Capac Jack go now. Devil safe with us," he said.

Rafe swallowed and closed his eyes tightly. Thus he did not see the enormous wink that Manco gave Jack. The master of Temford Castle wasn't to know it, but no further harm was going to befall him at the Indian's hands. Unless, of course, he was guilty of further misbehavior.

However, Rafe was not to have the opportunity to slip away into the safety of exile because he was arrested later that very day. Sir Quentin's lengthy missive to the commanding officer at the barracks prompted an immediate and sharp response, and as the midday sun was at its autumn height, a large detachment of soldiers rode across Temford Square to take over the castle.

Word soon traveled, and by nightfall the whole area rang with supposition and rumor. The army searched the castle from dungeons to battlements without finding any proof of Rafe's treason; indeed, he might have gotten away with it, except that Sir Quentin's letter named the exact volume of French poems that had been burned, and Jack could produce the incriminating sheet of paper. Another copy of the book was duly obtained, the traitorous message decoded, and Rafe's dishonor exposed in all its ignominy.

On Bonfire Night, instead of announcing his betrothal to Emily, Sir Rafe Warrender languished under lock and key in the barracks' guardroom. He awaited certain representatives of His Majesty's Government, who were coming north from London with all haste to interrogate him about his disloyal activities. While he slumped dejectedly in his cell, Shropshire society—excepting the denizens of Fairfield Hall—danced and made merry at the Royal Oak, and then marveled at the wonderful bonfire and display of fireworks. No one mourned Rafe's absence; indeed, no one even had a good word to say about him.

34

It was a fine day in late spring when Emily Fairfield became Mrs. Jack Lincoln. They married very quietly in the chapel at Fairfield Hall, with only the servants to witness their union. Everyone else, including Peter—and, to his immeasurable joy, Archie Bradwell—had sailed for Peru, where awaited the majestic Andes and the hidden treasures of the Incas. The boys would eventually come back, but Cora's stay was set to be a very long one. She had become Mrs. Felix Reynolds, united at last with the man she had adored for most of her adult life—a man who, it must be said, had become considerably rejuvenated by the arrival of his secret love!

Emily's remarriage did not go uncelebrated in the town of Temford, however, and a fine wedding breakfast was held at the Royal Oak. But as the sunny May afternoon wore on, the bride and groom slipped away from the celebrations and drove back to Fairfield Hall to be on their own. The wedding landau was drawn by four white horses and had its hoods down. It was garlanded with spring flowers, greenery, and white satin ribbons, and made a very romantic sight as it drove beneath the canopy of young leaves. A cuckoo called, hawthorn blossoms filled the air with fragrance, and here and there drifts of bluebells swathed the clearings.

Emily wore a gown of golden silk, with a matching lace pelisse, and she had discarded her flower-adorned bonnet to let the sun shadows dapple her hair, which she still wore short because that was how Jack liked to see it. A posy of rosebuds lay on her lap, and she rested her head contentedly against Jack's shoulder as the landau bowled slowly along the drive. Her white-gloved hand rested in his, and he moved his cheek against her hair, his eyes closed as the sunlight flashed through the leaves.

He wore the bridegroom's almost obligatory coat of royal blue with wide brass buttons, and with it he had a white silk waistcoat, breeches, stockings, and buckled black shoes. His starched neckcloth was a masterpiece of fashion, and on it shone a bright blue sapphire. The breeze stirred his blond hair as he slipped an arm around his bride. This was undoubtedly the happiest day of his life, a day when everything was right at last. All past injustices had been eradicated, he was master of his birthright again, and he had just taken to wife the most adorable, matchless, wonderful woman in all creation. And tonight they would lie together between lavender-scented sheets, making love until dawn . . . The only thing to mar the perfection of such a day was that in spite of the clearing by the pool having been searched and searched again, the Agincourt ring had not been found. If he could have worn it at his wedding, then absolutely everything would have been perfect. But what did it really matter, he mused, when everything else was so incomparable?

Suddenly, Emily sat forward with a gasp, her bouquet rolling from her lap onto the carriage floor. A flash of memory had returned, like the sun piercing the leaves above their heads.

Jack was startled. "What is it?"

"I . . . I've thought of something . . . Stop the carriage!" she called out to the surprised postilion, who immediately reined in the lead horses. She turned swiftly to Jack. "We must go to the clearing!"

"Now? But you are in your wedding gown!"

"That doesn't matter. Please, Jack, it's important!" She began to open the landau door, and Jack hastily did it for her and alighted. Then he assisted her down as well. "We can easily return after we've changed—" he began, but she would not hear of it.

"No, we must go now!" She caught his hand and began to hasten through the woods.

The pool was silent and still, and the May sunshine brightened the new leaves to a thousand shades of green. Ferns were unfurling, wildflowers added their hues to the undergrowth, and a tench broke the surface, sending rings across the mirrored water. Emily led the way to the spot where she remembered falling from her horse. "This is where I lay, wasn't it?"

Jack nodded, puzzled. "Yes, but—"

"And my head was about here, facing the fallen tree." Emily closed her eyes, trying to remember exactly what she had seen as she lost consciousness—something small and bright shimmering against the mossy trunk. Catching up her wedding skirts, she made her way through the soft grasses and primroses, not taking her eyes from the spot on the tree trunk. She reached it, but saw nothing, just gnarled bark, moss, and the moving shadows cast by the oak tree from where Peter had so often tried to catch fish.

"What are you looking for?" Jack asked. He could think only of the Agincourt ring, but he knew how often it had been sought without success.

She looked more closely, taking off her glove in order to pluck at the bark. Suddenly, a piece fell away, and something else fell too, making a tiny metallic sound as it disappeared into the ferns and flowers. With a triumphant cry Emily bent to retrieve it. Then she straightened, holding out her palm. The Agincourt ring lay there, its gold shining against her skin.

Jack stared at it. "But, how did you know . . . ?"

"When I fell from my horse that day, I saw something glint as I was passing out. I had quite forgotten it until a few minutes ago." She took the ring and made him take his left glove off. Then she slipped the ring onto his fourth finger. "Your treasured heirloom is where it belongs at last, Mr. Lincoln," she whispered.

He smiled and drew her into his arms. "Oh, I do love you, Mrs. Lincoln."

She lifted her lips toward his, and they kissed for a long, long moment, then she took his hand again and led him to the edge of the water. "Manco said that if we ever wished him to know we were happy and all was well, all we had to do was both throw twigs into the water. Do you believe in such things?"

"Oh, I believe in Inca magic, for I have seen it." Jack bent to take two twigs from the ground. He gave one to Emily. "Together now. One, two, three."

They tossed the twigs onto the water. Ripples went out widening more and more until they reached the edge of the water. But then Emily felt as if they continued somehow, spreading farther and farther across the earth. Across the oceans too . . .

It was midmorning in Lima, and summer had turned to autumn. The weather was unexpectedly fine, and the Andes' cordilleras soared in white-capped magnificence against a sapphire sky. The hacienda was quiet. Peter and Archie, now fast friends and quite inseparable, were at their lessons with the English tutor Cora had engaged. Felix had accompanied Cristoval out on his land, where a boundary dispute had arisen with a neighbor.

Cora was in the garden, seated on a chair beneath the evergreen branches of the molle tree. She wore a warm rose woolen gown and had a heavy knitted shawl around her shoulders because there was a definite chill in the air. She was reading an American newspaper that happened to have come into Cristoval's possession, he having found it at his club in Lima. It was several months out of date, but contained news she had not known.

Word of Admiral Nelson's death at Trafalgar had reached Shropshire before they departed, but she did not know about Bonaparte's huge victory over the Austrians and Russians at Austerlitz, or the Christmas peace the Austrians had signed with him three weeks later at Pressburg. Nor did she know that the great prime minister, William Pitt the Younger, had died in January, in reality because of an addiction to port wine, but it was said the cause was a broken heart because of the news from Europe. Now it seemed Britain was governed by a coalition under Lord Grenville, of whom she had never held a very high opinion.

It did not bode well for her homeland, she thought as she turned the page. But then a name immediately leapt out at her. Sir Quentin Brockhampton! She read the brief column. It seemed that Rafe's grand accomplice, and in many ways his equal in guilt, had made good his escape to America, where he had soon succumbed to the essentially dishonest streak in his character. This time, however, he had not escaped retribution, and had been sentenced to a considerable time in Walnut Street Prison, Philadelphia. Cora drew a deep breath. She supposed it was a fitting fate for him, rather than the much heavier price Sir Rafe Warrender had paid. Traitors were not treated leniently at the best of times, let alone during a war.

She settled to continue reading, but then cast a rather dark glance toward Manco, who was seated cross-legged on the ground by the silent fountain. He was playing his wretched flute again, and while she appreciated his talent, she did wish he would play something more cheerful. Were all Inca melodies sad and fit only to pluck at the heart? she wondered.

Manco was enjoying his flute playing; in fact, he was enjoying everything about being home again. Oh, the thanks he had given to Viracocha when he came ashore at Callao after another five-month voyage. No Inca had ever danced more wonderfully, or paid more homage. The great god was pleased with him and had smiled upon all his prayers since then. Life was good.

Suddenly, a slight splashing sound came from the pool of water around the fountain, which was not operating today. Manco stopped playing and turned his head to look. He saw rings rippling across the surface and lapping against the stonework, as if something had just fallen in, or a fish had come up from below. But there weren't any fish, and he knew nothing had fallen in. An odd sensation spread through him, a knowing feeling that he knew had traveled to him from the other side of the world. He smiled and looked at Cora.

"Capac Jack and Palla Emily well and happy," he said. "From beginning both hearts easy conquest, and today they marry."

"Mm?" Cora was absorbed in something in the newspaper. The Inca repeated his words, and she looked up then. "Married today? Come now, sir, you surely don't expect me to believe that you know this? *C'est impossible!*"

"It's true. Manco quite certain." He pointed to the pool, where the ripples were still just visible, then he picked up his flute to play again, but this time the music he chose was much happier.

If Cora had but realized, it was an Inca wedding song.